"A clever plot, a vibrant Cleveland and rural Ohio setting, and a realistically drawn hero make this series one to watch. It exudes much the same sort of charm as the early Spenser novels did."

—*Booklist* (on *Pepper Pike*)

"Roberts handles the private-eye format with aplomb and takes full advantage of his Cleveland scene . . . Best of all is his Slovenian sleuth, vulnerable and fallible, whom we are likely (and would like) to see more of." —*San Diego Union* (*Pepper Pike*)

"Fast-paced and smoothly narrated."

—*Washington Post Book World* (*Full Cleveland*)

"Another smooth page-turner from Roberts, who keeps the action moving and still fits in some wry observations on parenthood, teenagers, and marriage." —*Kirkus Reviews* (*Deep Shaker*)

"Roberts combines a strong character and a clever plot with the ethnic diversity that Cleveland provides. He proves that Midwest private eyes can hold their own with the best ones from either coast."

—*Des Moines Register* (*Deep Shaker*)

"There's an affection for Cleveland and an insistence on its ethnic, working-class life that gives vividness to the detection. Roberts writes with sharp wit, creates action scenes that are drawn with flair, and puts emotional life into a range of people."

—*Washington Post Book World* (*The Cleveland Connection*)

"Roberts is one of the best crime writers around, and *The Cleveland Connection* is his best effort yet. The plot has all the right ingredients—danger, suspense, intrigue, action—in all the right amounts; Milan Jacovich is the kind of guy we want on our side when the chips are down; and Roberts even makes Cleveland sound like a swell place to live. Don't miss this one." —*Booklist*

"Packed with unusual heroes, villains, and political twists and turns . . . a mystery that defies predictability."

—*Midwest Book Review* (*The Lake Effect*)

"A real treat . . . If you've somehow missed this series, definitely give it a try . . . If you're already a fan, this book will delight you even further.

—*Mystery News* (*The Lake Effect*)

"A corker of a whodunit ... Gritty, grim, humorous, sentimental—a perfect 10."   —*Chicago Sun-Times* (*The Duke of Cleveland*)

"The characters are vivid, and the plot goes in unusual directions, but ultimately it's Cleveland that captures our hearts."
                —*Pittsburgh Post-Gazette* (*The Duke of Cleveland*)

"Roberts affectionately weaves in the history and rich ethnic mix of Milan Jacovich's Cleveland turf."   —*Publishers Weekly* (*Collision Bend*)

"Roberts is a wordsmith of high order, and *Collision Bend* is a terrific novel of the mean streets."   —*Meritorious Mysteries*

"Roberts certainly creates a sense of place. Cleveland rings true—and he's especially skillful in creating real moral and ethical choices for his characters."   —*The Plain Dealer* (*The Cleveland Local*)

"Jacovich [is] one of the most fully realized characters in modern crime fiction ... Roberts is a confident writer who knows his character well and who has made him complex enough to be interesting."
                —*Mostly Murder* (*The Cleveland Local*)

"[Roberts] tells his tale in spare and potent prose. His Cleveland stories get better and better, offering far more than regional insights and pleasures."   —*Publishers Weekly* (*The Cleveland Local*)

"A series that gets better and better ... strongly recommended for those who like their detectives cut from the classic mold."
                —*Booklist* (*A Shoot in Cleveland*)

"[Milan Jacovich] is a hero one can't help but like. Roberts's polished prose, inventive plots, and pleasantly low-key style add extra appeal to his long-running series."   —*Booklist* (*The Best-Kept Secret*)

"Page turner of the week ... narrative comfort food ... a nifty spin on a classic P.I. formula."   —*People* (*The Indian Sign*)

"Brilliantly plotted, with a powerhouse climax."
                —*Booklist* (*The Dutch*)

"[A] roller coaster ride of a mystery ... Roberts speeds the reader through an investigation offering plenty of delicious twists and turns without ever compromising credibility."
                —*Publishers Weekly* (*The Irish Sports Pages*)

THE DUKE OF CLEVELAND

The Milan Jacovich mysteries
by Les Roberts:

Pepper Pike

Full Cleveland

Deep Shaker

The Cleveland Connection

The Lake Effect

The Duke of Cleveland

Collision Bend

The Cleveland Local

A Shoot in Cleveland

The Best-Kept Secret

The Indian Sign

The Dutch

The Irish Sports Pages

THE DUKE OF CLEVELAND

A MILAN JACOVICH MYSTERY

LES ROBERTS

GRAY & COMPANY, PUBLISHERS
CLEVELAND

Copyright © 1995 by Les Roberts

Gray & Company, Publishers
1588 E. 40th St.
Cleveland, Ohio 44103
www.grayco.com

Library of Congress Cataloging-in-Publication Data
Roberts, Les.
The Duke of Cleveland : a Milan Jacovich mystery / Les Roberts.
p. cm.
ISBN 1-59851-006-1 (pbk.)
1. Jacovich, Milan (Fictitious character)—Fiction. 2. Private investigators—Ohio—Cleveland—Fiction. 3. Artists—Crimes against—Fiction. 4. Cleveland (Ohio)—Fiction. 5. Missing persons—Fiction. I. Title.
PS3568.O23894D85 2005
813'.54—dc22   2005011235

ISBN 1-59851-006-1

Printed in the United States of America

10 9 8 7 6 5 4 3 2 1

For Sam Miller, who is the REAL Duke of Cleveland.

THE DUKE OF CLEVELAND

CHAPTER ONE

The wonderful thing about art, I suppose, is that it doesn't really have to do anything. Like the Gateway Arch in St. Louis or the *Mona Lisa* or Rodin's *The Kiss*—all that is asked of it is that it be beautiful.

It doesn't work that way with people.

Which was too bad for April Delavan, because she was beautiful, all right. Eighteen years old or so, with none of the Drew Barrymore seen-too-much-too-soon look that many of today's young people affect. Blonde curly hair framed a porcelain-smooth face that needed no makeup and that was punctuated by a delightful dimple just to the left of her mouth. Her eyes were remarkably large, the irises cornflower blue surrounded by dark rims; they gave her an ingenuous look of perpetual astonishment. Her aquiline nose had never felt the knife of a cosmetic surgeon but was actually genetic, and she possessed a pink rosebud mouth that couldn't seem to make up its mind whether to be heartbreakingly innocent or heart-stoppingly sensuous.

But in today's demanding world more is required of even the most beautiful people than just showing up, and as she sat across the desk from me in my office, I looked into those incredible blue eyes and ascertained sadly that no one was home.

I didn't think she was on any drugs. But April Delavan had that vague, bemused sort of look people get when subjected to a classroom lecture on the political and social currents of six-teenth-century Austria, and I finally realized she simply wasn't paying much attention.

She told me she had found my name in the Cleveland Area Consumer Yellow Pages under Detective Agencies. I'm not the first listing—I call my business Milan Security after my first name, which I pronounce the Americanized way, *My*-lan, rather than the way they'd say it in my parents' native Slovenia, *Mee*-lan, or the city in Italy, Mi-*lahn*. My last name, Jacovich, is simply too tough for most people to pronounce: the *J* sounds like a *Y* and the accent is on the first syllable. I could have simplified everything and called myself Ace Security, or Acme or Zenith, but I thought using my first name was a comfortable compromise.

I suppose April Delavan chose me instead of one of a dozen other detective agencies listed in the directory because of my proximity to where she lived. My office, the front room of my apartment at the top of Cedar Hill, where Cedar Road and Fair-mount Boulevard triangulate, is only about a two-minute drive from Coventry, the colorful section of Cleveland Heights where she apparently spent much of her time and from where she had made the call. I heard loud rock music blasting in the background when she'd called, and for all I knew she could have been using the pay phone at the noisy, cheerful little saloon called Pepper Ridge, except I didn't think they were open quite that early in the morning.

The only question she'd asked me on the phone was "Do you find people that are missing?" When I admitted that I did, she asked for an immediate appointment. She sounded young on the phone, younger than she was, and being a sucker for kids in trouble, I told her to come right over.

I wasn't quite prepared for April Delavan, though. She wore an olive drab army-surplus fatigue jacket, a swirling print peas-ant skirt, and a tank top that was really just a sleeveless under-shirt worn over not much, or for the seventeen small dangling pewter earrings she wore in her left ear, three in the lobe and fourteen along the top of the ear hanging from holes punched in the cartilage. Her hands—small and delicate with long, tapered fingers—were work-roughened, and the unpolished, not-quite-clean fingernails were bitten down almost to the quick. Her feet were encased in gray sweat socks and brown loafers. Nothing matched.

There had been a brief period in the spring of 1993 when the style mavens tried to foist the "grunge" look on American women, but I didn't assume April's getup was on the cutting edge of fashion—I think she just dressed that way because she was too lazy to do otherwise.

But then, when someone is that beautiful, they can wrap themselves in the help-wanted section of the *Plain Dealer* and people are still going to stumble all over themselves just trying to catch a glimpse of them. April Delavan possessed the kind of beauty that could alter world history.

And it was the month of April, the day after All Fools' Day—fitting, somehow. We had suffered through one of our longer winters, and March had been gray and rainy. But toward the end of the month the weather turned clement; the sun had come out of its long winter hibernation to bless us with its benevolent and warming rays, and Clevelanders were squinting like moles breaking the surface and seeing sunlight for the first time since early October. Cleveland is nicknamed "the Forest City," which not many people know, and as if living up to the sobriquet, all her trees were starting to awaken and bud, giving at least the illusion that rebirth was right around the corner.

April Delavan called me just after nine o'clock on a Tuesday morning and showed up a few minutes before ten. I'd made a fresh pot of coffee, and when she arrived I poured us each a large mug and settled in behind my desk to watch her dump four packets of sugar into hers. Morning sunshine streamed through the window, turning dust motes into dancing fairy trails and picking up all the golden highlights in April's hair. I hoped it wasn't picking up all the bare spots in mine; I share the curse of many Slovenian men and fight a never-ending battle with thinning hair, although my problem stabilized about the time I turned forty and is now in a holding pattern. I never bother trying to comb my hair artfully over my scalp, since that never fools anybody, but looking at April I was suddenly aware of the march of time and the equally relentless retreat of my hairline.

I wasn't proud that the presence of an impossibly beautiful eighteen-year-old in my office was making me self-conscious about my thinning hair, but there it was. I'm normally not a vain person, but I'm sure that April made lots of men think and behave in peculiar ways.

"Before we start," I said, "You should know that I get fifty dollars an hour or three hundred per day, plus expenses."

She held her mug in both hands while she slurped her coffee like a little kid drinking milk, compounding the effect by smacking and licking her lips after each gulp. "I've got money," she said. "Don't worry about that."

There was a flat, almost dead quality to her voice, as though she were parroting words in a foreign language, words she had learned phonetically but whose meaning she didn't know. I peered closely at her eyes again to make sure she wasn't on something, because I have a strict policy against getting involved with druggies, even beautiful ones with seventeen earrings.

I uncapped a felt pen and pulled a yellow pad toward me, writing April Delavan's name on the top line. "Okay. Tell me how I can help you."

"I haven't seen my boyfriend for two weeks," she said, looking around the room, out the window, at the ceiling, almost everywhere except at me. "He just dropped out of sight, and I'm getting worried about him."

"Who's your boyfriend?"

"His name's Jeff Feldman."

"Where does he live?"

She gave me an address on Euclid Heights Boulevard, west of Coventry, a stretch of street in Cleveland Heights lined with old stone apartment buildings, atmospheric and moody as hell. The kind of buildings that have names like the Saxony Arms etched in stone over their entryways.

"You live there too?"

"Sometimes," she said, her eyes focused on a galaxy far away.

"When's the last time you saw him?"

She had to think about it. "Two weeks ago Friday."

I wrote down *2 1/2 wks* and then underlined it twice and put three question marks after it. Had it been my lover, I wouldn't have waited two weeks and four days to get worried, but then that's just me. "Where was this, April?"

"What?"

Impatiently I tapped the point of the pen on the pad, leaving a Seurat-like pattern of dots—An Afternoon on the Grande Jatte in Cleveland Heights. The young woman and I were obviously operating in different time zones. "Where you last saw him."

"At Arabica," she said. "We were having a coffee and then he left, and that was it."

There are several Arabica coffeehouses in town, serving fancy coffee brews and health-conscious pastries. The one in Coventry, which I assumed she meant, caters to a mix of elderly bearded intellectuals, baby boomers from the surrounding neighborhood, young professionals in stylish jogging outfits, and the postteen counterculture who favor Mohawk hairdos, blue hair dye, and jewelry in their noses. The Coventry Arabica is known as Ara-freak-a, whereas the one in more fashionable and upscale Shaker Square that draws the wealthy young married crowd, the rich kids from Shaker Heights High, and the hip blacks from nearby Buckeye Road is locally nicknamed Arachic-a.

April Delavan seemed to me to have a claim on both of them. She dressed and acted the part of the Coventry street rat, but there was something aristocratic about her, a nobility of bearing that hinted of a background closer to that of the Shaker Square crowd. There was nothing of the streets in the way she formed her words, and a lot of the Hawken School. She took a crumpled pack of generic cigarettes from the pocket of her field jacket and lit one, not inhaling but blowing the smoke out of the side of her mouth in a fierce jet, once again looking like a little girl trying to act grown-up.

"Something must've happened to him," April said. "Otherwise he would have called."

"Why would something have happened to him?"

"Because he's just the kind of asshole that gets people mad

enough at him to do something about it." The vulgarity was simply offered, like something on a tray of canapés, and was even more unsettling emanating from that angel's face.

"Has he been to his job? What does he do?"

She waved a vague hand in the air. "He's got a loft in the East Thirties just off Superior. He's a potter."

I hesitated, felt pen hovering.

"A ceramic artist," she explained. "He makes clay pots and sculptures. And I'm trying to be a painter—so that kind of explains how we first got together."

I put down the pen. "April," I said as gently as I could, "are you sure he just didn't take off? Kids do that sometimes."

She laughed, although the twist of her mouth made it more sardonic than amused, and the silvery earrings tinkled like Chinese wind chimes. "He's not a kid. He's forty-two. I think. Or -three."

Older than I am. Not by much, but older, and running around with a toddler who had not yet stopped biting her nails.

"Still," I said, trying to suppress my judgmental side, "artists get moody sometimes. You mean he walked out of Arabica that Friday and hasn't called you since?"

Maybe he'd grown tired of playing in the sandbox with children, or maybe his feelings for April were more shallow than hers for him. I wanted to make some sense out of it before I had her sign a contract, took her money, and committed myself.

"I mean he hasn't called, hasn't even been around." She sounded irritated, offended. "Not at all. Not to the apartment, not to his studio, not to any of his friends'. Nobody's seen or heard from him. He just vanished." She took another puff on the cigarette and blew smoke in my direction. "Don't patronize me, okay? I'm a kid, but I'm not stupid."

"Sorry." I waved the poisonous fumes away. I smoke myself, so I don't feel I can tell others they can't—we Americans spend too much time minding other people's business anyway. But I can think of more felicitous hobbies than having to eat the exhaust from April Delavan's plain-wrap cigarettes. It smelled like someone smoking kohlrabi in the stall of a Greyhound terminal men's room.

"I don't have much to go on, April," I said. "Can you give me the names of some people to contact? People who know him, who might have seen him."

"He shares a loft and a kiln with two other potters—they haven't seen him either," she said smugly. "I checked."

"What about his family?"

She shrugged. "I think his parents live in New York."

"New York City?"

"I don't know," she said. "Look, we never got into long discussions about families and stuff. We didn't talk very much at all, tell you the truth. We just . . . hung out."

"But you live with him?"

"Some of the time." She gulped down the rest of her coffee, again holding the mug with both hands, the cigarette between her second and third fingers almost singeing her hair when she lifted the mug to her face. Cohabiting with someone she knew virtually nothing about didn't seem to disturb her.

"And what about the rest of the time?" I said.

She looked directly at me, those bluer-than-blue eyes as steady as a laser beam. "I live with my parents. In Gates Mills." She waited for me to process the information and then she blinked, like a huge frog waiting for a fly to get within tongue-flicking range.

Gates Mills in the Chagrin River Valley is one of the prettiest towns in Ohio—or anywhere else, for that matter. The houses are painted white and set on rolling, heavily wooded parcels of land that are, by law, a minimum of three acres. The river cuts through the middle of it, and up on the hill on the other side of Mayfield Road is a fairly new tract of homes selling for upwards of two hundred thousand bucks each that the old-liners in the valley witheringly refer to as "the Projects." Zoned for horses, Gates Mills is one of the places the polo-and-fox-hunting set hang their hats. Pretty high-rent district for a kid from Coventry.

"I'd like to come by the apartment later this morning, April," I said.

"What for?"

"To look around. You never know what you're going to find."
She didn't seem interested one way or the other. "Whatever," she
said, making it two words.

"Do you have a photograph of Jeff?"

She screwed up her mouth as though the very idea was preposterous. Pictures in the wallet were definitely for the picket-fence-
and-pressure-cooker crowd. I don't have any in mine either, if
you don't count the publicity photo of Maureen O'Hara that came
with the wallet, which tells you how many years ago I bought it.
I've never had the heart to remove it.

"How will I know him if I find him, then?"

She cocked her head to one side, prettily. Archly, as a matter of
fact, self-awareness flowing from her like liquid sunshine. April
Delavan might be a New Ager, living among the rebels and cast-
aways talking about karma and vibes and searching for themselves and the meaning of life in the dregs of fancy coffee in a
cardboard cup on the sun-dappled sidewalk in front of the Centrum Theatre near Coventry, but she knew damn well how good-
looking she was and used it every chance she got.

"Let's see, now." She pretended to think hard. Then, brighten-
ing, "You have a pencil and a piece of paper?"

I got a sheet of white typing paper out of the bottom drawer
and took a pencil from a plastic Cleveland Indians mug bear-
ing the likeness of the Tribe's politically incorrect mascot, Chief
Wahoo.

"What are you going to do?" I asked, pushing the stuff across
the desk at her. "Draw me a picture of him?"

She picked up the pencil and raised a sardonic eyebrow at me.
"What was your first clue?"

It took her about five minutes or so to complete her work, and
I busied myself sneaking a glance at the sports page of the *Plain
Dealer*. Baseball season was just around the corner, and already
the Indians' replacement players were struggling through another spring training in Florida. Losing in spring training doesn't
mean a damn thing, we tell ourselves every season. Especially in
a strike year.

When she finished the sketch she handed it over to me with a flourish that might have been born of pride. I guess I looked impressed, because she was smiling when I glanced back up at her.

"This is very good, April."

"What'd you expect?" she said.

Whatever I expected, it wasn't such a detailed piece of work. She had drawn a dark, curly-haired Semitic-looking man with a graying beard and aviator glasses. The hair had receded at each temple, the brows were shaggy and uneven, the chin weak even beneath the beard, the nose prominent but straight. A mean smile drew up one side of the mouth. It was the eyes that got me, though. Behind the glasses they were hard and unloving. Look at them one way and you'd see scheming and calculation, another way and they showed fear. With the set of his jaw and the supercilious arch of the heavy brows, they could also be classified as cruel eyes.

The drawing was remarkably skillful, especially done from memory, and so quickly. But it was also sketched with unforgiving anger, mocking cynicism, almost—as in the deep creases beside the nose and the sag of jowls beneath the jawline—vengefully. Every pouch and wrinkle of a dissipated middle-aged man had been penciled in.

"I didn't get it quite right," she said. "He's not that good-looking. He thinks he's pretty hot shit, but he's not much, when you get right down to it. In his dreams he wishes he looked like that." She lit a new cigarette from the glowing end of the old one and stubbed out the butt in my ashtray. She still hadn't inhaled any of it, and from the smell of it I believe it was a wise decision. "He's about five nine," she said, "but he walks around like he's six four."

I held the sketch by its edges so as not to smudge it; I'd get it photocopied later in the morning. "You don't sound like you like him very much."

She stopped to consider that for a while, staring up at the molding around the ceiling and blowing smoke at it. Then she stuck the cigarette between her lips; it wobbled comically as she spoke. "I guess I don't, when you come right down to it."

I sat back in my chair, studying her. She looked like a pouting, grouchy three-year-old with a cigarette hanging out of her mouth, one eyebrow raised in a kind of quizzical disdain.

"Then why do you care if I find him?"

She turned those amazing eyes on me, and in spite of myself I felt something flutter inside me somewhere between the heart and the groin. Instant dirty old man.

"Because," she said coolly, "he owes me eighteen thousand dollars."

CHAPTER TWO

He needed it.

That's why she gave it to him. He said he had one of his big-bucks deals brewing—he'd told her it was a sure thing—but he needed the eighteen large as seed money. He promised he'd make it back twenty times over. Maybe I'm better at math than April, but a quick mental calculation in my head told me that was in the vicinity of three hundred sixty thousand dollars. So little April, whose only knowledge of money was that it was always there for her whenever she wanted it, simply dipped into Grandma's trust fund and handed it over to him. In cash. She explained to me that she didn't have a checking account and had no idea how to get one.

She hadn't asked him why he needed it. Jeff Feldman apparently had a big deal brewing several times a month, and though none of them ever came to fruition, he touted each one to her as "the big one," the score that would put him on easy street.

There must be a million guys like Feldman—in the arts, in business, in every other field as well, including those slightly shady or even downright illegal. Always dreaming about the megabucks without ever stopping to figure out that most people who have money either earned it or managed to get themselves born with it. And it never ceases to amaze me how the hustlers and dreamers and risk takers and users, who appear pretty transparent to most people, always manage to attract beautiful and slightly vacant young women like April Delavan.

But in one of her more lucid moments April figured he'd taken her to bed until he got tired of her, then ripped her off for eighteen grand and disappeared into the sunset. And she was mad enough to hire me to find him and get her money back. Most of my business is industrial security, but it's a pretty dependable pattern that when I do get what I call a domestic case, the bottom line is almost always revenge.

After April left my office, the smell of patchouli and cheap tobacco lingered, a deadly combination that was making my sinuses ache. I gave the room a strong squirt of Lysol country fresh, opened the bay window that looks out across Fairmount at Russo's Stop-N-Shop market and the Mad Greek Restaurant, and took a whiff of the cool spring air. Then I sat down at my desk to review what I had.

She'd given me the sketch of Jeff Feldman—she'd even signed it April at the bottom, with a big circle above the *I* in lieu of a dot—along with a description, and a short list of his known hangouts. Besides Arabica, they included the Lonesome Dove Cafe on Mayfield and Lee, where I sometimes had breakfast if my work headed me in that direction, the Bop Stop, a mainstream jazz club just east of downtown, and Jerman's Cafe, an old-time saloon and current arts hangout on St. Clair.

April had also supplied the names of Feldman's closest associates—the two ceramic artists with whom he shared a studio loft and kiln on East Thirty-sixth Street, and an ex-girlfriend who made jewelry in a converted schoolhouse in the old Slovenian neighborhood where I grew up. She had then signed my standard service contract. And she'd left me a fifteen-hundred-dollar retainer.

In cash.

Not a lot to go on, I thought, as I made out a bank deposit slip. I usually use the ATM for most of my banking, but with a lump of currency this size—two Franklins and the rest in twenties, all of which she had stuffed into the pockets of her fatigue jacket like wads of Kleenex—I was afraid I'd jam the machine, so I parked at the bank and stood in line to hand it over directly to a living breathing human being. Who counted it briskly and gave me a receipt without looking very impressed.

I wondered why a Coventry kid, even one from a rich family, like April Delavan, was running around loose with that much money in her pocket. Surely she knew there are predators on the street who'd kill you for one percent of that.

Someone might have decided to do just that to Jeff Feldman while he was carrying her eighteen grand, in which case it was as gone as gone could be, disappeared into the mist like Brigadoon. You'd think he was old enough to be more careful. But if he'd managed to evade the raptors, where was he? Street crime is most often random, and the smash-and-grabbers don't usually make advance plans for disposing of the evidence—or the corpse.

I went downstairs to my car, got in, and drove up Euclid Heights Boulevard to the apartment where he and April had shared very small pieces of their lives.

It was one of a series of dark brick buildings west of the newly renovated Centrum Theatre. As I crossed the tree lawn to the sidewalk I noticed someone had chalked the letters OYOYOY on the cement. Sorrowful Jewish graffiti? In this particular neighborhood, perhaps. Most of the Jewish population of Greater Cleveland lives in the eastern suburbs of Cleveland Heights, Shaker Heights, University Heights, and Beachwood. Feldman was usually a Jewish name, but one can never be sure.

From an open window somewhere the sound of a tinny rehearsal piano and a robust baritone voice singing "There's a Boat That's Leaving Soon for New York" floated out over the flowering dogwood trees on the median strip. Coventry is a magnet for young creative types in every field of artistic endeavor. By day they work their nine-to-five jobs, if they are lucky enough to have them, and in the evening they sit around Arabica and drink coffee and spin dreams of sheer gossamer.

Feldman's apartment was on the second floor. I rang and was buzzed in, and found April waiting for me at the top of the stairs.

She'd gotten rid of the fatigue jacket—I'd see it in a few moments crumpled up on the floor in a dusty corner—and was now bare-foot, but otherwise she looked the same as she had in my office an hour before. She led me into the apartment, which held absolutely no surprises at all.

A boom box had been set on the hardwood floor and was cranked up loud enough to make the windows rattle. The parlor furniture was old and worn, although once it had been of good quality. The style was eclectic, as in a-free-couch-is-a-free-couch, and some of the pieces dated back to the fifties and sixties, including a two-tiered coffee table roughly in the shape of a boomerang. The plaster moldings around the ceiling were sculpted to look like grapevines. A big archway between the living room and the bedroom did nothing to conceal the queen-size mattress and box spring on the floor. The mattress was covered with faded blue and white striped sheets in an unsightly tangle and a sorry-looking army blanket.

Posters took up most of the wall space. One of them, a photographic close-up of a delicate piece of ancient Japanese pottery that I'd seen before somewhere, was mounted between two flat sheets of clear hard plastic and hung on an actual picture hook. The others, inexpensive art reproductions or photographs of Grecian urns and English porcelain, were either matted in cardboard or simply Scotch-taped up. They seemed not to reflect April's tastes very much, but maybe I was simply out of touch, and today's teenage girl thinks pictures of pots are totally bitchen.

Strewn all over the apartment were dirty foam containers that would survive in landfills for a hundred years, the residue of fast-food dinners consumed long since. There was a half-eaten plate of cheese and crackers on the coffee table. The place looked like a bed-and-breakfast for cockroaches.

A bookcase fashioned from decorative cinder blocks and raw plywood planks stood against one wall. On the top shelf was a sprinkling of the classics, Melville and Twain and *The Upanishads*, as well as several works by Philip Roth, Saul Bellow, Isaac Bashevis Singer, and a tattered copy of *The Catcher in the Rye*. The second shelf, which was several inches higher to accommodate large-format books, held volumes with titles like *The New Potter's Companion*.

On nearly every flat surface, including the floor, there were ceramic pots, bowls, mugs, and various other creations, many of them done with a rough sand-colored glaze, a few painted with blue and white quasi-Indian symbols. A couple of the smaller pieces had been used as ashtrays, and the now familiar smell of patchouli mixed with toasting kohlrabi fouled the already close atmosphere of the apartment.

"Did Jeff make all these?" I asked.

April nodded. She didn't waste a lot of words.

But I couldn't see a single sketch or drawing that might have been April's work. In fact there was little visible evidence in the apartment that she'd spent any time there at all. On a table near the door was a pile of unopened mail, all addressed to Feldman. Bills, personal letters, a package of discount coupons from Carol Wright, all neatly stacked. Apparently April had not even been curious enough to open it.

I went through the archway into the bedroom, stepping over a pair of jeans that had been shucked off and left on the floor—I guessed they belonged to her because white lacy underpants were still in them. Next to the bed was what had once been a coffee table; on it were a drugstore plastic alarm clock, a box of tissues, and another ceramic ashtray that probably hadn't been emptied since the Indians last won a World Series. On top of a dresser across the room was a TV set with a rabbit-ear antenna old enough to be in the Museum of Broadcasting. The TV was tuned to a talk show on which a group of women with Bronx accents were complaining about men who take their phone numbers in singles bars and then never call.

There was one closet in the room; a full-length mirror from which some of the silvering had faded was affixed to the door. The building was ancient, built in simpler days, when people had one dress-up outfit, one set of working togs, and one overcoat and kept whatever else they wore in a big steamer trunk or cedar chest. Closet space is at a premium in an old neighborhood like Cleveland Heights.

I opened the closet door to a smell part old sweat and part old dust, as though the clothes inside had been worn and then hung back up without cleaning or laundering. On a shelf that ran along the top of the closet were a variety of men's hats in a neat row, some caps with the logos of local sports team, one wide-brimmed job that must have come from a 1945 French gangster movie starring Jean Cabin, a crumpled canvas fishing hat I'd bet had never been within five miles of a trout stream, and a pricey Stetson for an urban cowboy riding the Cleveland range.

On the floor, along with enough dust bunnies to start a rabbit farm, were a pair of desert boots with reinforced toes, some Birkenstock sandals, rubber flip-flops, Puma cross-trainers, and a pair of black wing tips covered with a thin powdery film of neglect.

So many garments were hanging from the metal pipe in the closet that it probably would have buckled with the addition of one more pair of pants. Except for a few print dresses like your grandmother used to wear pushed off to one side, hung crookedly on the hangers, with one shoulder higher than the other, the clothes were men's, and casual.

Not a good sign. People who disappear voluntarily don't generally leave all their clothes in the closet, their pictures on the wall, and all their own ceramic art all over the apartment. But I didn't mention that to April.

"These are Jeff's?" I said, indicating the male clothing. She nodded again—silently, solemnly. Her pupils were larger than when she'd been in my office, and I figured she'd taken something to make her feel better in anticipation of my arrival—or more likely just for the hell of it.

I felt some of the jacket pockets to see if he'd left anything in them, but except for a few matchbooks, a disposable cigarette lighter, and thirty-eight cents in the pocket of a khaki raincoat, no sale.

"Did he have an address book or Rolodex, someplace he kept important numbers?" I asked, closing the closet door.

She shook her head.

"Everybody has an address book, April."

She shrugged her shoulders as if it wasn't her responsibility. "Maybe at the studio," she said.

I don't often find myself on Superior Avenue in the East Thirties. It's an old industrial section, factories and warehouses, some of which have been abandoned years before, squat, dark buildings like a series of fortresses protecting downtown Cleveland but more realistically keeping the downtowners from the suburbs. If you like turn-of-the-century architecture the way I do, the neighborhood is a visual treat. Otherwise you'd probably consider it ugly. Industrial blight is in the eye of the beholder.

Jeff Feldman and others like him had obviously beheld the old behemoths that now housed their studios with a kindly eye. Strapped for cash like artists since the beginning of time, they had converted the interiors of the buildings to creative work space without spending any money at all on exterior cosmetics. They looked pretty much the way they had for a hundred years or more, solid and functional. But like the steel mills that define the banks of the Cuyahoga River, the semideserted factories near downtown Cleveland have a terrible beauty. They stand for an era that has practically faded from consciousness, the days when the industrial Northeast and Midwest set the pulse of America, and her immigrant sons and daughters made her sing.

Feldman's building, the rearmost of a complex occupied by several small packing and industrial firms, had no cornerstone to date it, but I was sure that if there had been one, the first two digits would have been 18. It looked like a prison at first glance, huge dark stones blackened by time and weather forming a foreshortened C. The courtyard in the middle was almost half a block square. I was later to find out that the building's first incarnation was as a barbed wire factory. Begrimed industrial windows turned blind eyes in all directions.

I drove to the back as April had instructed, rumbling and jostling over broken and uneven asphalt and hanging onto the wheel like a Brahma bull rider. My car had been in an accident the previous fall, its door sheared off by a passing truck, and the frame hasn't been the same since.

I wheeled into a sort of covered parking bay under one wing of the building. The ground there was unpaved, a distinct improvement over the potholes and fissures of the asphalt in the courtyard, and moisture had leached through the cement overhead, forming the kind of stalactites usually found on the roofs of caves. Rubble from what looked like a dismantled building lay in the shadows along one wall, which after a second glance proved to be unconnected to the building proper, part of some other structure that went up about twenty-five feet. Water dripped down the side leaving brownish streaks, like the tears of a giant running through rusty mascara.

I parked in one of the vacant spaces. Under the leaky overhang there was hardly any light at all; a manmade cave a stone's throw from downtown. I checked the names in my notebook and then headed for the only doorway I could see, a big metal one with a small, filth-covered window at eye level.

There was a chill inside the building that went right through to the bone. I found myself looking at a flight of poorly lit concrete steps against one wall, opposite a large elevator. The elevator, obviously used for heavy freight during the age of the dinosaurs, was a three-sided steel mesh cage; floor-to-ceiling wooden gates met to form the fourth side. On its ceiling a forty-watt bulb burned merrily. It was big enough to accommodate a Honda Accord. On the whole it seemed safer than the stairway—at least the lighting was better, which gave some comfort—so I climbed in, closing the gate behind me.

It took me a minute to figure out how to work the damn thing. There were no buttons or floor indicators, just a lever mounted on a swinging plate. There were two arrows, one pointing up and one down, and even a techno-boob like me could puzzle that one out. I spent some time searching for the little catch under the handle that released the mechanism.

I finally found it and pushed the lever in the direction of the up arrow. The car lurched a few feet upward and then stopped, and I had a nervous moment until, with a groan of machinery from overhead, it started again. It kept going up in a herky-jerky fashion as long as I left my hand on the operating lever, grinding gears singing a protest in an ear-shattering soprano. I wondered what happened to the ancient and honorable profession of elevator operator. Obsolete now, with the advent of elevators that are fully automated, unlike fossils like this one. I made a mental note to take the stairs on my way out.

In front of my face the view turned to aged brick as the car rose, the only light that of the overhead bulb, and I had a momentary flash of claustrophobia, remembering Fortunato walled up alive in Poe's "The Cask of Amontillado." Then the cage and I emerged into startling, dazzling sunlight and the elevator bumped to a halt.

I opened the gate and stepped out onto a rooftop, one very tall story above street level. The tarred surface was tacky beneath my feet, sucking at my shoes, but brittle at the same time from a long hard winter. Over on one corner of the roof was what was left of a pigeon, not much more than sad feathers stirring in the gentle breeze.

From here I could see what the rust-stained concrete wall downstairs supported. It was a railroad spur line; a trestle from the Conrail tracks about a block to the north ran right up to the building. From the amount of trash and other detritus on the tracks, I reasoned it hadn't been used in decades.

"You must have a death wish." The voice was a deep, rumbly baritone behind me, and when I turned around the person I saw standing in the doorway leading to the loft didn't fit it. He was a potbellied five foot six and balding, with a scraggly gray beard that made him look as if he spent his spare time hiding under bridges to frighten the Billy Goats Gruff. He had what I think of as a "pinchface"; it looked as if someone took a large handful of his features and squeezed, and they had remained that way, all a trifle too small and too close together. He wore a pair of dusty jeans and a white Dacron shirt with the sleeves rolled up.

"Anybody uses that old elevator takes his life in his hands," he said. "Half the time when you open the door the elevator isn't there and you find yourself staring down into the basement. You looking for somebody?"

I consulted the scrap of paper in my hand. "I'm looking for either Tydings Belk or Alys Larkin," I said.

"Why?"

Strange question, I thought. "Because they share this space with Jeff Feldman."

Either the short guttural sound he made was a laugh or else he was clearing his throat. "What I'd have to say about Jeff Feldman is all four-letter words. I'm Belk. Alys Larkin isn't here right now." His single eyebrow, which went the width of his forehead with no discernible break and swooped upward at each end like the wings of a crow, lowered over his eyes. "Neither is Feldman." He blocked the doorway, his arms crossed over his barrel chest, glowering at me like the mean old man in the haunted house down the street. "Most visitors use the stairs."

"I guess I'm into living dangerously," I said. "My name's Milan Jacovich." I moved across the rooftop toward him and handed him one of my business cards. He gave it a quick glance and pocketed it.

"Private investigations?" Okay, so he read fast. "This is a joke, right?" he said, looking around for the hidden camera. "Where's Allen Funt?"

"I'm afraid it's no joke. Can we talk for a few minutes?"

"I don't want to buy anything, all right?"

"I'm not a salesman, I'm a—"

"Private eye," he finished for me. He screwed up his face, giving him the pugnacious look of Charles Laughton as Captain Bligh. "How baroque of you."

I was close enough that he had to crane his neck to look up at me. I was a defensive lineman at Kent State, and I'm big enough that I don't get intimidated easy. My size sometimes helps me out because people figure it's easier to cooperate with me than to get me angry. Then there are other times when being big causes problems—when a certain kind of guy takes it as a challenge. I could see Belk calculating in his head, figuring that because of the vast differences in our size he could get away with just about anything without fear of retaliation.

"Can we go inside and talk?" I said.

"Why can't we talk right here?"

I glanced over at the feathery corpse. "Because dead pigeons make me creepy."

He almost smiled but opted not to. Instead he turned on his heel and walked into the building. I hadn't been invited, but I followed him anyway.

The hallway I found myself in was a wide, high one. Stacks of broken lumber, its jagged ends sticking out at crazy angles, spilled over from either side. There were quite a few flattened cardboard cartons, some four feet square, and virtually endless rows of racks I was sure were used for drying and cooling newly made pottery. A fine white dust covered everything, including the tall industrial windows that almost entirely made up one wall. The sunlight had to battle through the grime to get in.

In the middle of the corridor stood a homemade-looking kiln about ten feet high, constructed of raw yellow flameproof bricks. Asbestos material was stuffed into the cracks between the bricks, and there was an opening in the front just large enough to allow a medium-size man to walk inside. On the floor beside the opening—I couldn't really think of it as a door, although leaning against the side of it was a hinged asbestos panel—was a blowtorch, probably used to light the damn thing. You wouldn't want to use a match. A large stack of the yellow bricks stood off to one side. Sitting on the ledge just over the entrance to the kiln was a ceramic doll about eight inches high resembling a Hopi Indian fetish. It had round holes for mouth and eyes, which gave it a quizzical expression.

Through a doorway whose double doors were gone, there was a huge loft that must have once been used for manufacturing, with fourteen-foot ceilings and windows. It was divided into three smaller spaces, each big enough for a family of five to live in comfortably and each containing a potter's wheel, a large sink, various scarred tables, more racks and shelves, and more clay pots, vases, trays, and whatnots than I'd seen in a lifetime.

It was fairly easy to spot which of the three work spaces had been Jeff Feldman's. The ceramics there, on the right side of the huge room, were similar in style and color to the ones I'd seen in his apartment. The ones in the center were larger and more abstract, and those on the left more elegant and functional—serving dishes, salad-size bowls and the like.

Tydings Belk turned around to face me again, once more crossing his arms across his chest like the guardian of a seraglio, a role for which he was at least eight inches too short. But the body language was defensive. "I'm pressed for time," he said, "so if you could expedite this, we'll get along better."

Getting along with him was my dream. "Fine. I'm trying to find Jeff Feldman."

He scratched his beard, and a few flakes of facial dandruff drifted down onto his shirtfront. "If you're a private detective that means someone's paying you to do it, right?" He screwed up his mouth and shook his head in disbelief. "I can't imagine why anyone would spend good money to find that sack of shit."

I took note of his hostility and then ignored it. "As you probably know, he's been gone for more than two weeks."

"My heart aches with missing him," he said dryly.

"You haven't seen or heard from him either?"

"No," he said. "But I've been on vacation for three weeks. Yesterday was my first day back." His tone sharpened. "And I'm way behind on my orders, hint, hint."

"Any idea where he might be?"

"Who cares? Feeding his nose, probably. Or between the thighs of some barely pubescent nymph. Or more likely making one of his endless deals."

"Deals? What kind of deals?"

"How many kinds are there?" he said. "Jeff is always looking to make a quick score. To him, it beats working."

"Score? You mean drugs?"

"I don't know that for sure," he said. "I do know he uses—I've seen him do it right here. He probably doesn't have any nasal passages left. As for selling the stuff himself, I wouldn't put it past him. Anything that'll put a fast buck in his pocket. Consultant deals, finder's fees, any kind of scam you can think of. Mostly related to art in some way, of course, because that's what he knows best."

"You know of any deal he was working on before he disappeared?"

"He didn't share confidences with me." Belk almost sniffed, the unmistakable sound a person makes when their feelings are hurt and they'd rather die than admit it. "He wouldn't even share materials here in the studio. Not a sharing kind of guy, unless there was something in it for him. He'd sell his mother to Arab slavers if it came to that."

"You don't like him very much."

"Is that a crime?"

"Only if you did something about it."

"I wouldn't give him the satisfaction," he scoffed. He was a supercilious, arrogant, patronizing little bastard. "What would I do about it? I split the expenses of this loft with him, him and Alys Larkin. It's economically feasible. At least, it always has been. But as you can see"—he swept a hand toward the workroom like an old-time Texas cattle baron indicating the scope of his land from horizon to horizon—"it's plenty big enough that we don't even have to talk."

"What do you mean, at least it always has been economically feasible? Isn't it anymore?"

"It would help if Jeff paid his third of the rent," Belk said. "We've been carrying him for the past three months."

"Would it be possible for me to look around a little?"

"For what?"

"I won't know until I find it," I said.

He stood as tall as he could. "Uh-uh. Not when he's not here."

"I'm not going to steal a pot or anything."

"That's not the point. I don't like Jeff, and if he ever shows up I'll squeeze the back rent out of him and then boot his ass. But he has a right to privacy like anyone else."

"Maybe there's something here that'll help me find him—in which case you get your money faster."

He shook his head. "Nope. You're wasting your time."

"It's my time," I observed.

"It's mine too—and you've taken up enough of it. So I'll say goodbye, Mr. Jacovich." He mispronounced it, using the hard *J*, like in Jack.

"It's Jacovich," I told him, saying it the right way. "Pretend the *J* is a *Y*."

"Pretend I'm somebody who gives a shit," he said.

CHAPTER THREE

The Coventry area of Cleveland Heights has as colorful a history as any neighborhood in town. During the sixties it was the Cleveland equivalent of San Francisco's Haight-Ashbury or New York's East Village, home of the rebellious youth of the counterculture. When hippies went out of style, the biker gangs claimed the turf as their own for a while, and on Coventry Avenue the evening air was shattered by the roar of Harley hogs.

Now, in the nineties, the kids have taken over again, and many of them look like they were frozen in time back in 1968, even though none of them were alive back then. The rest have Mohawk hairdos in bright pink or green, and some sport earrings in their noses or cheeks or other even more painful places you wouldn't expect to find earrings.

And they all flaunt sports team jackets or sweatshirts. Most of the Coventry kids wear the gear of local teams, the Browns or the Cavs or the Indians, but many others show eclectic tastes. The Dallas Cowboys are well represented, especially since the Browns cut quarterback Bernie Kosar in midseason in 1993 and he signed with Dallas and earned a Super Bowl ring. The other popular teams seem to be the Chicago Bulls, with or without Michael, the Chicago White Sox, and the Los Angeles Raiders. I doubt if many of these kids are fans of the teams whose colors they wear; the jackets are either much more cool than those worn by our home-town athletes, or the colors are also those of local gangs.

In any case, Arabica looked as if an NFL locker room had ex-ploded.

At nine o'clock on a Tuesday evening there were lots of people having coffee. Some of them had just come from the Centrum Theatre next door—three screens and the city's best popcorn stand—and some were waiting for the next show to begin, but most appeared to be there just to be there. And to be seen.

Arabica's walls are unfinished brick from which the noise bounces, and there was a good bit of it, the friendly, human sound of intense conversation. It's the kind of place people come to talk, to connect, to exchange ideas, and to meet people like themselves. You hear a lot lately about the resurgence of the coffeehouse in the nineties, but Arabica has been around a long while, long be-fore it became newly trendy. It's kind of a Cleveland tradition.

I go there sometimes, usually for a breakfast coffee. I could count on the fingers of one hand the times I've been in there at night, and I've been living in Cleveland Heights for eight years. So I had no way of knowing who the nighttime regulars were, the people who had fixed on the coffeehouse as their home away from home and spent every spare moment there. Except for their choice of drinks, they didn't really seem any different than the blue-collars who hung out at Vuk's Tavern a few blocks from where I'd grown up in the old neighborhood.

The after-dark Arabicans were about twenty years younger than the morning crowd, on average, and I let my eyes roam, resting for a moment or two on each customer, wondering if they might know Jeff Feldman, if they could help me locate him, or for all I knew, if they might be the reason he was missing in the first place.

I was in the coffee line behind two young people who were either artists or trying to look like it. The braless woman—you hardly ever see that anymore since the seventies limped into his-tory—was in her middle twenties. Her face was devoid of makeup and her hair, frizzy and dark and looking like a home permanent gone wrong, was pulled up into two enormous fat ponytails at the sides of her head. Dark half moons of pigment were embedded beneath her fingernails, and she was wearing grandmotherly round spectacles. A five-foot-long wool scarf was knotted around her neck and trailing over one shoulder; she should have been going door to door caroling in the snow in a Dickens novel.

Her companion was somewhat younger than she, and even taller than I am, although I must have had fifty pounds or more on him. He was dressed in paint-spattered overalls and a red T-shirt, which made him look like a gigantic toddler. His face was almost pretty, his complexion very pale, and he wore his dirty-blond hair in a modified Prince Valiant cut; he kept combing it out of his face with the fingers of both hands. He was talking too loudly, to attract as much attention as possible, the way so many young people do, as though what they have to say is of the gravest import and everyone in the world will want to hear it. The conversation seemed to be about gouache, and he used the word in every sentence like a mantra. I don't imagine too many people within earshot were impressed. Even I know that gouache was a technique for painting with watercolors, and the Arabicans all probably knew it too, but the young man seemed hell-bent on making everyone aware that he possessed some sort of insider's knowledge.

I took a table next to them near the window and drank my coffee, which was flavored with hazelnut. I'm one of the world's leading consumers of coffee, but I'm not a big fan of the flavored kind. However, hazelnut seemed to fit the mood of the moment.

Both of them chain-smoked furiously as if they were being paid by the puff. I eavesdropped openly on what the young man was saying so that he couldn't fail to notice my interest. He glanced over at me and smiled. It was an open smile with no hesitation—Arabica is the kind of place where strangers can connect without the bristling suspicion that is the most common symptom of our urban paranoia.

"How's it goin'?" he said, pleased he was getting some of the attention he'd hoped for.

"Hi," I answered, and toasted them with my coffee cup. "You're an artist, huh?"

Suddenly he ducked his head shyly, Henry Fonda as a boy, and his hair made curtains on each side of his face. "I'm trying to be. Actually I'm still in high school. Until June."

I tried to remember back to the Pleistocene Era when I was in high school. Sometimes when you hit forty it seems like your joints are slowly stiffening while the rest of the world is watching MTV, mainlining Clearasil, and waiting for its voice to change. I smiled back at him and the woman with him, who didn't seem quite so friendly. "You study art in school?"

He raised both hands palms upward as though he was weighing meat. "Nah. They don't pay much attention to art in public school. The budget and all that. But when I graduate I'm going to go on to art school." He lowered his voice a little. "If I can talk my parents into it."

I moved my chair closer and sat on it sideways so I could look at both of them. "I'm interested in art."

The woman regarded me through a narrow-eyed squint, whether caused by the smoke from her Marlboro or her growing suspicion that I was a possible chicken hawk, I didn't know. She had a wide, thin mouth like a bear trap.

"Yeah?" He seemed genuinely pleased. "What kind?"

"Ceramic pottery, actually."

Disappointed, his smile dimmed down, but not by much. "Oh," he said. "I'm not into that now. I'm a watercolorist. I'm into gouache." He pronounced the word with pride.

"Actually I'm looking for a potter."

"I know a couple," the kid volunteered.

"No, a particular one. His name's Jeff Feldman."

The woman stiffened as if hit with an electrical charge, and then her shoulders slumped, causing the tail of her red scarf to fall limply into her lap. "Oh, man," she said with a rising inflection.

"You know him?"

"You're kidding, right?" She gave me a Fellini bored-with-it-all look and blew smoke in my face. "Everybody knows Jeff Feldman," she informed me in the low raspy voice of someone who smokes too much. "There's hardly anybody in town he hasn't either borrowed money from or screwed, literally or otherwise." She gulped her coffee like she was knocking back straight rye whiskey. "Feldman stinks the big stink."

I'd hoped to find some of Feldman's friends at Arabica, and this woman hardly qualified. But she might be willing to talk for the very reason that she seemed to hate his guts. "Seen him recently?"

She pondered it for a while, then shook her head. "Now that you mention it, I haven't. Not for a few weeks at least. Funny, I'm mostly not that lucky."

"I haven't seen him either," the kid chimed in. "He usually comes in every two or three days, but he hasn't been around lately."

The woman looked carefully at me. "Why are you so anxious to find Feldman? Bill collector? Or jealous husband?"

"Nothing that exotic," I said, and when I didn't elaborate she nodded her head knowingly, folded her arms across her chest, and sat back in her chair.

I looked around. "Anyone else in here who might know him?"

"I told you," she said, "everybody knows him. It's a pretty close-knit community, Coventry."

"Sure, but any particular friends of his?"

The boy looked around the crowded, smoky room and then pointed at a pretty young woman sitting at a table against the wall by herself reading a hardcover book. "You could talk to Nicole over there. She used to know him real well."

His companion glowered and kicked him under the table and made him jump. He looked guiltily at her and then amended, "But they haven't hung around together for quite a while."

"Nicole, huh?"

"Look," the woman said, pointing a bony finger directly at my heart, "I don't think it's such a good idea going around bothering people about Jeff Feldman. I mean, does she look like she wants company?"

"You never know," I said.

I stood up and nodded a goodbye at them and made my way across the room to where the young woman named Nicole was sitting. Up close I saw she was quite attractive, with a prominent jaw and large brown eyes. Her blonde hair was cut to just below her ears and it looked soft and silky, bouncing prettily when she moved her head, like a model's in a TV commercial for shampoo. She was nearer my age than most of the other patrons in the Coventry Arabica, probably in her early thirties.

"Excuse me," I said. "Are you Nicole?"

She looked up from her book, which I saw was *The Morning After* by Katherine Roiphe, and she frowned a bit as though she was trying to recall whether she'd ever met me before. "Yes, hi," she said pleasantly.

I told her my name and my occupation, which raised an eyebrow. It always does. Most people aren't used to talking to a private investigator—they think we only exist in the movies. I try not to take it personally.

"Can I sit down for a minute?" I said. "I won't take up much of your time at all."

She glanced around with some apprehension. Apparently when she thought I'd just wandered over to make conversation it had been okay; now that she knew I was a PI I'd suddenly become vaguely threatening.

"I'm hoping maybe you can help me." I sat down across from her and put my coffee mug on the table. "I'm looking for a guy named Jeff Feldman," I told her. "I understand you know him."

Something in her eyes darkened, as if a cloud had passed across the face of the sun. "Who said so?"

I pointed across the room at the young watercolorist and his friend.

She sighed, rueful. "Some people just get off on minding other people's business."

I shrugged. "It's what I do for a living."

"I think it's what those two do, too," she said, her disapproval of the pair obvious. "From the soon-to-be-released motion picture, 'Get a Life.'"

"You do know Feldman, then?"

She closed the Roiphe book and put it face down on the table as if she didn't want me to see its title. "You might say that," she said, her tone suddenly brittle. "He lived off me for about four months."

"When was this?"

Her mouth grew thin and hard as if she was planning not to answer, but then she changed her mind. "Year, year and a half ago—no, more like two years. He stayed in my house, rent free, and I bought all the groceries. Then he just split. Without even saying goodbye. For greener pastures, I suppose." She lowered her eyelids slowly. "He left me a note. I was pretty glad to see him go, if you want to know the truth. I was getting as bored with him as I guess he was with me. Even though I'd loaned him some money that he never paid back."

"How much money?"

"If I tell you, will it help you find him?"

"No," I said.

"Then let's just say it was enough that I'm royally pissed off about it and not so much that it left me penniless." Then something dark and secret pulled downward at the corners of her mouth. "What do you want with him? Is he in trouble? Never mind, silly question—of course he is. He's always in trouble. It's a way of life with him."

"What kind of trouble?"

"Money trouble, more often than not. But woman trouble too. And artistic trouble."

"What kind is that?"

"He's really not very good at what he does, and underneath all his arrogance and bullshit, I think he knows it. And it eats him up alive."

"Have you seen him recently?"

The eyes opened wide; unadorned by makeup, they were soft as a fawn's. "Not hardly. Oh, I see him around—this is a pretty small town, when you get right down to it. But I try my best to ignore him when I run into him. Screw me once, shame on you— screw me twice, shame on me."

"He's not winning any popularity contests around here."

"That's because he's the most self-centered person I've ever met. He's the worst kind of user. He's so obnoxious that at first you're deliberately rude just to get him to go away. Then you get the guilts because you were mean, and so to make amends you try to give a little, and you wind up getting taken."

"You wouldn't have any idea where I could find him?"

She looked away and shook her head. "Except for his studio, Jeff doesn't stay in one place very long."

"I've checked out his studio."

"Then I can't help you. Last I heard, he was living with some kid. I think her name is May or June." She attempted another smile, with limited success. "Some month."

"April. I know about her. She doesn't know where he is either. Are you a potter too?"

"Hardly. I'm a doctor."

I laughed, which called forth a dark frown from her. "Sorry," I said quickly. "That took me by surprise."

"Why? You can't figure out what a doctor's doing hanging out at Arabica?"

I hesitated, and she jumped in quickly. "Or you can't imagine one being involved with a creep like Feldman?"

"You're getting warmer," I admitted.

"I'm in neonatology. The tiny babies, the preemies. I keep them alive and healthy until they grow into themselves. But with adults?" She flapped her hands in the air. "I'm just as dumb as everybody else when it comes to relationships—they don't teach that in med school."

"I wish they'd teach it somewhere," I said. I took out one of my business cards and gave it to her. "If you should see him, I'd appreciate it if you could let me know."

She read the card, smiled. "Jacovich." She pronounced it correctly, which pleased me inordinately. "Croatian?"

"Slovenian. You must be a Cleveland native."

"I was born and raised in Bedford Heights. But I work at the Cleveland Clinic, and so I moved up here to minimize the driving time." She pointed out the window vaguely. "I live just down the street, on Kent Road."

"What's your last name, Nicole?"

"Archer," she said, and pantomimed pulling the string on a longbow. "Twang," she sang.

I stood up. "Thanks for your time. I hope I didn't spoil your evening."

"As a matter of fact, you brightened it considerably. I never met a private eye before."

I hear that a lot, and I never know what to say to it. I think people always expect me to pull my roscoe, take a slug of rye from the bottle in my bottom drawer, and crack wise out of the side of my mouth. "I never met a neonatologist before," I countered. "So we're even, Doctor."

"How'd you wind up being a private eye?" she said. "It isn't something a kid grows up dreaming about. Whatever possessed you, anyway?"

I leaned down to her. Her shampoo smelled of citrus. "Lauren Bacall," I whispered in her ear.

CHAPTER FOUR

The next morning I bought a ticket for the Ohio Lottery's eight-million-dollar drawing that evening. I thought of Clint Eastwood as Dirty Harry saying, "You feel lucky, punk?" and had to admit I didn't. But what the hell, shoot a buck.

I had breakfast at one of Jeff Feldman's local hangouts, the Lonesome Dove Cafe, reading the paper and keeping my eye on the door. I couldn't realistically expect Feldman to come walking in and sit down at the next table, but hope springs eternal. I asked the woman at the counter whether she knew him and if he'd been in yet this morning, and she said that, come to think of it, she hadn't seen him for quite a while. So far I was getting nowhere, but at least I was consistent.

After breakfast I found my way down to St. Clair Avenue in the East Seventies, what a lot of Slovenians call "the old neighborhood," even though their grandparents, who came here from Ellis Island to work in the steel mills in the early part of the century, still refer to it as "Chicken Village," from the days when they all had chicken coops in their back yards.

It was familiar territory for me; as a kid I'd roamed these very streets in a hunting pack, looking for some mischief to get into with my high school buddies Marko Meglich and Alex Cerne and Rudy Dolsak and Matt Baznik. It was on these sidewalks that Lila Coso and I had defied the traditional distrust between Serbs and Slovenes and begun courting, finally deciding to share our lives together. After a twelve-year stretch of slicing pieces of each other away until there was little left of either of us, the marriage ended in divorce, leaving two boys, Milan Jr. and Stephen, as survivors and spoils of our marital wars. Time with the boys is still endlessly fought over, even now that Milan Jr. is almost out of school and deluding himself that he's all grown up, and Stephen is going through that agonizing period between childhood and adolescence when he doesn't know exactly who or what he is yet.

Officially I see them every other weekend, although Lila has been known to relent a little when my *Plain Dealer* columnist pal Ed Stahl wangles me midweek summer tickets to Indians games; the reality is that I get less and less of Milan Jr. the older he grows, and when I have Stephen over on Sunday he often brings along a friend, leaving me odd man out.

Lila still lives in the house we'd bought together, sharing it now with a guy we'd both known in high school, Joe Bradac, who'd worshipped Lila from afar and waited until I'd gone before moving in. Give him credit for patience.

But don't get me started on Joe Bradac.

I pulled into the parking lot of the school building, which was no more than fifteen blocks from the home in which I'd grown up just off St. Clair. It dated from the turn of the century, and like so many others of its period it was a heavy, ponderous construction of dark and somewhat imposing brick. It hadn't served as a public school for years and had been slated for the wrecking ball until a neighborhood coalition rescued it and turned it into a unique residence-cum-workspace for artists of all kinds, who pay minimal rent for a place to live and create. Cleveland recycles old buildings instead of tearing them down, and the school was a splendid example of urban renewal and support for local culture at the same time.

Part of the playground had been covered with asphalt for resident parking, and brave landscaping attempts had been made around the rest of the building. Some young saplings, braced and trussed against the lake wind, had survived the winter and stood unsteadily amidst plots of grass and beds of spring flowers. It had rained during the night—not surprising in an Ohio April—and the morning was still misty. Beads of moisture clung to the leaves and sparkled on the grass.

I found the name I was looking for on the menu board by the door, entered the proper code on the keypad bolted to the wall, and was buzzed in. As I walked through the wide tiled hallways my footsteps echoed hollowly on the linoleum. There might even have been the ghostly sounds of exuberant children laughing and shouting as they ran between classes through the corridors of memory, but I didn't listen that hard. The place still looked like a grade school, with low drinking fountains and fluorescent fixtures set into the ceilings. Any moment I expected to hear a bell ring.

Down near the end of the hallway a door was open and a tall woman stood framed in the light, straight blonde hair falling to just below her wide shoulders. Apparently Jeff Feldman had a thing for blonde hair.

"Hi," I called. "Ms. Oakey?"

"Yes, but that sounds so stuffy. Let's make it Valerie, all right? Come on in." She stepped aside, and I walked past her into her studio apartment.

It was a converted classroom, and along one white-painted-over wall there was still a trough for blackboard chalk. The single large room was neatly divided into three parts. The living space contained a two-piece sectional sofa with a vaguely southwestern print, several pillows big enough to sit on, a dinette set, and even an upright Wurlitzer piano with several books of pieces by Czerny, the patron saint of the intermediate piano student, propped on its music rack. Over the piano was an inexpert pastel portrait of Valerie Oakey sitting on a stool, nude from the waist up, a blue throw sort of draped over her lap. I blushed a little, not sure whether I was supposed to look at it or not.

Just off the living room area was a small kitchen, partitioned off by wallboard. An afterthought bathroom had been added against one wall, and directly above it was a sleeping loft accessed by a sturdy wooden ladder. I could see the bed up there was unmade and covered with a rumpled homemade quilt.

At the other end of the huge room was a work area with a

scarred wooden table, drying racks, a sink, and a kiln not much bigger than a king-size microwave oven, atop which perched a little ceramic doll similar to the one I'd seen on the kiln in the old barbed wire factory.

"Thanks for inviting me on such short notice," I said.

She waved a large-boned hand. "It's okay, really. I almost never start working until later in the afternoon. Mornings are for getting myself together and getting my eyes open. Can I get you something to drink? Coffee or tea?"

"No, don't bother."

"It's no trouble—it's instant."

I shook my head. I'd rather stick pins in my eyes than drink instant coffee. It's one of those inventions like pantyhose and AstroTurf that has seriously diminished the quality of our lives.

"Make yourself comfortable then," she said. She indicated the sofa for me, and plopped herself down on one of the floor pillows, amazingly graceful for a woman so gangly and awkward-looking, all sharp knee and elbow angles. Valerie Oakey was not what anyone might call attractive; her nose was too flat and wide, her lower jaw undershot, her blonde hair too lank and straight, with little body to it, and her skin too sallow. Her eyes were nearly slate-colored, and the intelligence and kindness that radiated from them made the rest of her looks unimportant. I figured her to be close to forty.

"You said on the phone you wanted to talk about Jeffrey," she said.

I nodded.

"I don't know how much help I'll be to you. He doesn't check in with me and give me his schedule." She looked embarrassed. "He didn't do that even when he was living here, he just came and went as he pleased. He didn't handle responsibility very well." She spoke as if she was discussing somebody else's ex-lover. "I don't think I've seen him in a month."

"Nobody has. I've been hired to try and find him."

"By whom?"

I smiled to take the sting out of it. "It's kind of unethical to tell you that."

"No problem." She shifted around on the cushions, extending one long leg from under her full skirt. "I imagine it's someone he owes money to."

I started to say something, but she stopped me. "Educated guess—you don't have to tell me," she said airily, waving a hand. She did that a lot, talking with her hands, perhaps because they were her best feature, slim and beautiful, with long, artistic fingers. "So what do you want from me? I'm a friend of Jeff's—as much as anybody can be his friend. But we haven't been together for almost three years."

"I've been told all that," I said. "But I know that you still see a lot of him, and I was hoping you could point me in the direction of someone else who might know where he is."

"I can't think who."

"Anyone he did business with?"

She smiled, covering her mouth with her hand in a gesture that seemed curiously Asian. I think it was to hide her teeth, which were long and unevenly spaced. "Jeff 'does business' with anyone who's willing to give him money."

"Selling his work?"

She hesitated. "That, too, but not often. He's not terribly good, to be honest. But he has art world connections both here and in New York, and sometimes he acts as a broker if someone wants to buy a collection, or even an individual piece, if it's valuable enough. And then he takes a commission."

"A percentage?"

"Sometimes. But usually a flat fee. Enough to keep him alive until the next one. Or the next woman he can hustle out of a few bucks." Said with no rancor or bitterness; there was something very centered about Valerie Oakey.

"You mind a personal question?" I said.

She drew her knees up and hugged them against her chest, modestly wrapping her skirt around her thighs. "If you want to know how much he's into me for, I can't even remember anymore. A few thousand over the years, I'm sure."

"And he never paid you back?"

"Ten bucks here, twenty there. Never enough that I noticed

it." She rocked back and forth slowly. "Jeff's a rat, and makes no bones about it, which is kind of refreshing if you think about it. He uses women and then tosses them away, but he's always pretty up-front, so I went into it with my eyes open. And it's not that he's exactly the world's greatest lover, either; frankly he hardly even makes the effort. But there's an inner drive, a magnetic intensity about him that draws people at first—especially women. I suppose they all think that they'll be the one to finally tame him, which is the ultimate in kidding themselves. Then they're bitter when he leaves them. And leave he does."

"But you're not bitter. You're still his friend."

She stretched her legs out straight in front of her and wiggled her feet, which were encased in thick gray athletic socks and soft leather running shoes. "I guess I'm a sucker at heart. Behind the bravado, Jeff is a charter member of Losers Anonymous, and for all the lousy things he does he's more to be pitied. Not many people feel that way about him. I think I'm the only friend he's got. Isn't that sad?"

Sadder for her than Feldman. "You mentioned that he sometimes acts as a broker for expensive ceramic pieces."

She nodded. "Because of his New York connections he sometimes knows about really rare pieces or collections."

"What New York connections?"

"His mother, for one. She has a gallery in TriBeCa."

"What's the name of the gallery?"

"He never told me. Or if he did, I forgot. And his father is a professor at City College." She frowned, trying to remember. "In the art department."

I took my notebook from my inside jacket pocket and clicked open my pen. I jotted down CCNY.

"He didn't particularly get along with his parents," she went on. "He used them when he needed them, that's all."

"These customers of his—where does he meet them?"

"Collectors," she corrected me. "He meets them all over. Different places."

"That's not very specific."

"I'm not sure I can be more specific than that. There are just as many rich people at Arabica as there are at Giovanni's or Sammy's," she said, mentioning two of Cleveland's pricier restaurants. "And he hangs around the local galleries a lot, striking up conversations with the browsers who look like they might have money. He impresses hell out of them with his knowledge and expertise—and whatever anyone thinks of Jeff, he knows his ceramics. Of course it really cheeses the dealers when he aces them out of a sale, and then he's persona non grata in that gallery, but mostly they don't find out, because he arranges to meet his customers later, sometimes at their homes or more often at some restaurant where he can cadge a dinner out of them."

My pen hovered over the notepad. "Do you know the names of any of these galleries?"

"Sure," she said. "He used to go to the Wickersham on Larchmere when he was living here. And Dorian's."

"Where's that?" I said, writing the names.

"On Murray Hill," she said. "In Little Italy."

My ballpoint pressed so hard on the paper that it almost tore it.

I stay away from Little Italy these days like most people avoid dark alleys or sleeping in a draft. Not that I don't love the Italian food that's served in some of the great restaurants there like La Dolce Vita or the Baricelli Inn, but I've had enough run-ins with the mob boys from Murray Hill to last me several lifetimes. I don't know why I'm still walking around, to tell the truth.

Maybe it's clean living, good karma, and that I'm a Capricorn with Scorpio rising, whatever that means. Nevertheless, I dutifully wrote down the name of the gallery.

"Those are two he goes to a lot, because they sort of specialize. But I imagine he's sniffed around everyplace in town that deals in ceramics and pottery—and there's lots of them. Galleries, antique stores, art cooperatives."

"How about the collectors? Any you can remember?"

She shook her head. "Jeff guarded those names as if they were the secret code that could unleash nuclear missiles aimed at Russia. He didn't want anyone cutting in on his action."

"He wouldn't even trust you?"

"Not even me. Trust isn't in Jeff's vocabulary, unless it has the words Morgan Guaranty in front of it."

"You must know some collectors in town. After all, you're a ceramicist too."

She uncoiled herself from the cushions, stood up, and came over to me with her hand extended. "Come here," she said, "and I'll show you what I do."

I got up and allowed her to lead me over to the portion of the big room that housed her kiln and work materials and several corkboards propped against the wall with colorful little ceramic and cloisonné pins stuck on them.

"I make jewelry," she said, stating the obvious. "I sell to a few galleries here in Ohio and in the Pittsburgh area, but mostly to gift shops and boutiques. And I hit all the craft shows within a two-hundred-mile radius, like the Yankee Pedlar in Canal Fulton, the Gift Show at the Convention Center, the Cain Park Art Festival." She went on the defensive. "It's not much of a living, but I get by. And the best part is, I get to do what I love."

"That makes you one of the luckiest people alive," I assured her. I examined the pins and necklaces more carefully. "These are beautiful. You do nice work."

"Want to buy one for your wife?"

"I don't have one of those."

"Oh. Sorry."

"Nothing to be sorry about. I guess I'm getting to the point where I like it that way." I pointed at the little doll atop the kiln. "Who's this little guy?"

She smiled, relaxing. "That's my kiln god. All serious potters have one, to ensure good spirits for the firing."

The doll wore a curiously dopey expression for a god. "Does he have a name?"

"I never bothered to give him one. Maybe I'll call him . . ." Her eyes twinkled. "What's your first name again, Mr. Jacovich?"

"Milan," I said, laughing, "but that's a hell of a name to lay on a kiln god."

"Then I'll call him . . . Seymour."

"Seymour?"

She arched her brows. "Sitting up there he gets to see more than he should sometimes."

"I think Seymour is an exceptionally noble name."

From the worktable she picked up a crudely made clay pot about the size of a small cereal bowl. "Here. A present."

"I can't take this," I said. "Or at least let me pay you for it."

"Nonsense. It's an end-of-the-day pot." She saw my quizzical look. "There's always a bit of clay left over and we potters hate to let it go to waste, so we always throw one last pot. For the road." She turned it upside down and showed me the initials VLO scratched into the bottom of it. "It's even signed. Please—I'd like you to have it."

I took it from her outstretched hand. It felt heavier and more substantial than it looked. I figured I'd use it on my desk as an ashtray. "It's very nice. Thanks."

"Maybe it'll inspire you to find Jeff. It worries me he's been missing for so long."

"Well, he might not exactly be missing," I said.

"No?"

"To his friends he might be, because no one's seen him around. But in all probability *he* knows where he is."

She crossed her arms. "That'll be the first time, then," she said.

CHAPTER FIVE

I headed east up Fairhill Road.

Aptly named, it climbs from the southwestern quadrant of University Circle up to the part of Coventry Road that slices through Shaker Heights. It's curvy and slippery as hell in the wintertime, but now its trees were beginning to show that kind of frozen-peas green that signals the onset of spring. I turned south to Larchmere Boulevard, where antique shops and art galleries and antiquarian bookstores coexist peacefully with several pizza joints, a few new upscale restaurants, and the smoky old Academy Tavern with its big juicy hamburgers, all just a few steps from the Rapid tracks on Shaker Square.

The Wickersham Gallery was small and unobtrusive, with only a little polished-brass nameplate on its brick frontage to identify it, probably on the theory that if you didn't know where it was in the first place you didn't deserve to. Its one window was draped in beige velvet and displayed four pieces of exquisite English porcelain. The discreet price tags next to them were exquisite, too.

Gold-leaf lettering on the glass door proclaimed that visits were BY APPOINTMENT ONLY, but I went in anyway. Live recklessly, that's my motto.

Even though the temperature outside hovered somewhere in the high fifties, the heat in the gallery was in its winter mode, and I immediately felt suffocated by the hot air that blew from several vents in the floor.

The man who came quickly out of the rear of the shop was in his late forties, tall and hearty with startling blue eyes in a ruddy face. He wore a black wool suit with velvet lapels and a collar-less, tie-less, blindingly white shirt buttoned at the neck, an outfit for which he seemed too large. The black and white would have made him look a little like a priest if not for his white hair, which was pulled back into a Eurotrash ponytail that curled under itself at the back of his neck. He smelled of Calvin Klein's Obsession for men.

He gave me a thorough, professional once-over and apparently decided that my suit hadn't cost enough for me to be desecrat-ing the hallowed ground of his establishment. "We're really not open to the *public*," he said without much warmth. His speech was fussily precise.

"I'm not exactly a customer. Are you Mr. Wickersham?"

"There is no Mr. Wickersham," he announced, stretching his chin out as if his shirt was buttoned too tightly around his neck. "My name is Edgar Curtin—*I'm* the owner here." Mr. Curtin was the kind of person who spoke in italics.

I handed him my business card, which he regarded as he might an obscene photograph. "Private security? I'm sorry, we already *have* a security system in place." He tried to return the card, but I backed up, leaving him holding it out awkwardly.

"I'm not selling anything," I said. "I'm on an investigation, looking for a man named Jeff Feldman. I'm told he sometimes comes in here."

Edgar Curtin's ruddy face got a little more ruddy and he rolled his eyes heavenward. "To my everlasting sorrow, *yes*."

"When was the last time?"

"Probably a month or so ago," he said too readily. "I can't re-member. It *wasn't* something I marked down in my memory book." He flicked some imaginary lint off his sleeve. "Why do you want Feldman?"

"It's a private matter."

He gave me a haughty look. That's a word I never thought I'd use, *haughty*, but it fit Curtin like a spandex workout suit. "So I'm supposed to answer *your* questions but you won't answer *mine, is* that it?"

"Not at all, sir." The respectful "sir" made him unbend just a little, and he fluttered his eyelids like a silent-movie vamp. I dislike being obsequious, but the object of the game is to get the job done, after all, and Curtin struck me as the kind of man who'd do just about anything for you if his vanity was stroked. He probably spent more time than he cared playing lickspittle to all his wealthy and demanding customers and wanted to get some of his own back. "But I know you're busy, so I won't bore you with a long drawn-out story."

He crossed his arms and gave me a little knowing nod. "I'll bet he owes someone money. That doesn't surprise me. He's *always* borrowing money. Not from *me*, of course, I'm not that stupid. But he's a—well, I think, it would be charitable to call him a 'hustler.' And he always needs money for his little *schemes*."

"What kind of schemes?"

Curtin looked away from me, out the window. "I'm sure I wouldn't know." He uncrossed his arms and shot his cuffs. "I'm an art dealer—a *legitimate* dealer. I have no interest in Jeffrey Feldman or in his sordid little doings, which I'm sure are mostly *beyond* the letter of the law."

"Why do you say that?"

"Because I know Jeffrey." He said it as if no one else in the world did. "Easy money is his middle *name*."

"That's not my concern," I said. "I'm just trying to locate him."

"Oh, drat!" he said ingenuously. "I was hoping he was under *arrest* or something."

"I'm not a policeman."

"More's the pity, then."

"Sounds like you don't like him."

"I don't know anyone who *does*." Curtin adjusted the lapels of his jacket. He fiddled with his clothes a lot. "He's *not* a very likable person."

"Why do you let him hang around the gallery, then?"

"He doesn't *hang around*."

"But you said he does come in here a lot."

"It's a public place."

"No it isn't, Mr. Curtin. You just told me you're not open to the public."

"Yes, but . . ." He sighed. "You wouldn't understand," he said, as though there were a lot of smart, classy, sophisticated people out there who would understand but I wasn't one of them. Sometimes my job wreaks havoc on my ego.

I decided I'd live with it. "Try me," I said.

He looked down his long, patrician nose at me, but since he was about three inches shorter than I am, to do it he had to bend his head back so far that I could see his nose hair. "I don't want to bore *you*."

"I don't bore easily."

"Well, *I* do. And I have *many* things to attend to, so I'm afraid I have to cut our little audience short."

Audience. Like with the queen of England. Like with the pope. Edgar Curtin thought a lot of himself. But I have a pretty highly developed sense of self-esteem too, and I wasn't going to be dismissed like an underbutler after he'd served high tea.

"Just one more thing. Are there any of your regular customers that Feldman is particularly close to?"

His laugh came out more like a snort. "*Surely* you don't imagine for *a moment* that I'd answer *that* question!"

"One can only hope."

He spoke slowly and clearly, and somewhat loudly; perhaps he'd decided I didn't understand English. "I've no *intention* of involving any of our patrons"—I ducked my head dutifully, accepting the correction—"in whatever Feldman's gotten himself mixed up in. I wouldn't last in business ten *minutes* if I disclosed their identities to just *any—*"

"They'll never know I heard their names from you," I assured him, cutting off what was certain to be an insult.

"That's because you *won't*. Now I must excuse myself, Mr., uh . . ."

He consulted my card, holding it at arm's length. He treated me to another supercilious sneer; I think he'd seen too many old

George Sanders movies. "Unless I could *possibly* interest you in some seventeenth-century English porcelain?"

I leaned very close to his face, close enough to startle him out of his oh-so-proper composure and back him up a few steps. "Not until payday," I told him.

I didn't get to Little Italy until about two in the afternoon. Dorian's was about half a block south of Mayfield Road, with its fragrant bakeries and Italian markets, its pasta restaurants and private social clubs, the Holy Rosary Cathedral and the Mayfield Civic Theatre, which had stood empty for years. I drove partway up the red-cobbled street called Murray Hill, my tires singing over the bricks, and miraculously found a parking place across the street from the little gallery.

There are many galleries on Murray Hill, ranging from reasonable and accessible to horrendously expensive. Each year they hold an Art Walk to kick off the summer festival season.

I could see through the window that Dorian's was brighter and less formal than the Wickersham Gallery, and the ceramic pieces were more colorful and considerably more whimsical. And it was open to the public—every Wednesday through Saturday, according to the card inside the glass door. I went inside.

The man who put down an art catalogue and rose from his desk to greet me was somewhere between chubby and seriously obese, with several sets of jowls surrounding a moon-shaped face out of which sharp blue eyes peered. He was coatless and wearing a pair of maroon slacks and a maroon and gray tie, and the vast expanse of white shirt across his chest and belly was like the face of K2. He had even less hair than I did, but he deluded himself into thinking that letting one side grow long and combing it flat across his head in long black swirls could camouflage serious pattern baldness. His chipmunk cheeks were red and raw-looking, as if he shaved extra close to tame a heavy beard. In any case, from clear across the room I could smell the Old Spice he'd splashed them with. The price of their respective aftershave wasn't the only thing that distinguished him from Mr. Curtin.

"Hi," he said. "Browse all you want, and let me know if I can answer any questions for you."

I don't get good openings like that very often. "As a matter of fact, you can, if you're the proprietor here."

He bobbed his large head to acknowledge that he was, and his chins kept moving long after his head stopped. He didn't look like a Dorian, but then Edgar Curtin's name wasn't Wickersham, so very likely he wasn't one.

"I'm trying to locate a colleague of yours," I said. "His name is Jeff Feldman."

"Dorian" didn't make any pretense of not being surprised. The smile went out like a light bulb whose time had come. "He's not my colleague."

"But you do know him?"

His face was closing up faster than a corner bar at quitting time. He spread his Polish-sausage fingers wide. "I might. I know lots of people. Where'd you get the idea to come here? And why are you asking, anyway?"

"I'm sorry," I said, and fished out a business card. "My name is Milan Jacovich—I'm a private investigator."

He stared at the card, and his red cheeks turned the drab gray color of the skies over Lake Erie in February, and his eyes got hard and piggy. I suddenly got the feeling that Dorian wasn't quite as soft as I'd first thought.

"Uh-huh." A fine sheen of perspiration popped out on his forehead. Then he glanced around nervously, as if hoping the cavalry would come riding over the hill, but sadly there were no bugles.

"Well, Mr. Jacovich," he said finally, pronouncing my name as if he'd been doing it all his life, "I'd be glad to talk to you, but I'm a little busy right now."

I looked over at his desk, which had nothing on it but the art catalogue and a mug half full of a bright orange tea. Maybe if he didn't finish perusing the catalogue before the end of the day he'd have to pay a penalty.

"When would be a better time?"

He looked around some more, his jowls swinging with each pivot of his head. "To talk? Uh, five o'clock," he said. "How about five o'clock this afternoon?" His laugh was frantic and high-pitched, although no one had said anything remotely amusing. "That'll give me some time to get out from under all my, uh, paperwork." He fumbled my card in both hands, like Oliver Hardy doing his trademark tie twiddle.

I checked my watch, wondering what to do with the next two and a half hours. "I won't take up much of your time . . ."

"Five o'clock," he said again, as if the saying of it brought him a kind of peace. He was nodding for some unknown reason, perhaps in approval of his own perspicacity and cunning. He moved his head around a lot. "That'll be a good time. To talk. You come on back at five o'clock, all right?"

"Five o'clock," I repeated dutifully, but felt no inner peace at all.

His relief as I walked out of the gallery was almost palpable. As I turned to pull the glass door shut behind me, I saw him sink heavily into the chair at his desk, pick up the telephone, and punch out a number fast enough to win second prize in a speed-dialing contest.

CHAPTER SIX

T he practical thing for me to do was go home, so that's what I did. Little Italy is less than five minutes from my apartment, and I figured I could get some paperwork of my own done, and maybe straighten up a little instead of killing two hours in some bar.

I collected my mail and shuffled through it as I ascended the stairs to the second floor: an invitation to join a record club. A sales pitch for health insurance. An envelope congratulating me on being a first-round winner in a sweepstakes I'd never even entered. My auto club renewal. This week's *Time*. A catalogue from someplace in Colorado that sold personalized address labels and notecards. Nothing I really wanted to open right away. I started thinking perhaps I needed to perk up my life a little.

I took off my jacket and loosened my tie, unbuttoning my top shirt button so I could breathe again. I should have chosen a profession that allowed me to work tieless. That's what comes of not planning ahead.

I put Valerie Oakey's end-of-the-day pot on my desk and sat down; it looked nice there next to the telephone, as if it belonged. I pulled out my accounts receivable file, which was fatter than I would have liked. Then I sorted out the accounts that were past due and set about sending out second notices, without much optimism. The phone interrupted me.

"It's that time of year again," Ed Stahl said when I answered. He never says hello or identifies himself when he calls—he simply figures I'll know.

"What time is that?"

"The Indians' home opener, Milan. Against the Red Sox. It's next Tuesday."

Ed Stahl writes a daily column in the *Plain Dealer*, adorned at the top with a photo of him that cuts off the crown of his head just above his Clark Kent glasses, giving him the appearance of a petulant owl. Ed is probably the best friend I have in the world, since I've managed to alienate most of the others at one time or another. The fact that he never alludes to his celebrity status in town, nor to the Pulitzer Prize that gathers dust in the back of a closet somewhere, endears him to me even more than his value as a source and a sounding board. To say nothing of the fact that he can get tickets to sporting events like the Tribe's opener, or to Browns games—seats on the fifty-yard line—or for the Cavaliers when they play a hot team like the Chicago Bulls or the Charlotte Hornets and no one else in town can get near the Gund Arena.

He's also one of the few single guys I know, giving us something else in common. Cleveland is a very married town.

"Are you saying you've got tickets, Ed, or are you just calling everyone in town to tell them baseball season's starting, just in case they don't read the paper?"

"Everybody reads the paper," he said. "Or else I'm out of business. Four tickets, right behind the first-base dugout. You and me and your boys, all right?"

"It's a school day. Lila'd cut my throat if I pulled them out of classes for that."

"Oh, right." I could hear him puffing his malodorous and ever-present pipe. "Okay, why don't we bring dates?"

"Since when do you have a date to take to a ball game?"

"I don't," he said. "I thought maybe you could fix me up with someone."

That wasn't even amusing. I hadn't been out with a woman in months. I guess I'm not very good at dating. After my divorce there'd only been one woman I'd lasted with for any length of time—Mary Soderberg, the head of sales at Channel 12, who had dumped me for a romance with her boss. There've been a few since, most notably a nice lady named Kellen Charles, an advocate for the homeless out in Lake County, but her single-minded devotion to her job had eventually left me out in the cold. Literally. Our relationship had begun in a blizzard and had stretched over the winter. By the time the weather turned warmer and the pansies and crocuses were beginning to blossom, it had fizzled and gone out.

"That's like asking a man with no legs for tap dancing lessons," I said.

"We'll figure something out then," Ed said. "Meantime I'm going to pencil you in for Tuesday."

"For the Tribe opener you can pen me in," I told him. Opening Day of the baseball season is special all over the country, but I think in Cleveland it's more so, especially since we began playing in our new stadium. We haven't had a winner here for so long, each home opener is a rekindling of hope.

And hope is what keeps us all going, Tribe fans and lottery players and newspaper columnists, secretaries and social workers and even private investigators. Maybe especially private investigators. Without hope there's not much point in hauling your aching bones out of bed in the morning, much less going to the trouble of brewing coffee and making toast. Even the ones who crawl out from under a rock, like Jeff Feldman; they do it with the hope that things will be better in the sunshine than they were beneath the rock.

So I hoped I'd find a date for the ball game, and that the Indians would win. I hoped the lottery ticket folded neatly inside my wallet would bring me eight million bucks. And I hoped I'd find Jeff Feldman and get little April her money back.

Toward that end, I called Feldman's studio, hoping I wouldn't have to talk to Tydings Belk, who struck me as a truculent ass at best—and he probably wasn't at his best very often. But for a change I lucked out. Alys Larkin answered the phone, and when I explained who I was and what I wanted, she agreed to talk to me.

"Is there someplace we could meet besides your studio?" I asked. "I don't think your partner likes me very much."

"He doesn't like anybody very much," she said. She had a low, masculine voice, and her speech was abrupt and staccato. "All right. You know where Mitsy's is? Jerman's Cafe on St. Clair. Seven-thirty," she said, and before I could tell her that seven-thirty was fine, she hung up on me.

With the exception of Nicole Archer and Valerie Oakey, everyone who'd ever come into contact with Jeff Feldman was insufferably rude.

I finished dispatching the due bills and glanced at my watch. A quarter to five, still time for the last mail pickup of the day. I went downstairs, dropped the envelopes in the box across the street, and then drove back down to Murray Hill.

The rotund gallery owner seemed surprised to see me. He jumped out of his chair as if it had been electrified, looked at his watch, then at me, then out the window. "Um. Hi. You're a little early."

"Five minutes," I said.

"Right, right. Well, have a seat, make yourself comfortable," he told me, indicating one of two chairs opposite his desk. "I'll be with you shortly." He bustled into the back room and closed the door. You've probably never seen anyone that size bustle. If you had, you'd not soon forget it.

I didn't sit down as invited but walked around the gallery, inspecting the work on display. Some of the ceramic and glass pieces were tacky and dull, but most were imaginative and well crafted, at least to my untrained eye. The prices weren't nearly as shocking as those at the Wickersham Gallery, i.e., they were somewhat less than my monthly income.

I noticed one of the buttons on the telephone console light up: the owner had gone into the rear of the gallery to make a phone call. It stayed lit for only about thirty seconds, then went out again, but he didn't reappear, so I continued my perusal of the stock. I especially liked an eccentric ceramic water pitcher and matching basin done in bright green and blue. Sixty-five dollars. I wasn't going to buy it—my apartment was too crammed with stuff as it was, and my budget doesn't allow for whimsy. But it was an attractive piece, and I admired it for a few moments, wistfully aware that I had no one I could give it to as a present.

Finally Dorian came out of the back, pulling his jacket on. It was a gray tweed, and I breathed a sigh of relief. I'd worried that it was going to match his maroon slacks.

"Well, now, Mr. Jacovich, thank you for waiting," he said, wheezing noisily. "Sorry I had to inconvenience you, make you come back and all, but you know, the middle of a working day . . ." He flapped his arms ineffectually, seeming almost disoriented. He was like a car engine that hadn't had sufficient opportunity to warm up.

"Something to drink?" He asked as if the fate of the world as we know it depended on my answer. "Coffee, or tea?"

"No thanks," I said.

That seemed to stun him. "I'll just . . . get myself some then— ah, if you don't mind."

He went back into his inner sanctum, and I heard the clinking and clanking of a spoon hitting the sides of a mug. Then he returned, slowly, carrying the mug as if it contained molten gold, and gave me that weak, prissy smile again. I could see he was stalling for time. What I didn't know was why.

I found out a few moments later when the front door of the gallery opened and Victor Gaimari came in. I'd rather have seen the guy with the leather face and the chainsaw from that old movie. Hannibal Lecter cranky because dinner was late. Cujo in a bad mood. Anybody but Victor Gaimari.

The world sees him as a stockbroker, Ohio State graduate, ballet and Play House and Cleveland Orchestra patron, and according to the "Mary, Mary" society column in the *Plain Dealer*, one of our town's most eligible bachelors.

Victor Gaimari is the Duke of Cleveland.

He's also the nephew and heir-apparent of the septuagenarian Don Giancarlo D'Allessandro—the Old Man, the boss of bosses of the northern Ohio branch of what most cops refer to as "the outfit," what Marlon Brando fans call "the family," and what the rest of us know as the mob.

"Hello, Milan," he said in that surprisingly high-pitched voice of his, extending a soft, well-manicured hand, his white teeth sparkling against his seamless health-club tan. With his dark hair and mustache Victor looks a lot like Cesar Romero in *Carnival in Costa Rica*. "Nice to see you again."

That's right, *again*. Victor and I seem to cross paths and purposes a lot. Maybe Cleveland is too small and intimate for you to avoid your enemies forever, but it seems that for the last few years, every time I get involved in a case that turns out sticky and dangerous, with layers upon its layers that when peeled back reveal the corruption beneath, Victor and his uncle are always hanging around on the sidelines, calling the plays.

So we're old acquaintances. Like the Indians and the Red Sox are old acquaintances. Like the Browns and the Steelers. Like North and South Korea.

"Victor," I said, giving him the most unenthusiastic handshake I could muster without being totally cold-fish about it. I noticed he was alone. That's always a good sign; when Victor is up to no good he frequently drags his hired muscle around with him. Today he seemed to be in his respectable businessman mode: dark gray pinstripe suit, white shirt, muted blue and gray tie. He's just an old smoothie, Victor.

"How are you, Milan?" he said, sitting down easily in the proprietor's chair and adjusting his trousers so they wouldn't wrinkle. God forbid they should wrinkle.

"I hang in there, Victor. I'm like Jason. No matter what they do to me, I keep coming back."

A thin vertical line appeared between his perfectly arched brows. "Jason?"

"It's a movie. Forget it."

"Ha ha," Victor said, and showed his teeth again. That's the closest he ever comes to actually laughing.

"What brings you here?" I looked at Dorian. "Besides a phone call."

He inclined his head slightly, giving me credit. "You don't miss a lot, do you?"

"I get paid not to."

"Of course. Well, you've got me dead to rights. Mr. Diorio called me this afternoon and told me you'd been around."

"Mr. Diorio?"

Victor indicated the gallery owner. "Alphonso Diorio—Dorian to the art world. This is one of the most successful small galleries in Cleveland."

Dorian almost bowed, beaming in the warmth of the approval of his patron.

"Does he call you every time a customer walks in?"

Victor smiled, his dark eyes like a snake's. "Only when they're as famous as you. You're not unknown up here on the hill, Milan. Among my family, and friends. You and I go back a long way, don't forget."

"How could I forget, Victor? You're one of the stars of my high-light film."

He inclined his head slightly to accept what he perceived as a compliment. Very ducal, Victor. "So when Dorian heard your name, he rightly took the precaution of talking to me before he started answering any of your questions."

"I haven't asked any yet."

"I know." Victor spread his hands expansively. "But I'm here now, so ask away." He crossed one leg over the other; his oxblood cordovan bobbed distractingly. "I can't wait to hear what this is about. You always get involved in such interesting situations."

It's hard not to be put off by Victor Gaimari. He's a master at making you feel awkward and stupid. "What have you got to do with Jeff Feldman?" I asked.

His perfect tanned forehead wrinkled with what appeared to be genuine puzzlement. "Jeff Feldman?"

I nodded. "That's who I'm looking for."

Victor chuckled; he was way too young to chuckle, and it sounded phoney. In frustration I made a fist, and the two men exchanged a glance as my knuckles cracked.

"Can we get on the same page here?" I said. "I thought Dorian called you because I was inquiring about Feldman."

"He called because you were here, period. He knew that you and I have had our—moments—in the past, and he didn't want to be indiscreet. So he wisely called me, and here I am." The smile kicked in all the way. "And to see you again, of course. Always good to see you, Milan."

"Then you know Jeff Feldman?"

"Sure I do," he admitted. "I'm something of a collector of fine porcelains, and there are few people in town as knowledgeable on that subject as he."

I turned in my chair so I could see Diorio. "What about you, Mr. Diorio?"

"Dorian," the fat man gurgled. "In the gallery everybody calls me Dorian."

If, like his namesake in the Oscar Wilde story, this Dorian had a magical portrait in the attic that got old and ugly while he stayed young and beautiful, he needed to have it restored.

"Feldman's just a guy, that's all," he went on. "He's a hustler, he hangs around some—"

"Just a moment." Victor stood up and looked down at me. I hate being looked down on, especially by Victor, so I stood up too. "Will you excuse us for a minute or two?"

"Sure," I said. "Take all the time you need, get your stories straight."

Victor breathed my name in a sigh of exasperation, and I watched them disappear into the back room together. I could hear the sound of their voices through the wall. Dorian was doing most of the talking, and his tone sounded agitated. Victor's higher-pitched voice interrupted occasionally to ask a question.

It gave me a chance to continue my browse of the gallery. The favored colors seemed to be shades of black and gray, variations of pink and burgundy. Most of the pieces fit my definition of art— they only existed because they were pretty. There wasn't a damn thing I could think of to do with any of them.

I did see a couple of Valerie Oakey's ceramic pins mounted on a velvet board, priced at twenty dollars each.

They came back in less than five minutes, Victor leading the way. When we'd both sat back down in our respective chairs, Victor looked up at Dorian and said, "Go ahead and tell him." Dorian cleared his throat and straightened his shoulders in the manner of a second-grader called upon to recite the Pledge of Allegiance. "Jeff Feldman has been coming in here pretty regularly for the last few years. He shows up for all the special events like show openings and cocktail parties, or else about once every couple of weeks. More often if he's got something interesting or unusual to peddle."

"What does that mean, interesting or unusual?"

Dorian's expression became pained, and he tried to explain with his hands but was unsuccessful. Finally he said, "Older pieces. Maybe even historical."

I nodded and tried to look thoughtful and intelligent, but I didn't know what the hell he was talking about.

"He meets my customers," Dorian said, "he finds out what kind of stuff they collect. Sometimes he makes his own private deals with them."

"Doesn't that cut into your action?"

Dorian looked at Victor, who just lowered his eyelids. He has long black eyelashes, like Elizabeth Taylor.

"We take a percentage," Dorian said.

"A substantial percentage," Victor added.

"Victor, you're a wonder."

That got his full attention. "I am?"

"Is there anything in this town—or anyone—that doesn't have your fingerprints all over it?"

"I'd like to think not," he admitted, and I had to admire his candor. "But actually there are lots of things. For instance, when the Browns cut Bernie Kosar and let the Dallas Cowboys have him, I was against it. No one asked me, though."

"I'm surprised. Now let me get this straight. Feldman comes in here and co-opts your patrons, and you take a cut."

"They aren't my patrons, they're Dorian's. And I probably would put it a little more gently." The corners of Victor's eyes crinkled. "But in theory I think you have it down right."

"But he's just a no-talent sleazebag running around the East Side living off one woman after the other," I said. "Why put up with him? Why not deal direct? You don't need him. You're an established gallery."

Dorian cleared his throat. "Sometimes the pieces he has—"

"Are suspect," Victor finished.

"Fakes?"

Victor shook his head. "There's no question of their provenance. But most countries have very strict laws restricting the exportation of their antiquities. Dorian's wouldn't dare touch them. Jeff Feldman has certain—connections—that occasionally allow him access to pieces we as a legitimate gallery might not be able to acquire. And it's on these occasions that he becomes, ah, valuable to our business."

I rose and leaned over the desk, getting right in his face. "What you're saying is that Feldman fences stolen ceramics to you."

"You really do have an absurdly narrow view of the world," Victor said. "A fence is a guy a burglar comes to when he's knocked off a wealthy home in Pepper Pike or Beachwood. The fence pays ten cents on the dollar for the stolen goods and then peddles them elsewhere. Jeff Feldman is no fence."

"If it walks like a fence and quacks like a fence . . ."

"It's a broker. Look, no one is getting hurt, all right? Nobody's house gets robbed. It might not be legal—and I suppose in your book that makes it one of the Seven Deadly Sins. But it's just another way of doing business, that's all."

"What about these countries trying to protect their heritage?" I asked, straightening. It sounded lame even when I said it.

"Oh come on," Victor said, showing annoyance for the first time. "Not even you can really be feeling sorry for repressive regimes like the People's Republic of China. Or Greece. Or certain countries in Africa or Latin America that are run by thieving despots." He shook his head, thoroughly fed up with me. "Do you take Flintstone vitamins to keep you from ever growing up?"

"Only the green ones. Where is Jeff Feldman?"

"I'd like to know who suggested you look for him here."

"Just about everyone conversant with the art scene in Cleveland knows he hangs out here, among other places."

Victor's shoulders tensed. "What other places?"

"Lots of them. But no one's seen him. Have you?"

"That depends what you want him for."

"I don't. But somebody else does."

"Who?"

I shook my head. "Not a chance, Victor."

He looked at me. So did Dorian, with wide, unbelieving eyes. Victor wasn't used to hearing the word *no*.

Except from me. Finally he stood up. "Well, I haven't seen Feldman for several weeks. I don't know where he is, either." His hand caressed his silk tie. "I wish I did," he said almost wistfully.

"Why?"

"Because." He started for the door, and Dorian almost fell all over himself getting there first to open it for him. "He's got something that I want," he said without turning. "Very much."

And then he was gone, before I could ask him to elaborate. I think he liked the idea of leaving me hanging.

CHAPTER SEVEN

It's one thing to jerk an air-headed rich kid like April Delavan around, or an impoverished artist like Valerie Oakey, or to stiff your studiomates for your share of the rent. It's quite another to get on the wrong side of Victor Gaimari. Victor ought to wear a surgeon general's warning that pissing him off can be hazardous to your health.

He'd been remarkably forthcoming, at that. Maybe it was due to our long association, during which I had never screwed him, even though I've had many chances. Maybe it was because he just didn't consider me much of a threat. But he'd given me some information I didn't have before, and I was grateful to him, even though it ground my guts to admit it. Now, however, I had another appointment. I found my way back down to St. Clair Avenue and grabbed a quick but delicious roast pork dinner at Maria's Restaurant. Then I headed for Jerman's.

Jerman's Cafe has been a fixture on St. Clair Avenue since 1908, under the same family management, and in an era where change for the sake of change is the order of the day, I find that nothing short of remarkable.

The decor inside is what Mitsy, the ever smiling white-haired Slovenian owner-bartender, refers to as "old joint." The walls, ceiling, and moldings are covered in stamped tin, the kind you can't get anymore, and the big storefront windows looking out over the avenue are shaded with big bamboo blinds. The juke-box in the corner plays the great big-band stuff like Glenn Miller and Tommy Dorsey. Behind the long wooden bar are several ancient mirrors advertising various beers and whiskeys, and there is a back room containing both a pool table and an old upright piano. Beyond that is the family kitchen, looking bright and warm and homey.

The only nod to the modern age is a small TV set in the far corner. It's always on, but nobody ever looks at it.

Being in the old neighborhood, most of Mitsy's clientele are the Croatians and Slovenians who live within walking distance. But there are lots of younger people, too, artists and poets and writers who've found inexpensive living and studio space in the St. Clair–Superior corridor, and it's not unusual to see them sitting at a table drinking Mitsy's beer or whiskey and eating a pizza or sub they've brought in from somewhere else, earnestly discussing their art.

Alys Larkin, who shared the studio with Jeff Feldman and Tydings Belk, looked more like a sculptor than a ceramic artist. Her hands were large and strong, with thick, square fingers, and the cardigan sweater she wore with the sleeves pushed up to the elbow revealed powerful, sinewy forearms. Her dark curly hair was chopped short, the kind of hairdo that can be styled by running your fingers through it after your shower.

Her manner was very no-nonsense, and I got the feeling that she had lots of other things she'd rather be doing than talking to me. A yellow and black Subway bag and the remains of a sandwich were on the table next to a half-empty bottle of Guinness stout. I ordered a Stroh's.

"If you want to know whether I'm concerned that Jeff just disappeared, the answer is no," she said after we'd introduced ourselves. "I don't like having to eat his share of the rent, but otherwise he's not really a part of my life."

She took a slug of Guinness, straight from the bottle, and wiped her mouth. She was pretty brittle, on the outside, anyway, and I imagined she would intimidate the hell out of Jeff Feldman.

"I'm talking to everyone that knew him," I said. "So I appreciate your seeing me."

"I had to eat anyway," she said, and tore off part of her sandwich with her teeth. "I don't smoke, but if you want to, feel free. This is a saloon, after all."

"Thanks," I said, and took out my Winstons. I shook one out of the pack and fired it up. "I'm basically looking for a direction. No one I know of who knows him has seen him. I'm hoping you could give me a nudge toward someone I don't know."

"I assume you've already talked to all his women," she said. "The blondes. Oakey and the baby doctor and that little twit of a child he's been humping for the past few months—I can't even remember her name."

I nodded.

"Well, that takes care of all his friends."

"What about his enemies?"

She took another slug of stout and grimaced, but the expression had nothing to do with what she was drinking. "Get hold of the Cleveland phone book and start with *A.*"

"Isn't that a little severe?"

"Only if you didn't know him. Jeff's a liar and a cheat, and he'd sell his little sister's braces right out of her mouth."

"He has a sister?"

"Not that I know of. It was a figure of speech."

"Anybody he did business with?"

She snorted. "Business—that what you call it?"

"What do you call it, Ms. Larkin?"

"Hustling. Hondeling. Grubbing for dollars." She rubbed her hand over her face, scrubbing it, but since she wore no makeup, there was no damage done. "Wasn't there a TV show by that name once? *Grubbing for Dollars?*"

"I think it was 'bowling.'"

"Feldman'd do that too if he thought he could make a buck at it."

"How did he make a living? Selling his ceramics?"

"Partly," she said. "There must be a lot of undiscerning people in the world, because his stuff was pure crap. Mostly he sold other artists' work."

"Yours?"

Her look could have withered a peony bush. "No thanks, I'd rather peddle my ass on Prospect Avenue." She blew out a mouthful of air and waved a hand in front of her to disperse the smoke from my cigarette, so I stubbed it out half finished, permission or no. "Jeff had pipelines to some really fine collections in New York and Los Angeles, and even in London, and he dealt them to very select and very rich connoisseurs here in town."

"Like who?"

"I don't travel in those ritzy circles, so I don't remember too many of their names."

I opened my notebook. "How many do you remember, Ms. Larkin? How many names?"

"Ah, you're going to make me work, aren't you?" She put an elbow on the table, made a fist, and rested her chin on it for a moment like Rodin's *Thinker*. "A west-side attorney named Richard Hover. A surgeon, a Dr. Keighley—I can't remember the first name. A downtown stockbroker, Victor Gaimari."

I wrote down Victor's name dutifully. The way she identified him as a stockbroker led me to believe that she didn't know of his other activities, and I'd be just as happy if it stayed that way.

"Mrs. Albert Gramm," she continued, and lifted her beer bottle with her pinkie fully extended, "who's some sort of patron of the arts who lives in Bratenahl, on the lake." The pinkie went down and she took another swallow. "And a real estate developer from Gates Mills, Chase Delavan."

My hand froze with the pen poised over the notebook. "Delavan?"

"Right," she said. "Those are the only names I can think of offhand."

I closed my notebook. It couldn't be a coincidence—Delavan is just not that common a name. "Thanks. You've been more than helpful."

"Let me be even more so." She slammed the brown bottle down on the table. "You're spinning your wheels."

"Why do you say that?" I asked, startled.

"Because my guess is that he finally screwed the wrong person and figured it would be healthier to get out of town. Far out of town. I doubt he'll ever show his face in Cleveland again, which is a good break for all of us."

"Interesting guess," I said, thinking of the gallery on Murray Hill.

"You're welcome to it. I hope to hell he's in trouble," she said. "I hope to hell he gets burned. He's a small man, Mr. Jacovich. Small-thinking, small talent." She jutted out her jaw at me. "Small dick, too, if you must know."

I guess that raised my eyebrows, because she continued, "Once. One time. I'd been drinking. And that's the only reason, believe me."

"I believe you," I said.

"It's not that I didn't remember the next morning. Just that it was unimportant enough to forget about right away. I'm not one of the long string he leeched off and then dumped."

She looked at her watch. It had a plain canvas band and looked like it told the time, the weather, and for all I knew, the dew point. "We through now?"

Not the most polite dismissal I've ever received, but I accepted it with more grace than it deserved. "I think so." I handed her my business card and stood up. "Thanks for your time. I'll get the tab."

"I already paid for mine," she told me.

I'd known from the start that April Delavan came from big east-side money. Wealth and privilege was in her look and her bear-ing—you could almost smell it on her. And it isn't unusual for rich people to collect fine art of one sort or another. You can only have so big a house, so fine a car, take so many vacations abroad, and you've got to spend that money somehow. But her father's doing under-the-counter business with Feldman was something I hadn't considered.

There was always a chance it might not be monkey business, of course. I imagined Chase Delavan was a legitimate and respected collector. But from what all Jeff Feldman's friends and associ-ates had told me, especially Victor Gaimari and Dorian and Mr.

Curtin from the Wickersham, I was fairly certain everything he touched was just a trifle tarnished.

There was no listing for Delavan Realty or anything like it in the yellow pages, but it was way past business hours anyway. A perusal of the residential book was fruitless, too, and when I called information I found that Chase Delavan's home phone was unlisted. "At the request of the customer," the recording said. As if somebody else could request that your phone not be listed.

I could have called April at the Euclid Heights Boulevard apartment she'd sometimes shared with Feldman and asked her, but I didn't think she'd much relish the idea of my talking to her parents.

So I did what I always do when I'm in a bind for information: I called Ed Stahl at home.

If there was anyone who'd know where to find a rich big shot like Chase Delavan, it was Ed. But then Ed would also have a line on a steelworker named Stanley Pilsudski, and he'd be able to put his finger on an office supply salesman named Harvey Greenstein. If you live in Greater Cleveland and Ed Stahl doesn't know you, or know who you are, chances are you don't even exist.

"You're interrupting me in the middle of a poker game," Ed complained. "As you well know, because you were invited."

"I had to work," I said.

"Don't give me that, you're self-employed—you can make your own hours. I've always envied you that, Milan. You, and real writers."

"You're a real writer."

"I'm a journalist," he said, "which is a polite way to say newspaper hack. Real writers have their work in the Library of Congress, and they go to bookstores and sign autographs for fans. With me, people say no comment and hang up on me, and they use what I write to train the puppy to pee on. Now what's so important that you interrupt my betting rhythm?"

In the background I heard the mutter of male voices and the clicking of plastic chips. I tried envisioning them all sitting around Ed's dining room table, friends and acquaintances of mine, and some that I had little to do with beyond Ed's Wednesday night poker soirees. "I figured you'd be losing anyway, like you always do," I said, "and that taking you away from the game for a few minutes would be an act of mercy."

"As it happens, I'm up nineteen dollars and change, you bastard. What do you want?"

"Chase Delavan. Know him?"

"Chase Delavan," he repeated, and I could almost see him smacking his lips, savoring the taste of the elegant name on his tongue like a wine fancier would a fine cabernet. "Yes, it rings a bell, but it's a distant one. Is this a pop quiz, or do I get any hints?"

"He's a real estate developer."

"Ah!" Ed often says "Ah!" like that when light dawns. "Right, I've got it now. Sure I know who he is, although I don't think we've ever met. Calling Chase Delavan a real estate developer is like calling Michael Jordan a basketball player. Both are accurate enough descriptions, but they don't quite tell the whole story."

"I'm sure you're going to," I remarked.

He cleared his throat, ready to recite. Ed spends so much time expressing himself on paper that whenever he has the chance to expound orally on any subject, he warms to it. "If memory serves, Delavan is in the final phase of raping some beautiful woodlands to create a tract of homes—oh, excuse me, luxury estates—down around Hudson. He's also done extensive developing in Bainbridge Township in the past couple of years, and I think he had a lot to do with building up some other little minitowns in Geauga County, which used to be really beautiful before he got hold of it. His second car, I think, is a bulldozer. Delavan is the most formidable enemy of trees since Rin Tin Tin died."

"Like any other developer."

"Yeah, but Delavan deludes himself into thinking he's enhancing the natural beauty, not screwing it up. You know what the price tags are in that rarified neighborhood, don't you?"

"I can't count that high."

"Lots of people can, though, especially some of those trickle-down Republicans from the eighties who made sure that damn little trickled. And they're smart enough to know you can hardly go wrong putting your money in real estate."

"It's the land, Katy Scarlett," I said, affecting a Thomas Mitchell Irish brogue. "So Delavan is a heavy hitter?"

"So heavy that if Hank Aaron hit ahead of him, Aaron would bunt."

"Where do I find him? I know he lives in Gates Mills, but his phone's unlisted."

"Why don't you call his office tomorrow?"

"I don't know where he works. There's no Delavan Realty or anything. Why do you think I called you?"

I could hear Ed puff on his Kaywoodie briar and then sniffle. Frequently his pipe smoke drifts up under his glasses and makes his eyes tear. Ed lives in a tulle fog of smelly blue smoke. "I don't have my files here at home, and the old memory isn't what it used to be."

"Too much Jim Beam is hell on brain cells."

"So is too many klobasa sandwiches and pierogis, but it hasn't seemed to affect you any." I heard him humming softly under his breath. "I'm trying to remember now, Delavan's firm has kind of a funny name. October Homes? November Homes, maybe? Something like that."

"April Homes?"

"Right! April Homes. Yeah, they have a really treacly company motto, something like, 'It's always springtime in an April Home.'"

"Please, I'm getting a sugar rush."

"It sells houses though. Apparently. Unless Chase Delavan hit the Super Lotto." He paused, puffed, and then I heard him swallow something, and the tinkle of ice cubes. "April Homes, yeah. How'd you know that, Milan?"

"Shot in the dark," I said.

CHAPTER EIGHT

hagrin Falls is a little jewel of a village set eighteen miles southeast of Cleveland. Its namesake river was either christened after a French fur trader, bears an Indian name meaning "clear shining water," or was so called due to the fact that the founder of our city, Moses Cleaveland—don't ask me where the extra *a* went—was exploring navigable waterways and discovered the falls to his chagrin, depending on which oft-told tale you prefer. One thing about the Greater Cleveland area, there are always several pieces of conflicting folklore to enliven our history, and you can pick the one you like.

The bragging points of Chagrin Falls include a beautiful waterfall right on its busiest street, a rustic gazebo in the village square, a quaint little popcorn shop that sells more flavors of candy and ice cream than you've ever imagined, and an old-fashioned hardware store in which, the locals boast proudly, television comedian Tim Conway once worked when his name was still Tom Conway. Its swooping hills and verdant riverbanks dotted with Western Reserve–style homes surrounded by sumac and maple and oak trees, Chagrin Falls is one of the places northern Ohioans always take their out-of-town visitors to see.

When I tracked down the address I had for April Homes, I found its headquarters in a big frame building by the Chagrin River and within earshot of the falls, but it lacked the lavish over-

stated elegance characteristic of similar establishments downtown. In fact, the only indication that it was an office at all was a
seven-foot-long model of an upscale housing tract under a clear
plastic box on a table in the reception room. It was marked with
the legend APRILWOOD. The houses were all two-and three-story
Georgians of the type usually described by eager realtors as "emotional."

I had secured an appointment, when I finally got through to
Mr. Delavan on the phone that morning, by telling him I wanted
to talk to him about Jeff Feldman, so when I arrived the recep-
tionist, a pleasant, fiftyish woman with a yellow designer suit and
an early nose job, whisked me into his private office.

I'm sure that the elder Delavans had called their little boy
Chase with the unwavering conviction that he'd eventually become a handsome, tanned, well-built, silver-haired millionaire
with country club memberships, a manicure, and a thousand-
dollar suit—and not one to disappoint, he had grown into the
name. He was that rare breed of man who would not look ridiculous in hunting pinks.

His office didn't look much like an office, though. There was
a small desk against one wall, very French-looking and possibly
the very desk at which Empress Josephine had written notes inviting friends over to celebrate her husband's latest conquest of
Europe. The rest was furnished as a country gentleman's living
room. Delavan and I sat facing on a pair of couches that flanked
a well-used fireplace, although the weather was a bit warm for
a crackling hearth. The coffee was served in delft cups and sau-
cers, with a sugar bowl and creamer to match. All that was missing was the bourbon and branch water, but after all, it was only
eleven o'clock in the morning.

"Well then," he said, taking a hearty breath. I had a feeling he
started most conversations that way, exuding bluff confidence as
well as complete control. He was in his middle fifties, and his
voice was cultured and carefully modulated, the result of childhood elocution lessons, I imagined, and a four-year tenure behind ivy-covered walls. Not Yale or Harvard—he wasn't quite that
tight-jawed. Princeton, perhaps, or Brown. And the haircut must

have set him back at least eighty bucks. He had a trim, whipcord type body that I was certain he took good care of. Nothing plebeian like iron pumping or aerobics, though; He moved with the careful precision of a martial artist.

"You spoke on the phone of Jeff Feldman, Mr. Jacovich."

"That's right. I'm told you know him."

"Of course I do. I've done some business with him—art business. I'm a collector of fine porcelain, among other things, and Feldman, being an artist in his own right and the son of a noted art educator, is something of an expert in the field." The speech sounded rehearsed, as if he'd decided to give me a rush of useless information right off the bat so I wouldn't ask any questions of my own.

So I didn't, at first. I simply said, "I'd enjoy seeing some of your collection."

"Good lord, I don't keep any of it here in the office. It's in a bank vault, where it won't get broken." His hand touched his black and gray silk tie as though assuring himself it hadn't fallen off. As if it would dare.

"When's the last time you saw Feldman, Mr. Delavan?"

"I couldn't really say with any degree of accuracy. A month ago, perhaps. Maybe two. We don't get together socially. Just for business reasons."

"Art business."

His blue eyes glinted in the diffuse sunlight filtering through the window. They were not the cornflower hue of his daughter's—more like the cold, blue metal of a cop's service revolver. "That's right, art business." He stroked his chin the way the British actor Jack Hawkins used to do. "You're a private investigator, is that right?"

"Yes, sir."

"May I ask in whose behalf you've come here?"

There was no way I was going to tell him I was working for his daughter. "I'm afraid it's unethical for me to answer that, Mr. Delavan."

"I see," he said. "Well, I'm not sure that I should even be talking to you, then. I mean, what's in it for me?"

"Does there always have to be something?"

He waved a hand around his elegant domain. "You're damn right there does. I didn't get where I am by giving things away," he said. "All right, since you're here anyway, what the hell. What about Feldman? What is this all about?"

"He seems to have disappeared."

He frowned. His eyebrows were dark in contrast to the silver of his hair. "I'm truly sorry to hear that," he said. "We were working on a—project."

"A real estate project?"

He laughed as though the very idea was preposterous. "An art project. He's attempting to locate a very rare piece of pottery I'm anxious to own, and he's supposed to be acting as a factor for me. He's done it before—helped me acquire a fabulous Red Anchor scent bottle of Nicholas Sprimont's from the famous Chelsea factory. I assumed that I hadn't heard from him for a while because his search was so far unsuccessful."

"Then you didn't know he was gone?"

"Certainly not. As I said, we weren't close."

I had to ask this next one very carefully, choosing my words the way I'd pick out fresh fruit from the produce bin. "Were you aware, sir, that your daughter April knows him?"

He made a little kiss shape with his mouth. "Naturally. How did *you* know?"

"Comes with the job," I said.

He waited for me to elaborate, but I didn't. "As a matter of fact, they met through me. That is, Feldman came to our home, and she was there." He looked the way people do when they smell something bad. "One of those magical moments, I suppose."

"That doesn't bother you, what with the large difference in their ages?"

His hands were lying in his lap, and now he raised them a few inches and then dropped them again. "Certainly it bothers me. But April is what used to be known in polite circles as willful. She refused to even consider college, she dresses like a bag lady, and she runs with a wild crowd. Unfortunately, last year she gained access to quite a substantial trust fund from her grandmother, so now she has fifty thousand a year to do with pretty much as she likes. Her mother and I gave up trying to control her years ago."

Considering she was only eighteen I found that to be a pretty reprehensible admission, but I didn't say so. Everyone tells me I'm too judgmental, even Ed Stahl. So I kept my mouth shut.

"I'm just hoping it's a phase and that it will pass in time," Delavan went on. "Other phases have. Buddhism when she was fifteen. Dating black boys in high school. Wanting to join the Peace Corps. You think my hair got this color by accident." He studied his well-buffed fingernails. "You have children, Mr. Jacovich?"

"Two boys."

"Well, raising a girl is a different proposition, I'll tell you." He lifted his shoulders and his dark eyebrows at the same time. "You just go with the flow and do the best you can."

I didn't think he was doing his best as a parent, but again I failed to tell him so. I was pretty proud of my self-discipline. "Your daughter is . . . seeing Feldman, but you didn't know he'd disappeared?"

If he perceived disapproval, he chose to ignore it. "April is, uh, noncommunicative at best, and downright secretive most of the time. And we certainly don't talk much about what she does and with whom she does it."

"She lives with you, doesn't she? At your home, I mean?"

He shrugged. "Sometimes. And sometimes she stays elsewhere. In any case, she rarely discusses her personal life with me, and I've learned not to ask, because number one, I hate confrontation, and number two, I'd just as soon not have to hear the grisly details. And I don't think she's mentioned Feldman twice since she began seeing him." He sighed. "Which is fine with me."

"Just what is this rare pottery Jeff Feldman is trying to find for you, Mr. Delavan?"

A frown darkened his handsome face. "I couldn't very well tell you that."

"Why not?"

He looked at me as if I were simple. "If I let it get around that it's available, every collector in the country would try to outbid me, that's why not."

"It's that rare?"

His eyes got almost misty, and he floated off for a moment into his own private reverie. "That rare and that exquisite, yes."

"I won't tell anyone," I said, weary of his patronizing. "Scout's honor."

He smiled easily, not knowing he was being put on. "That's very touching, Mr. Jacovich, but it's still quite impossible."

"Is he trying to acquire this piece from his New York connections?"

He ignored my question and stood up, smiling insincerely. He was only about five foot ten, but he carried himself like a much taller man. "I'm afraid we have to bring our little chat to a close now. I have some homes to build."

I stood up too, very straight, emphasizing the five inches I had on him, and he backed off a step. I tried picturing Chase Delavan with "homes to build," wearing a hard hat and overalls, sawing lumber and hammering nails, but the image came too hard. I shook his outstretched hand, and it was soft and smooth; I'd have bet the farm it had never even held a hammer.

I had a late breakfast at a downtown Chagrin Falls restaurant called Dink's, where they serve real Geauga County maple syrup on their pancakes. Dink's acquired a certain cachet a few years ago when an elderly male patron who ate there daily died and left a teenage waitress a small fortune, but the big draw for me is always the pancakes.

It took me half an hour to get back to my apartment, where I immediately tore off my tie and exchanged my jacket, slacks, and dress shoes for a sweatsuit and Nikes. I sat down at my desk, switching on the green-shaded desk lamp that Mary Soderberg had given me once for Christmas and reached behind me to turn on the inexpensive little boom box I keep on a shelf for company. The velvety voice of Dee Perry on WCPN came at me. Dee plays the best radio jazz in town, a nice mellow background without too much talk, just right for working. Then I pulled a fresh stack of plain white three-by-five index cards out of the top drawer and began inscribing them individually with a felt-tip pen:

FELDMAN

APRIL

CHASE DELAVAN

TYDINGS BELK

ALYS LARKIN

NICOLE ARCHER

I lingered over that one a minute, and then added *M.D.* after it, remembering Dr. Archer's soft eyes and the way she'd said "Twang!" to make sure I remembered her last name. Then I continued:

VALERIE OAKEY

EDGAR CURTIN

DORIAN/VICTOR

There was a perverse satisfaction in not allotting Victor Gaimari a card of his own. Childish, I admit, but it was a small indulgence I allowed myself, and it felt good.

I lit a cigarette and tossed the burnt-out match into Valerie Oakey's end-of-the-day pot. I was getting to like it. Then I gathered up my notebooks and transferred all the jottings I'd made during my interviews onto the cards. It's the way I always work. If I have all the various components of a puzzle on index cards, I can shift them around on my desk to see if any pattern emerges.

Feldman's card went on top. Directly beneath it I spread those of the three women he'd used, putting Chase Delavan's card beneath his daughter's. Belk and Larkin got their own row, as did Curtin and Dorian/Victor.

By this time it was past two o'clock—it's tough reaching people between noon and two because of lunch breaks. I dialed New York City information to get the number of the City College of New York.

Or "Siddy Collitch of Noo Yawk," as the operator answered. We Clevelanders don't exactly speak like Oxford dons, but next to native New Yorkers we sound like Sir John Gielgud doing Shakespeare's Ages of Man.

"I'm trying to find Professor Feldman in the art department," I said.

"Moment." The dentalized *T* at the end popped like bubble gum.

She put me on hold, and syrupy dentist's-waiting-room music oozed out of the receiver, clashing horribly with a latter-day Dizzy Gillespie version of "Night in Tunisia" on WCPN. I couldn't turn down the phone, so I exercised my only option and clicked off the radio. Reluctantly. I love "Night in Tunisia."

"Dr. Feldman's office," a cheery female voice said. She was probably an art major.

"Is Dr. Feldman in?" I asked. "This is Mr. Jacovich calling from Cleveland, Ohio."

"Will he know what this is in regard to?"

That's the world's most irritating question. It'd be one thing if it were the mayor's secretary doing the asking, or the chief of staff's at the Cleveland Clinic. A woman answering the phone of an art teacher in a municipal college was quite another thing. I wanted to ask her if the professor was psychic, in which case he might very well know. Instead I just said, "I don't know, I'm not psychic. Why don't you put him on the line and we'll ask him?"

I heard her sharp intake of breath, and felt a little bit lousy for intimidating a college kid—but only a little bit. Teach people manners when they're young, before rudeness becomes a way of life.

"Hold on," she said shakily, and the canned melodies kicked in again. Probably an album entitled *Footlight Favorites* or something, because the violin section was moaning out "The Music of the Night" from *Phantom of the Opera*. Listening to the music of Andrew Lloyd Webber is like being stuck in a stalled elevator.

After almost a minute I finally heard a human voice. It sounded old, weary, and more than a little cranky.

"Mr. Jacovich? Have I got that right? From Cleveland?"

"Yes. Professor Feldman?"

"What can I do for you that's so important you had to send my girl into an emotional malaise?"

I figured her malaise would deepen if she heard him refer to her as "my girl," but I didn't imagine telling him so would do my inquiry much good.

"I'm sorry to bother you at work, sir, but I'm trying to locate your son."

His only answer was a sigh that came over the line sounding like a Gulf Coast hurricane.

"I haven't been able to find him here in Cleveland," I told him, "so I took the liberty of calling you, in case he might be visiting."

"Jeffrey doesn't visit. He swoops. Calls from LaGuardia and says he's in town and we should get his room ready. He stays one or two days, enough to do his business, and then he's gone again. He thinks we're the Feldman Hotel. But he hasn't really lived here since he was twenty-five years old, so you're asking the wrong guy." He spoke as if he had a mouthful of food, which may have been the case; college teachers often eat at their desks. Knowing New York, I figured I was listening either to a corned beef sandwich or hot pastrami. On hard Jewish rye—any other kind of bread would be unthinkable.

"What," the professor went on, "he owe you money or something?"

"I'm just trying to get in touch with him. I'm a private investigator."

"Oy!" he said, lowering his voice a register or two. "That sounds serious. He did something wrong?"

"I wouldn't know that, Professor. My job is simply to locate him."

"And you can't do that in Cleveland?"

"Not so far, no, sir."

I heard him chewing, then swallowing. "I don't like the sound of that."

"I don't mean to alarm you."

"Too late," he said.

"There's nothing to worry about—he could very well be staying with a friend. But I just wanted to check with you. When's the last time you heard from him?"

"Maybe a month ago. This is bothering me, Mr. Jacovich, that nobody can find him in Cleveland."

"It's early days to get worried, Professor. He might be just about anywhere in the world, on business. But you're sure he hasn't been to New York?"

"He hasn't been in touch. Like it would break his back to call his mother once in a while. For all I know he might have been in town, but he didn't call or stay with us. He was here in March for three days, and the only time we saw him was at breakfast for a quick coffee, and then he skeedaddled till all hours of the night. We found a note on the kitchen table. 'Gone back to Cleveland. Love.'" He made a snorting sound and then coughed. "A note to his mother, he leaves. 'Love.'"

"Do you happen to know why he was in New York?"

"Not to see his parents, I can tell you that," he said, bile behind it.

"Did he tell you who he was seeing?"

He made a whiny, humming sound in the back of his throat. "Some gallery or other."

"Do you know why?"

The timbre of his voice dropped once again. He sounded worried. "One of his big deals, I suppose. Jeff is a real big dealer. Big shot, dot the *i*."

"You remember the name? The gallery name?"

"No, not offhand. Wait . . ." He breathed softly into the phone. "We found a business card crumpled up on the dresser in his room after he left. My wife stuck it someplace, I think. Maybe I can find it tonight."

"If you do, can you call me?"

"Sure, yes. Whatever I can do."

I gave him my number, and he repeated it to make sure he'd copied it down correctly.

"I appreciate your being so cooperative, sir."

"What's not to cooperate? Jeff's a real putz, he always has been, and it grinds my behind trying to think where we went wrong. But hey, he's my son. You got kids, Mr. Jacovich?"

"Two sons."

"Then you know. Blood tells, am I right?"

"You're right," I said.

CHAPTER NINE

I f Jeff Feldman's vanishing act was bothering his father, it was literally gnawing at me. People just don't become invisible. Even factoring in his considerable and varied debts, I was starting to think that perhaps Jeff Feldman had not disappeared voluntarily. He'd left his clothes in his apartment, he'd left a lot of admittedly not very good ceramic pieces in his studio, and he'd left a lot of loose ends of his life dangling. Add to that his father's ignorance of his whereabouts—assuming the professor was telling me the truth—and my inability to unearth anyone besides Valerie Oakey who even remotely liked him, and I was working up a good head of steam on a worry.

So I put in a call to Lieutenant Mark Meglich, the number-two guy in the homicide unit of the Cleveland P.D., at the old stone monster on Payne Avenue, which was once central police headquarters, before they built the Justice Center, and which veteran cops now call the Old Central.

Mark Meglich and I go back so far I can't remember a time when he wasn't there. It was somewhere in grade school that we'd first hooked up together, before he turned into a yuppie cop and Anglicized his first name, Marko, to Mark. We'd played football together in high school and had both wangled jock scholarships to Kent State, and then our life paths diverged. He went to the police academy, and I went to Cam Ranh Bay.

I came back from Southeast Asia relatively unscathed—I

hadn't suffered a scratch, and apart from some recurring night-
mares that had eventually trickled to a stop, I'd exhibited few of
the psychological horror symptoms that still haunt a large percentage of Vietnam vets. But I had no direction in my life. I'd
majored in business at Kent and minored in psych, but after seeing six-year-old kids rigged up as human booby traps and whole
villages of massacred civilians rotting in the fetid jungle heat, examining quarterly sales figures seemed a little beside the point.

So Marko talked me into becoming a cop. He guided me
through the rookie traumas and trials, keeping me from falling
all over myself and giving me sound career advice. In the New
York department he would've been my rabbi, in Chicago they'd
have called him my Chinaman, but in Cleveland there is no expression quite so colorful—I guess he was simply my mentor.

And that's where we butted heads. Because after a few years I
decided I didn't want to be a policeman anymore. A big-city police department, especially Cleveland's, is as political as a smoke-
filled room at a convention, and I've never been good at playing
politics. So I quit the department to open my own private security
agency, and Marko had found it nearly impossible to forgive me.

We never really broke with each other. When we were both
married we spent time together with our wives, as couples do,
and when our marriages collapsed at about the same time there
was a certain huddling together for warmth, a kinship in adver-
sity, I suppose, until I decided to heal quietly and in solitude and
he opted to outrun his own pain with a long succession of col-
lege-age girls in vain pursuit of his lost youth. But the issue of my
resignation still simmers just below the surface; it has for years.

"Milan!" he said when I'd identified myself. "How've you been,
big guy?"

"Fine, Marko," I said, leaning heavily on the name. It annoys
him to be called Marko, and I know it—just as he knows how I
hate being referred to as "big guy." That's the way our friendship
is, warm and loving but now peppered with little jabs and stings.

We talked of this and that, he asked about my boys, I asked
about his love life, and none of it meant much. The empty trap-
pings of artifice.

He finally said, "You must be on some sort of fishing expedition, Milan, or you wouldn't have called."

I felt embarrassed. Nailed. "Well . . ."

"What do you need?"

"How're you fixed for John Does?" I said.

He was silent for a moment. "Since when?"

"Let's say the last three weeks."

"Fair. But I think we've still got a couple of empty drawers in the cooler, so come on over and bring your toothbrush."

"That's cute," I said.

"Tell me what you've got in mind, and I'll see if anyone fits the bill."

I did, giving as much of a description of Jeffrey Feldman as I had: white, Jewish male, early forties, dark hair, about five foot nine, beard. I realized it could have been any one of ten thousand people. That's what's ultimately so sad about death, the very ordinariness of it.

"What makes you think he might be resting in one of our air-cooled luxury suites?" Marko said.

"Because he's not anywhere else. At least, not that I know of, and I've been looking for three days."

"Three days? Is that all? Sometimes it takes me that long to find my car keys."

"Mark . . ."

"All right," he grumbled. "Let me take a look. Can I get back to you tomorrow?"

"Taking the afternoon off, are you?"

"You've got some nerve, pal."

"If I didn't I'd be selling ties at Kaufmann's instead of doing this. Before you go home, okay?"

He sounded resigned. "If not sooner, right? Don't go anywhere."

I hung up, my hand still on the receiver. It suddenly occurred to me that I didn't have anywhere *to* go.

I sat for a while, studying my index cards, pondering their artistic and geometric arrangement as well as their logical relevance. Then I decided that Chase Delavan was in the wrong place on my desktop. His connection to Feldman was the business they did, not the Jeff-April relationship. I moved him next to the two gallery owners, Curtin and Dorian, which wasn't much of an improvement except that it made the pattern more symmetrical.

Until an idea clicked into my head. It wasn't one I liked very much, and I reached for the phone again with weariness as well as a certain trepidation.

It annoyed the hell out of me that Victor Gaimari didn't sound more surprised to hear from me. Almost as though he'd been waiting for my call. If I made a list of all my favorite people in the world in order of preference, Victor Gaimari would show up on about page 957, but underestimating him is one mistake I've never made. He's a smart, canny guy, and I have to give him that.

"Hi, Milan. How very nice to talk to you," he said. Matter-of-fact. Casual. As if I called him several times a week just to chat.

"I wonder if I could drop by your office after work this evening, Victor. Something I'd like to run by you."

There was a brief silence. "Is this in connection with what we talked about yesterday?"

"Yes, sort of."

"I said just about all that I have to say on that subject, I think. I'm not sure I can offer you anything new."

"I think you can."

"Oh?"

"Look, you said you wished you knew where Jeff Feldman was, and I'm trying to find him too. If we put our heads together and share our information, we may be able to expedite the process."

He took his time answering. "That sounds . . . intriguing, but I'm planning on leaving work early."

"Could we meet somewhere then?"

"I can't. I'm having a few people for dinner this evening."

"Damn!" I said.

"Wait, here's an idea. Why don't you come for dinner as well?"

The very thought gave me gooseflesh. "That's very kind, Victor, but no thank you. How about tomorrow?"

"I'll be in meetings all day." He sounded genuinely sorry. "So

I guess it's dinner tonight or it'll have to wait until Monday." I heard him turn a page, probably in his appointment calendar. "Or Tuesday, to be more realistic."

I didn't say anything for a moment. I knew I was being manipulated, and I didn't much like it.

"Come on," he said, "it'll be fun. We keep saying we have to get together socially—here's our chance."

We didn't keep saying that, *he* did.

"Otherwise I just don't see when we'll have a chance to sit down."

That was mob lingo, I knew, to "sit down." To negotiate. To carve up the spoils. But somehow I don't think Victor meant it that way.

"There'll he a lot of nice people. Corporate people, mostly. Very respectable." He waited a second and then played his ace. "And my uncle will be there too. You know how fond he is of you."

His uncle. It was getting worse.

"Cocktails at seven," he said, "dinner at seven-thirty. No fuss. Informal clothes."

In Cleveland's higher echelons an invitation specifying "informal clothes" demands a suit—for men, anyway. "Formal," of course, is a tuxedo, and the last time I wore one of those was to my high school senior prom. "Casual" means a sports jacket and tie. Any dress code less explicit than that is probably for a beer bust.

"And after dinner we can talk, just the two of us. I promise." He waited a moment. "Can I expect you?"

I felt like a lab specimen squished between two slides. "How can I turn down such a gracious invitation?"

"Terrific! I've been wanting to do this for a long time. You remember where I live, don't you, Milan?"

"I remember," I said.

I brooded for the next half hour, courtesy of a couple of cans of Stroh's from my refrigerator. I'm not the most social animal in the world, and trading inanities and drinking with upraised pinkie all evening with a bunch of people I don't know—especially the kind of people Victor Gaimari might have around—was a bleak prospect.

Yet it was something I almost had to do. I suppose I could have declined without hurting Victor's feelings too much, presuming he had any, but I was beginning to sense an urgency in the Jeff Feldman situation that hadn't been quite so apparent at the beginning. What gave me heartburn was the realization that Victor was becoming more and more adept at painting me into a corner as the years went by.

The phone ringing at my fingertips startled me out of my deep thoughts.

"Milan Security," I answered.

"This is Meglich Insecurity," Marko said.

"Of course it is. Who else but someone suffering from severe insecurity would go out with twenty-year-old girls?"

"Twenty-year-old boys?"

I thought about it. "Name me a twenty-year-old boy who's not insecure."

"Doogie Howser, M.D."

"You're watching too much television, Mark. Your brain is turning to Cream of Wheat. Did you go sightseeing in the morgue for me?"

"God no. That wasn't part of the deal. But I scanned my files and then I called the coroner's office. We currently have five registered guests who've come in within the last three weeks, and three of them seem to have had the same travel agent."

"Meaning?"

"They died from more or less natural causes."

"What's more or less a natural cause?"

"One heart failure, which goes on the books as a massive myocardial infarction. That's a weird word, isn't it, infarction? It looks like somebody misspelled 'infraction.'"

"It has to do with the cutoff of blood supply from a muscle or tissue, which is called an infarct."

He was silent for a few seconds. Finally he said, "How in hell do you know stuff like that?"

"I paid attention in biology while you were daydreaming about scoring touchdowns. What about the others?"

I heard him breathing through his once-broken nose as he looked, and I lit a cigarette while I waited. "One malnutrition, one ordinary old age."

"Forget the old-age one."

"Okay. Malnutrition, a Caucasian female in her late forties. Apparently a bag lady who just checked out under a railroad bridge on the Near West Side with enough Sneaky Pete in her system to keep her preserved for six months."

"And the other two? The ones who didn't die of natural causes?"

"Black male, around twenty, cause of death a gunshot wound, found in a vacant lot on Union Avenue. If he has family or friends, no one seems to miss him, because there's been no missing-persons report." He paused. "White male, near forty, drowned in the lake and washed up near Edgewater Park on March twenty-third."

The hair on the nape of my neck prickled. "Give me a little more on that one."

His sigh was put-upon, and I heard papers rustling. "Dark hair, around five nine, must've weighed around a hundred and fifty pounds when he was alive."

I chewed on the inside of my cheek. "Circumcised?"

"Who cares?" he snapped. "Jesus, Milan, what the hell kind of a question is that?"

"An intelligent one, I thought. Jeff Feldman is Jewish."

"Lots of people get circumcised besides Jews."

"But virtually no Jews don't."

"That's not much of a reason to—"

"Work with me, okay?"

"Wait." He hummed softly under his breath as he looked through his files. I wasn't certain, but it sounded a lot like "Memory" from *Cats*. You can't even get away from Andrew Lloyd Webber's music when you're talking to the homicide division.

"Here it is," he said. "Dick, condition thereof. Six point six inches in length, flaccid. Circumcised."

I took a final puff of the cigarette and crushed it in my new ash-tray. It didn't taste very good. "Can you meet me at the morgue?"

"Do I have to? I hate that place."

"Funny, most people like it," I said.

"You going to come down right now?"

I looked at my watch. "About an hour."

"Sure, I guess so. Why not?"

"Thanks, Mark."

"Hey, Milan?"

"What?"

"When we get there, will we have to look at his dick?"

CHAPTER TEN

Marko Meglich is a big man. Not as big as I am, but broad of chest and shoulder, and the years have added a little more to the mix, especially around the equator. Always a sharp dresser, it seems to me that in the last few years Marko has been overdoing it. On this particular Thursday afternoon he was wearing a lightweight double-breasted wool suit in a mocha shade, with a white shirt and a silk tie speckled with red, blue, and yellow spring flowers on a field of meadow green. He smelled gloriously of too much Brut. He started losing his hair much later than I did, but he's catching up with me fast.

He was standing in the anteroom of the county coroner's office, smoothing the big mustache he'd worn since his divorce and chatting up the pretty woman behind the counter, even though she was too old for him—she must have been all of twenty-eight.

"Hey, Milan!" He moved easily away from the counter and shook my hand firmly with both of his. In school he'd had a rep around the Division II circuit for having good hands, hands that could pull down overthrown passes into coverage. Now they get a weekly manicure, but they're still strong.

"You're all dressed up for the occasion!" he said, making as though to straighten my tie. "You think the stiff downstairs is going to care how you look?"

"I'm going to a dinner party."

"Must be some party to get you into your good blue suit." He went back over to the counter and spoke to the woman, whose name tag identified her as D. Poe. She picked up the telephone and punched out three digits, then said something in a tone too low for me to hear and hung up. She nodded at Marko.

He came back over to me. "We'll wait for our tour guide."

We lit Winstons—mine—to pass the time, discussing the Indians' need for bullpen pitching just as if they weren't on strike, wondering whether this would be the year they'd finally put it together. It's not easy being a Cleveland sports fan; the Indians have been suffering through pennant drought since 1954, a fact made only slightly more palatable because the Chicago Cubs have been pennantless since 1945.

A side door opened and a tall, rotund black man wearing a white smock over a light blue shirt and a navy tie appeared. His name tag read B. JOHNSON.

"Lieutenant?" Johnson said, looking from Mark to me.

"Yo," Mark said.

"Will you follow me, sir?"

There were no ashtrays visible, so we threw our cigarettes on the linoleum floor and stepped on them and followed Johnson through the door and down a flight of uncarpeted steps. The walls in the stairwell were made of cement blocks painted white, and the formaldehyde smell seemed to have penetrated to their very core. A slight wave of nausea tickled at the back of my throat.

In the basement of the building our footsteps echoed on the tiled floor of a long, sterile corridor with glass-paneled doors on both sides. Through one I saw an autopsy room, with two white-shrouded figures lying on gurneys. I didn't look into any of the other rooms.

B. Johnson led us to a door with no window in it, a steel one, and unlocked it with one of a mass of keys he kept on a fat key ring at his belt. He swung it open, and the strong smell hit us immediately, along with a blast of supercold air. It was almost like walking into a butcher's freezer.

They went in ahead of me. I hesitated for a beat and then followed them.

B. Johnson looked at me. "You all right?"

"Fine."

He shook his head crossly. "Don't pass out on me now, man," he admonished. "I've got too much to do today."

"I'm fine."

"Don't worry about him, Johnson," Mark said. "He used to be on the Job."

"That don't mean piss in the wind," Johnson said, going over to a wall lined with large steel drawers. "I've seen cops on the Job ten, fifteen years, they take a look in one of these drawers and they get all weak in the knees and white around the mouth. Or else they throw up their guts right on the floor." He put a long-fingered hand on one of the drawer handles and looked at me suspiciously. "Don't you toss your cookies, either. Better you should pass out than you barf and I gotta clean up your mess."

I squared my shoulders, despite the cold. "I said I was just fine, Mr. Johnson. And if I'm not, I promise I'll throw up on the lieutenant's suit."

B. Johnson allowed himself a small smile. "Well, that's all right, then," he said, and slid the drawer out about four feet. It made a horrendous squeaking noise. I didn't suppose they oiled the runners very often. The drawer was on the top row; its handle was at about the level of B. Johnson's shoulder. On its front brass numerals screwed into the steel identified it as number 17.

We moved forward to stand on the opposite side of the drawer from Johnson. Mark nodded, and Johnson carefully drew the sheet down as far as the opened drawer would allow and stood back almost proudly, like a used car salesman showing a couple of high school kids a cherry 'sixty-five Mustang.

The body was an allover pale gray, the lips and the desiccated nipples bluish-purple. It had been in the water for a while, and the attrition of decay and underwater fauna had rendered the features indistinct and unformed-looking, almost like a sketch someone had drawn, then erased, and not filled in again. The nose was slightly pug, the forehead high, the jaw almost prognathous. The beard was scraggly and dark brown.

My stomach doing a Fosbury flop, I stared down at what was left of the face. Then I took a copy of the sketch April had drawn of Jeff Feldman from my inside jacket pocket, unfolded it, and looked at it for a long while, then back down at the corpse. Wordlessly I passed the sketch to Mark, who examined it and then handed it back.

"You don't have a photograph?"

"Just this."

"A drawing."

"Uh-huh."

"Hard to tell from a drawing," he said.

I nodded.

"Hard to tell anything after he's been in the lake for a while. But if I were a betting man—and I'm not, of course, because I'm an officer of the law and betting's illegal—but if I were making a wager, I'd say this isn't your guy."

I nodded and folded the sketch back up and replaced it in my pocket as Mark motioned to B. Johnson to close the drawer. It squeaked on its runners again, and the clang it made as it slid shut was awfully final.

"I don't think it's my guy, either," I said.

It felt good to get outside in the fresh air, but the brisk breeze off the lake couldn't quite blow the smell of death away.

"I've got a question," Mark said. "I've gotta ask it. If this Feldman's been missing three weeks how come nobody filed a missing-persons report on him? His family or somebody."

"His family lives in New York," I said. "They didn't even know anything was wrong until this afternoon."

"No friends?"

The tobacco tasted bad again, and I tossed the cigarette away after two puffs, watching the wind pick it up in midair and send it skittering down the block. "No friends."

"Everybody's got *some* friends."

"You didn't know Jeff Feldman."

"I think I'm glad about that." He hunched up his shoulders and then flicked some imaginary lint from the lapel of my good suit. "You're lookin' sharp today. You sure you're not going off on some hot date and not telling me about it? So who's tossing this dinner party?" lie said. "Somebody I know?"

"The only people you know are murderers."

"So you're having dinner with some murderers, huh?"

I shrugged, uncomfortable with the question. I didn't answer him because I truthfully wasn't sure.

We said our goodbyes, and I walked a block and a half to where I'd left my car in a metered parking space, enjoying the architectural splendors of the early twentieth-century buildings downtown, trying to think of anything at all except the corpse I'd just looked at in drawer 17. It was rather like trying not to think about elephants.

The old good news–bad news dichotomy sprang unbidden into my head: the good news was that the cadaver in the drawer wasn't Jeff Feldman. The bad news was that he was still missing and I hadn't a clue as to where to look for him.

A gaunt, hunched-over figure shuffled toward me on the sidewalk as I got to my car, eyes on his scuffed shoes and spine curved into a question mark. If he'd straightened up he would have been well over six feet tall.

He was bundled up in some nondescript brown jacket, and even though it was April there was a long scarf around his neck, army green and faded.

"Can you spare some change?" he said, raising his head to look at me, and then recognition flickered in his bloodshot and dirt-caked blue eyes. "I know you," he said.

I reached into my pants pocket. "I don't think so."

"Oh yes," he insisted, and stood up a little straighter, "I saw you lots of times before." He rubbed his hands together as if he were holding them under one of those electric hand dryers found in public rest rooms. And then I recognized him, too.

He'd been a familiar figure around downtown Cleveland for at least twenty years, way back before anyone had ever heard the term *homeless*, when he was just a wine-crazed, panhandling vagrant with no place to live. On the rare happenstance that he was relatively sober, his speech indicated an education of some sort, but nobody knew just who he was and where he came from.

I'd fished him out of doorways many times when I walked patrol down here and taken him someplace warm for a cup of soup, and I'd busted him on two occasions when the winter weather was particularly severe and I figured he'd be better off in a cell than sleeping on a wet, steamy grating next to a big building that provided only minimum protection from the wind.

His name was Johnnie B. MacDonald, or so he told everyone, although it probably was one of a long line of aliases, and there wasn't a cop on the beat who didn't know and like him. Most took care of him in one sense or another, with a few bucks or a container of coffee so loaded with sugar that it would keep him nourished for part of the day anyway. When I'd ridden a patrol car I would sometimes put the heater on and drive him around for an entire shift, and once a few days before Christmas when he'd been stiff with cold and the hairs in his nose had frozen, he'd said to me, "Man, this weather just gets into my bones," and I'd given him the gloves right off my hands.

But that had to be fifteen years ago. Yet he vaguely remembered me, an amazing feat considering he probably couldn't recall where he'd spent the previous night. Long-term memory, they say, is the last to go.

Johnnie B. MacDonald lived on the pleasure of the city and county and off the kindness of cops and pedestrians, nourished by muscatel or whatever else he could find to drink—cough medicine, rubbing alcohol, Sterno, and other things you probably wouldn't want to think about.

"You're right, you do know me," I said. "You're Johnnie B."

He bobbed his head and grinned, showing the three brown and crooked teeth in his lower jaw; the rest had fallen out or been knocked out, but since he rarely ingested anything that wasn't liquid, I don't suppose it bothered him. It didn't seem to matter much where we had met before, so I didn't enlighten him. Too much to explain—I used to be a cop, I'm not one anymore, now I work private. I didn't imagine he'd care.

I took a careful look at him. His face was lined and leathery and dotted with healed-over scabs, his hooked nose bloomed with broken capillaries, his eyes were all three colors of the American flag. His hands, though covered with rough skin and sores and calluses, were slim and artistic-looking, with the tapered fingers of a violinist or painter, and they were always in motion when he spoke, drawing imaginary pictures in the air, two mesmerizing dancers weaving before his face. It was impossible even to estimate his age; he'd looked at least sixty when I'd first met him, although I'm sure he was younger than that, and his appearance hadn't changed much over a decade and a half.

"How are you, Johnnie B.?" I said, and put my hand around his scrawny bicep. My thumb and middle finger nearly came together on the other side.

"I'm good," he cackled. "Got busted out in Euclid just after New Year's for hangin' out in the 7-Eleven. I was in there warmin' up, and I didn't wanna go back outside—it was colder'n a witch's tit that night. So the boys picked me up and brung me in, an' that old hangin' judge out there, you know the one, he gimme sixty days in the lockup. I ate regular an' stayed warm, so except for nothin' to drink it wasn't all that bad." He lowered his eyes. "You haven't got any change, have you?"

I dug into my pocket.

"I hate t'ask you, because we were friends, but y'know how it is." He looked at me again, straining his memory. "We *were* friends, weren't we?"

"We were friends, Johnnie B."

He seemed to relax a bit; at least he knew now that I wasn't going to steal his shoes. "I knew it. Never forget a face, that's my advice. A man sometimes don't care if you recall his name, but if you forget what he looks like, that's an insult."

"My name's Milan," I said. "I used to be a cop."

"An' you ain't no more?"

"I ain't no more."

I gave him five dollars. He didn't even look at it but squirreled it away in his shirt pocket, the one with the button. He patted the pocket a few times as if it held a kitten.

I unlocked my car door.

"You headin' out east?" he said, his shaggy eyebrows twin arches of hope.

"Where do you need to go?"

"I gotta go over One-eighty-fifth." In blue-collar Cleveland, you "go down" to work, no matter where your job is geographically located, and you "go over" virtually everywhere else.

I checked my watch. It was five thirty-five. Where he was heading wasn't anywhere near my destination, but it wasn't far enough out of the way that I could refuse him. The sky was darkening already, and the lake breeze was kicking up, and all he had on to fight the chill was a lightweight jacket and that green scarf.

"Get in," I said. If I was late to Victor Gaimari's, so be it.

He didn't smell as bad inside the car as I thought he might; he'd probably slept in a homeless shelter the night before and enjoyed a shower. His clothes, while faded and and worn, were surprisingly presentable, and he sat easily in the corner of the seat, his back against the door and his thin hands clasped around one knee. A patch of bare skin poked out through a hole in his khakis, just below where his fingers interlaced. I clicked the automatic door lock shut so he wouldn't fall out.

Cleveland doesn't have a serious rush hour the way they do in Chicago or Los Angeles, but because it was the end of the workday and downtown was emptying quickly, I opted to stay off the Shoreway and instead headed east up St. Clair Avenue.

"What's going on over One-Eighty-fifth Street, John?"

"I gotta find a guy," he said.

"You're not in any trouble, are you?"

"Who, me?" he said, as if I'd just verbalized the unthinkable. "Naw. I just gotta find this guy."

We passed East Fifty-fifth; now we were in the old neighborhood. I glanced at the lighted Stroh's sign in the window of Vuk's Tavern, which is where I hang out when the mood strikes me, and I suddenly wanted a beer. Badly. But I wasn't going to march Johnnie B. MacDonald in there—Vuk would have taken it unkindly. Besides, Johnnie B. wasn't going to get any drinks from me. Whatever he bought on his own with my five dollars, however, was his business.

"This thing got a heater in it?" my passenger asked.

I reached over and flipped on the heat, and immediately warm air filled the car. He wriggled ecstatically and made a purring noise deep in his throat.

"I owe this guy some money," he said, "so I gotta go over One-eighty-fifth an' find him."

That worried me. "How much you owe him?"

He scrunched up his face, giving him the look of a particularly sappy hound dog. "Four dollars," he said. "He loan it to me last week, an' I gotta find him an' pay him back."

"You got it?"

"I had it before. Now with your five I can maybe buy me a flop and a sangwich too." He waggled a long, bony finger at me. "Always keep your credit rating good," he admonished. "And pay your debts."

I wanted to give him more, then—maybe twenty. But I didn't. The Muscatel Bottlers of America is not my favorite charity. "That's good advice," I said.

"Damn right. A man who don't pay his debts, he might as well dry up and go lay in the garbage for the trash men to collect."

It took about thirty more minutes in homeward-bound late afternoon traffic to get up to 185th and St. Clair, a colorful ethnic neighborhood where each summer they hold a street festival with button-box bands, amusement park rides for the kids, and enough booths offering pierogis, Italian sausages, bratwurst, Amish funnel cakes, Buffalo wings, and potato pancakes to clog your arteries for a month.

"Thanks, man," Johnnie B. said when I pulled up to the curb. "God bless you. And you take care of yourself now, you hear me?"

"I hear you," I said.

"You take care your health. Your health's a precious gift, y'know."

He climbed out of the car, made sure the door was securely shut, and gave me a discreet little wave before he moved away. I watched as he weaved unsteadily down the sidewalk, aiming for the nearest tavern. I didn't know whether he was heading for a drink or trying to find the guy whom he owed four dollars, so he could keep up his credit rating. Either way, there wasn't much I could do about it.

I headed south, toward Victor Gaimari's house in the tony eastern suburb of Orange, thinking about Johnnie B.

And wondering why a strict code of honor that so informed the behavior of a homeless wino had completely eluded a man like Jeffrey Feldman.

CHAPTER ELEVEN

The village of Orange is out near Pepper Pike and Solon and Hunting Valley, all rolling hills and stands of oak and pine and buckeye, with a few birches and sumac thrown in just for variety's sake. Victor Gaimari lives right in the middle of it on three heavily wooded acres, in an enormous gray-painted Cape Cod colonial that would be called a mansion just about anywhere else but in the elegant eastern suburbs is just another nice house. In any case, against the almost dark sky its windows were lit up like a scene on a traditional Christmas card, and as I cruised up the winding crushed-oyster-shell driveway at a quarter past seven, it seemed properly ducal.

At the top of the drive a guy was waiting to take my car, and I use the word "guy" advisedly. He didn't look like the usual kids who work for the valet parking services, but then of course Victor wouldn't entrust the parking of his guests' cars to strangers. He was around forty, with dark thinning hair, a thick left ear, misshapen knuckles, and a too-small-in-the-shoulders black suit he must have bought at a discount clothier. I figured he'd fought light heavyweight.

I think his associate just inside the door had been his sparring partner, and from the look of him I'd have wagered his name could be found somewhere on the guest registers of the state correctional facilities in Lorain or Mansfield. Shiny scar tissue thickened both eyebrows.

He moved easily into the doorway, effectively blocking it.

"Yes?" he said in a voice indicating he'd been hit too many times in the throat.

"Milan Jacovich."

My size, the Slavic cheekbones, and the dip in my nose, a souvenir of the football wars, evidently didn't sit right with him. He gave me a dose of attitude and didn't even try to be discreet about checking the list on a table near the door. "You're not on the list," he said.

"That's because I was invited by Mr. Gaimari only this morning."

He seemed to be having some trouble digesting that information. Finally he came toward me, hands in front of him. "Lift 'em up," he said.

I took a step away from him to give me some swinging room. "You're nuts if you think I'll let you pat me down at a dinner party."

"Your call," he shrugged, and dropped into a boxing crouch. It was about to get ugly when Victor came bounding up the three steps from the sunken living room, a bloody Mary in his manicured mitt. "Milan," he said as if he'd been waiting all his life for me to show up. "I'm so glad you could make it."

He took in the situation with one glance. "Trouble?" He's quick, Victor.

"Not quite," I said.

He glared at his muscle. "For Christ's sake, Angelo, where do you think you are?"

The big guy looked crestfallen. "Sorry, Mr. Gaimari."

"The guy's just doing his job, Victor," I said, and allowed him to lead me into the house.

We walked through the vestibule to the living room, which was approximately the size of the Old Arcade downtown. I'd been there once before, but it had been strictly a business visit, and I'd failed to notice that the house was filled with beautiful things, some of which belonged in the Cleveland Museum of Art, like a small, ornately framed pen-and-ink sketch by Matisse—I'm no art expert, but I know a Matisse when I see one—and a somewhat larger Bonnard. Graceful and powerful sculpture, both traditional and modern, rested on tables I was sure had first been dusted in the eighteenth century. There were delicate, luminous porcelain bowls and urns, and a striking bronze of the head of a wailing baby. And socializing in the midst of it all, beautiful, influential people. Victor spares no expense in surrounding himself with what he wants. He's one of those men who, while rarely deliberately cruel, truly believes that the rest of the world has been put in place for his own personal use.

The assembled guests looked like a print ad for fine Scotch whisky. The men were in dark suits, the women in dressy cocktail attire and a lot of understated jewelry. A musician installed at the ebony grand piano was all duded up in a wine-colored suit, maroon shirt, and flowered tie, and a toupee with luxuriant black curls seemingly made of vinyl that tumbled down the back of his neck. He'd covered up the gray in his beard with what looked for all the world like shoe polish. He was playing "Don't Cry for Me, Argentina." I should have known.

Victor guided me down among the guests for introductions, pushing me at a paunchy sixtyish man in a charcoal pinstripe. "You know Judge Pingitore, don't you, Milan?"

Of course I didn't, at least not personally, but I'd read about him for years. "Your Honor," I said.

"Jerry," the judge corrected me. "Say hello to my wife."

I turned and did as I was told; Mrs. Judge was a fast thirty-five, and I guessed she was the second Mrs. Judge.

I didn't need to wonder why a municipal judge was having dinner at the home of a mob boss. My mother didn't raise any stupid children. Victor propelled me on to meet the rest of the guests. The piano man had segued into "I Don't Know How to Love Him," from *Jesus Christ, Superstar*. Apparently we were in for an Andrew Lloyd Webber festival.

I met Victor's date, a well turned-out blonde whose name was familiar to everyone who read the society pages. Chickie Tattersfield was the ex-wife of the CEO of a *Fortune* 500 company in Cleveland. The divorce had been exceptionally messy, as I recalled, as divorces usually are when millions of dollars in property settlements are at stake, but it hadn't kept her from chairing several of the more creatively staged benefit parties in the last few years. I don't know whether her mother had named her Chickie or if it was one of those prep school nicknames like Pudge and Pidge and Muffy that somehow don't ever go away.

But I didn't have time to ask her before Victor steered me across the exquisite Persian carpet—a trek as long as a senior citizen's morning power walk—and into a large sunroom just off the living room.

"What would you like to drink?" he said on the way.

I knew what I wanted to drink, but I didn't think a can of Stroh's would fly in such a rarefied atmosphere. "Whatever you're having," I said, hating myself for wimping out.

The sunroom is where the bar had been set up. Unlike the parking attendant and the mug checking guests at the door, the young bartender looked like he knew what he was doing and hadn't learned it at hard labor at the expense of the state.

"A Mary for Mr. Jacovich," Victor told him.

That jerked my chain, and I wondered if he'd done it deliberately. I haven't really gotten over Mary yet—Mary Soderberg, who livened up my days for about a year and a half at a time when I really needed it, until she decided life in the fast lane with her boss was more exciting than with a slightly shabby Slovenian detective who used to play football.

He touched his glass to mine. "To old friendships and new, revitalized ones."

I nodded, pushed the celery stalk garnish aside with my finger, and took a gulp, trying not to make a face. I don't like either vodka or tomato juice.

"Come on, Milan." Victor was tugging my arm and pulling me away from the bar. "I'd like to introduce you to your dinner partner. I think you'll be pleased."

I was. She was about five foot five and had shoulder-length dark hair and quick, inquisitive blue eyes. She was probably close to thirty-five. Her clothes were expensively understated, and although she wore no rings—when I see an attractive woman I always check for a wedding ring before anything else—there was a diamond tennis bracelet on her left wrist. Like everyone else at the party, she moved and carried herself with the unshakable and specific confidence of the very rich.

"Cathleen Hartigan, Milan Jacovich," Victor said.

She took my hand in hers, squeezed slightly, and gave it back to me.

Our host excused himself by saying he would "leave you two kids alone to get better acquainted."

Yes, he actually said that. Sometimes I just don't believe Victor.

"Victor didn't have time to fill me in about you," Cathleen said, "since he only invited me this afternoon, but what little he told me was fascinating. He says you're a private investigator."

Lots of people think my profession is "fascinating," but then I imagined that Cathleen Hartigan would have said that if I'd told her I drove the salt truck that de-iced the streets in the wintertime.

"It's not exactly the way it is in the movies," I said. "What I do most is industrial security."

"What's that?"

"I keep employees from taking home too many paper clips."

She put a red-taloned hand on my arm. "You don't look like a paper clip counter. And what do you do when you catch them at it?"

"I have them flogged," I said.

She took her hand away. "Okay."

"What do you do, Cathleen?"

The look she gave me was almost a challenge. "I'm a lawyer."

Like a lightbulb appearing over a character's head in a comic strip, the familiarity of her last name kicked in. Hartigan. In a region where most politicians are either black, Irish, or Italian, the Hartigans are practically a royal family.

"Pretty famous name around these parts," I said. "Are you one of *the* Hartigans, or only a shirttail relative."

"If you mean is the judge my mother, is my uncle in Congress, and is my brother Kevin a city councilman, I guess I'm going to have to plead guilty."

I nodded. "My family was big in the steel business. My grand-father Stupar worked in the smelter at the LTV mill, my father Louis was the shop steward at Deming Steel, and my mother Marijanna, well, she was famous all up and down St. Clair Avenue for her pork roast with sauerkraut."

"And you broke with tradition and became a detective."

"Black sheep of the family—went to college and everything. You're empty-handed. What can I get you to drink?"

"A beer would be nice," she said.

"I doubt if they have beer."

"Are you kidding? Victor Gaimari probably has a better-stocked bar than the Ritz-Carlton. Come on."

She took my arm and we started for the bar. "Don't feel you have to drink beer just because you're with one of the great un-washed," I said.

She stopped and leveled a gaze at me that was as sharp as a laser beam. "Mr. Jacovich, I think you're a snob."

"Me?"

"Sure, you. A reverse snob, which is the worst kind. You're feeling put-upon and defensive because you're in a room full of rich people, so for protection you come on as some sort of noble peasant."

"I didn't mean—"

"The hell you didn't!" Her eyes were shining, but she didn't really seem angry. More amused, I thought, which was a thousand times worse. "You haven't even known me for five minutes, but I'm here at a Victor Gaimari dinner party and I have a family that gets into the papers a lot, so you immediately make judgments. You think I walk around in a party dress and diamonds all the time dropping the names of my influential relatives? Come off it, pal. A week ago Friday I was eating a pierogi in the basement of a Polish church in Tremont, and I watched the final game of the season between the Browns and the Oilers from the Dawg Pound and damn near froze my ass off. Now are you going to get me that beer or are we going to stand around all evening trading bullshit?"

"Wow," I said. "You kiss your mother with that mouth?"

She laughed. "Let's go!" she said, and pushed me in the direction of the bar.

I shoved my barely tasted drink at the server and asked for two beers.

"Would you like Samuel Smith Pale Ale or Taddy Porter, sir?" Cathleen Hartigan and I looked at one another and started to giggle.

That's when the Old Man showed up.

I knew he had arrived even before I saw him, because all conversation stopped, and the air actually got a little heavier. Like when you were a kid in school giving the substitute teacher a bad time and all of a sudden the principal walks in. The Old Man has that kind of presence. Nobody here, except the hitter checking guests at the door, was part of the "family," but they all knew who Don Giancarlo D'Allessandro was—and what he was. He had only to make an appearance to produce a kind of reverent awe.

He's a small man, his skin thin and gray and stretched tightly over his features like ancient parchment, but in Cleveland he casts a giant shadow. Victor apparently inherited his fashion sense from another branch of the family, because D'Allessandro wore a jacket with a black and white windowpane check, plaid pants, and a too thin black tie carelessly knotted under the collar of a white shirt with a pattern of tiny roses.

He posed stiffly in the entryway; maybe he was waiting for bows and curtseys. He was flanked by his driver, John Terranova, a man I knew, and a woman in her sixties who I'd never seen before. I knew that the don's wife had been dead almost twenty-five years and that he had reputedly kept company for some time with the widow of one of his closest associates, one Vincenzo Sordetto, known in certain circles as Vinny Sword, who had come to an untimely end in the parking lot of a *shvitz*, a steam bath, on Kinsman Road, courtesy of a car bomb that had blown out windows for two blocks in every direction. The bomber had never been found out, at least not by the Cleveland police, and nobody was ever able to pin down whether the bomb had been directed at the D'Allessandro family or whether they had indeed been behind it. I assumed that the woman, whose aspect was that of a proud, vigilant eagle, was Regina Sordetto. She watched over her charge with a protectiveness that bordered on ferocity.

Terranova scanned the room. When his eyes met mine, although my appearance there clearly startled him, he allowed himself a small and unobtrusive smile. We were hardly friends, but we weren't exactly sworn enemies either. I'd even served him a Stroh's at my apartment one night. So I nodded back, embarrassed for him that he was here in the capacity of little more than a servant.

Victor was at his uncle's side immediately, embracing him, kissing the hand of Regina Sordetto, and leading the two of them down into the living room, where almost all the guests except Cathleen Hartigan and myself had assembled to greet the newcomer.

Terranova waited until the don had navigated the wide steps, then disappeared, presumably into the kitchen with the other servants.

"We should go over and say hello," Cathleen said.

"You know him?"

"Sure, everybody knows Mr. D'Allessandro." She looked at me. "I'm sorry, it was me being the snob that time. Do you know him?"

"Everybody knows Mr. D'Allessandro."

We moved out of the sunroom and over toward the steps, where Judge Pingitore was kissing D'Allessandro's withered cheek. "You're looking fine, Mr. D.," the judge was saying. "How do you feel? You feeling good? You're looking good."

When D'Allessandro greeted my companion his eyes lit up, and he took both her hands in his. "Cathleen," he pronounced, his Mediterranean tongue bouncing gently off the Irish name. "Good to see you. You get more beautiful every time."

Then the old man saw me. He wasn't surprised; I'm sure Victor told him I'd be there. "Milan Jacovich," he said, and his mouth pulled back in a rictus the way it always did when he said my name. The hard consonants were alien to someone like the don, who probably still thought in Italian.

"Don Giancarlo." I shook his frail, dry hand. It felt like the claw of a bird.

"How long we know you, Milan Jacovich, and this is the first time we take an evening meal together?"

"Too many years," I said. "It's my pleasure."

Don Giancarlo released my hand and put his palm against my cheek. "I like this man, Victor. He's respectful." And he patted my face like I was his grandson.

I was pretty annoyed with myself for plugging into the mob's comedy of manners, which is as strict and formalized as in seventeenth-century France. I was, however, the only male present who didn't bestow a kiss on the old man. Everybody has a line that they draw, and that one was mine.

D'Allessandro was ensconced in a high-backed chair and given a large goblet of red wine, which I imagined came from a special supply Victor kept on hand. As opposed to most of the wines in his cellar, this one had probably been made somewhere in the garage of an old Murray Hill house by someone who had known the old man for fifty years.

I turned to Cathleen. "You and the don are buddies, it seems."

"I've known him since I was six years old," she said. "I know people say terrible things about him, but he's always been lovely and kind to my family."

I'll bet. "I haven't known him quite that long," I said. She nodded. "You're a friend of Victor's."

I started to say that I was no more a friend of Victor's than of Genghis Khan's, that I didn't have friends like Victor, but it seemed too much trouble, and ungracious, at that. I was in his home, after all, drinking his Samuel Smith Pale Ale and munching on his canapés.

"Funny I haven't met you before," she said. "At some party or benefit."

"Not really. I don't do the benefit circuit, and this is the first time I've been to Victor's house socially."

There was mischief in her eyes. "How do you like it?"

"What's not to like? What other private home could you go to and get the choice of Samuel Smith's Pale Ale or Taddy Porter?" And we tinked glasses.

After a few minutes Victor announced that dinner was served.

The piano player gave us all a break and went off to take his own dinner in the kitchen, and we filed into the dining room. It wasn't quite as cavernous and cold as the one in *Citizen Kane*, but the effect was the same. There were fourteen people in all, but there was room for eight more at the table, and all the chairs matched. In my apartment, if I have more than four people to dinner I have to set up a card table and folding chairs.

Cathleen Hartigan and I found our place cards a bit south of the middle of the table. Below the salt, I figured. Next to me was a pleasant, forgettable woman whose husband, seated across the table and down a few seats, did something in city hall in Mayfield Heights. Victor was at one end, with Chickie Tattersfield on his left and a statuesque brunette I found out later was a vascular surgeon on his right. The doctor's husband, a psychiatrist, was on Cathleen's left. But nobody sat down until Don Giancarlo did, and he made a kingly figure at the other end, Mrs. Sordetto on one side of him and Mrs. Pingitore on the other.

Two middle-aged white-clad women were busily serving mushroom broth, while another was circling the table pouring white wine into delicate goblets of Irish crystal. I didn't think even Victor Gaimari kept that kind of household staff, so I assumed the dinner was being catered.

"Victor," the surgeon said, running her strong, capable-looking hand around the edge of her dinner plate, "this service is exquisite. Nineteenth-century British, isn't it?"

Victor beamed. "You have a very good eye, Patsy. I came across it about two years ago at a wonderful moody old castle in Cornwall and decided I couldn't possibly do without it, so I had it shipped over. I'm glad you like it."

"Like it?" she said. "I'm green with envy."

Victor looked over at me. "Milan here has developed an interest in fine porcelain. Haven't you, Milan?"

My soupspoon was halfway to my lips and stopped there in a ludicrous moment of suspended animation. I couldn't believe he was going to draw me into a learned discussion on porcelain with someone like the doctor, who obviously knew what she was talking about. In the meantime I realized that I probably looked like

a candid photograph in a tabloid. I put the spoon down, aware
that everyone at the table was looking at me.

Giancarlo D'Allessandro raised a quizzical eyebrow. "Mr. Jacovich is a man of many interests, eh?"

Victor nodded, gesturing toward me like a model pointing to a
refrigerator on a game show. I was apparently his prime exhibit.
"It comes from having—what is it they say in those commercials?
An inquiring mind."

And then all of a sudden I knew why I'd been invited. Power.
Victor Gaimari is a powerful man and he likes to exercise that
power in unique ways. For reasons of his own that I'd never been
able to fathom, he'd been trying to buddy up to me for years, and
having to come to his home for an elegant and out-of-my-league
dinner party in exchange for information I badly needed was evidently the price I had to pay for not letting him become my best
friend. Now that I was here, he was going to squeeze a little.

Squeezing was Victor's hobby.

"And at the moment Milan's decided to inquire about the collecting of porcelain and ceramics. Haven't you, Milan?"

I picked up my wineglass. The delicate stem felt awkward in
my big hand. "That's right, Victor. I decided I couldn't possibly
do without it."

And I lifted the glass in a toast to mine host.

"Ha ha," Victor said.

CHAPTER TWELVE

I had to hand it to Victor, the dinner was superb. Chicken Cae-
sar salad, long-bone veal chops with some sort of cognac glaze,
and cheesecake with fresh strawberries. Of course there was
coffee, and of course it was strong and good.

The assembled guests carried on about how wonderful everything was except D'Allessandro, who ate a meal specially prepared for him, pasta with some sort of bright red sauce, and complained that the damn doctors who told him no more red meat
were going to kill him with boredom. He was also the only one
present who tucked his napkin under his chin.

Table conversation was pretty stimulating too. No sports talk,
no television chatter. Politics, for the most part, local politics and
the fabled renaissance of Cleveland's downtown area. Victor said
he was trying to talk Judge Pingitore into running for statewide
office.

The judge blushed, toying with his new potatoes, and nearly
tugged his forelock. "It's a little early to be talking about that now,
Victor. The election is a year and a half off. I'll admit I've been
thinking about it . . ." and here he actually chuckled. I've never
really heard anyone say "heh heh," before. Maybe he thought all
judges were supposed to talk like Andy Hardy's father.

"But I haven't made any firm decision," he told us.

"I hope you'll let us know as soon as you have," Victor said
playfully. "You know you have my support."

Pingitore ducked his head and allowed how very grateful he was for that fact, and for Victor's friendship, and Victor lifted his wineglass and proclaimed, "To next year's election, Judge—and Columbus."

I assumed Victor meant our state capital and not the fellow who discovered America. Poor old Chris isn't exactly a popular fellow these days, except perhaps in Italian households; a statue of him bigger than Miss Liberty in New York Harbor had been offered to Cleveland a few years ago and unceremoniously turned down. But I drank to him anyway, and not to the judge's own political ambitions.

The don simply smiled and nodded, twirling his fork against a tablespoon, and spooled pasta into his mouth, while his eyes glittered with approval and anticipation—you could tell he was smelling blood and the hunt was up—and I knew in my heart it was a done deal that Jerome Pingitore was going to be the next attorney general of Ohio, one with an eye on the governor's mansion five years down the line.

After dinner we wandered out into the living room again while the serving women cleared the table and the hardguy who'd taken names at the door circulated around with after-dinner cordials. The piano player, whose eyes had taken on a twinkle since last we saw him and who'd acquired a certain redness around the edges of his nostrils, resumed his station and unveiled another of his talents, singing. I wasn't at all surprised to discover he was a tenor, and that his first selection was "All I Ask of You" from *Phantom*. Or pleased, either.

I was spared the rest of the medley when Victor invited me into his study for a talk. "We'll have to keep this kind of short, Milan," he said. "After all, I have other guests."

"I appreciate that."

"Is this something my uncle needs to hear?"

"Not unless he can't possibly do without porcelain either."

I excused myself from Cathleen Hartigan, who was deep in conversation with the psychiatrist anyway, and Victor led me up the steps from the living room and down the hall, holding an enormous snifter of brandy in each hand. His study was behind double doors at the end of the long corridor, and when I opened the door and we went inside I wasn't surprised to find it was all dark wood paneling and leather furniture, with a cherrywood desk on which a family of four could have slept. A computer station in matching wood was built into the wall, and of course there was a fax machine. I'd have been disappointed if there wasn't.

He handed me one of the brandies, and we sat at either end of a long sofa made of soft beige leather, the cushions of which were like embracing arms. Victor ran his hand over the leather, caressing it. "I love to sit here," he said. "It feels like the skin of a woman, doesn't it?"

No woman that I ever met, but I dutifully agreed with him. I wondered if his housekeeper gave the sofa a twice-daily dose of Oil of Olay.

He leaned toward me and clinked his snifter against mine. "Here's to the skin of beautiful women," he said. At last, something I could drink to.

I'm not much of a brandy connoisseur, but what I sipped was sensational, unlike anything I'd ever tasted before, with a sort of prunelike undertaste. Victor seemed pleased that I appreciated it.

"Armagnac," he said. "It's an acquired taste, I suppose." He arched one perfect eyebrow. "Speaking of tastes, how do you like Cathleen Hartigan?"

"She's very nice," I said.

"And attractive."

"Very."

He smiled a satyr's smile, just a few kilometers short of a leer. "Any magic there?"

"Magic! Was this a fixup?"

"That sounds a little like junior high school, doesn't it?" he said. "No, not really. I thought you two would like each other."

"She's more your type than mine."

He pondered that. "True. And we did date for a brief time."

"Swell."

"But I think Cathleen would like to be married, and I've always thought you were a marrying kind of guy."

"Victor, you missed your calling. You should have been a matchmaker."

"You could do worse," he said. "She's a hell of a gal." He sat back against the soft cushions and carefully crossed one leg over the other. "So what's this business you wanted to discuss, Milan?"

"Jeff Feldman."

He exhaled impatiently, frowning. "I hardly know Jeff Feldman. And I feel about his whereabouts the way I do about Albert Belle's batting average. It interests me in a very abstract way, but it has no bearing on my life or well-being one way or the other."

"You said that he had something you want."

"You'd be surprised how many people have things that I want, but I hardly lose any sleep over it."

"Victor, let's not play games."

"Why not? That's what we do, isn't it? I mean, that's our contract."

"We don't have a contract."

"Sure we do. We all have contracts with everyone we know. Our family, our friends, our lovers. Each relationship carries its own special contract, its own set of rules and parameters, and if we break that contract it seriously ruptures the fabric of the relationship. Yours and mine is that we devil each other." He smiled, oozing charm. "Isn't it?"

"You mean you invited me to dinner tonight just to jerk me around?"

"No," he said. "I invited you because in a very strange way I like you. You've caused me a lot of grief over the past few years, and a bit of money, too. But you're a stand-up guy, as they say in Collinwood where my uncle grew up."

"They say it on St. Clair Avenue too."

"And I respect that in you, even though you're a pain in the ass. And so does my uncle. So I asked you here out of friendship. And respect."

"You guys are big on that, aren't you? Respect."

"'You guys.' We're just like anybody else. We're businessmen. To assume that everyone with a vowel at the end of his name is a gangster is insulting. It's not true, and you damn well know it."

"I wouldn't insult you in your own home while I was sipping your Armagnac, Victor." I gestured at him with my drink. "Look, you say Feldman has something you want. Right now nobody seems to know where he is, and that means you don't get what you want."

He smiled. "I hate it when that happens."

"Okay. I'm trying to find Feldman, and maybe you can help me. I'll be helping you too."

"I don't know what I can tell you," he said. "I don't know where he is either."

"But you know what it is he's got. That you think he's got, anyway. Tell me what it is, and maybe I can find him."

He considered it, delicately running a finger around the rim of his snifter. "I'm not sure that's germane."

"Why don't you let me decide what's germane?"

He glanced over at me, his nostrils flaring a bit. "Don't push it," he warned.

"I'm not. You're very good at what you do, Victor. Whatever the hell it is."

He couldn't keep from chuckling at that one.

"Well, I'm damn good at what I do," I went on. "Why don't you just let me do it?"

"I'm not stopping you."

"You're not helping me, either."

"I'm not sure I should."

"Why not?"

He preened his mustache. "I think you know me well enough to know that I'm a little competitive."

"More than a little."

He nodded. "Just as much so with my art collection as with anything else."

"So?"

"So Feldman has a line on a piece that I'd positively kill to own." He saw the look on my face and chuckled. "Just an expression, Milan."

"Uh-huh."

"If the word gets out that this piece is available and that I'm trying to acquire it, other collectors might try to buy it out from under me. That will send the price up significantly. And I'd like to avoid that. So it's probably better that you don't know."

"I'll find out," I said.

"How?"

"I told you, I'm good at what I do. Besides, it's hard to keep a secret. Sooner or later the word will get out, and your competitors will be running up your arm anyway. But if you tell me now, maybe I can find Feldman quickly and you can have your little bauble all to yourself."

"Little bauble," he murmured.

"I don't know what else to call it."

He stared into the depths of his snifter for almost a minute, inhaling the vapors, his nose at the rim. I tried it with mine, and it made me dizzy. Then he uncrossed his legs and leaned forward, elbows on his knees.

"You can call it the Helgenburg vase," he said, as though presenting me with a gift beyond price, and then he was quiet, his thoughts far away.

I didn't say anything, mainly because I was plumb out of questions. It's usually better to keep your mouth shut and listen anyway.

"Josephus Helgenburg was an Austrian porcelain maker, born just after the turn of the eighteenth century. A contemporary of Josiah Spode and Josiah Wedgwood."

I nodded. I had at least heard of them.

"Helgenburg had a small factory near Vienna, but his influence was widely felt all over Europe, because he was a master not only at creating fine porcelain but a pioneer in decorating it with gold leaf and semiprecious stones, a technique which was fairly rare and, as you can imagine, very expensive. You with me so far, Milan?"

"I went to college, too, Victor."

"Forgive me," he said, "but most people find all this a trifle arcane." He took a birdlike sip of his Armagnac and savored it for a moment before he continued. "Helgenburg's work came to the attention of most of the royal courts of Europe, and especially of Charles Edward Stuart. Know who he was?"

"I know the Stuarts were the ruling family of England, so I'd guess he was a shirttail relative of some sort. But I thought their line ended a little earlier."

"So it did," Victor said. "Their royal line. Charles Edward, the grandson of James the Second, was also known as 'Bonnie Prince Charlie.' Or, in unkinder circles, as 'the Young Pretender.' He was a lover of beauty, young Charlie, of beautiful women and beautiful things. And when he saw some of Helgenburg's work, he became his patron and commissioned him to design his table service. Understand?"

"Sure I do," I said, getting annoyed. "I commissioned mine from Wal-Mart."

He stood up, the better to let a sip of the Armagnac slide down his throat. "Jeff Feldman managed to locate a vase for me," he said, sighing his appreciation of the brandy. "A Helgenburg vase. One of only two that he created with a cabbage leaf pattern, circa 1745. There are photographs of it in several of the books on porcelain in the library. It's about sixteen inches high, and one of the only individual pieces of Helgenburg's—that is, not part of a larger set—in existence." He closed his eyes for a moment, I suppose envisioning it. "One of them is in the British Museum's permanent collection. The other was supposedly somewhere in Germany right after the war in a cache of art treasures that had been stolen by the Third Reich and squirreled away or buried. No one has known where it ended up until now."

"And where's that?"

"In New York someplace. Feldman wouldn't tell me exactly."

"Why not?"

"Two reasons, I imagine. First of all, whoever has it probably did not acquire it by the usual legal means."

"You mean it's hot?"

"You have a quaint way of expressing yourself, Milan."

"What's the second reason."

He looked down his patrician nose at me. "Because if I knew

where it was myself, I wouldn't need him to get it for me. Obviously."

"Obviously."

He began pacing the room. "Feldman is always on the lookout for rare and beautiful pieces for me," he said, "but when he said he'd located a Helgenburg, I couldn't believe it."

"Neither can I."

He stopped his pacing and stared right through me.

"All right, I get it, Victor. We're playing movie trivia." I got to my feet, too. "I'm Humphrey Bogart and you're Sydney Greenstreet. I thank you for the meal, but I'm really pissed off that you're trying to jerk my chain like this."

"You can look up Helgenburg in any library."

"The Helgenburg part might be on the up-and-up, but either you're trying to have a good laugh at my expense or you've gone Looney Tunes."

He sat down on edge of the huge desk, the balloon of Armagnac in one hand, one foot casually crossed over the other. "I assure you that I've never been in better mental health. And you've known me long enough to know I don't ever laugh where there's money concerned."

"So now Feldman's gone AWOL, after you gave him a big chunk of cash in advance to get this thing for you."

"On his word alone? Of course not," he scoffed. "I'm not stupid. I told him to check into it further, to bring me absolute proof that the item in question was bona fide, and that if he could convince me that it was, I'd make it well worth his while. I'm a dedicated collector, Milan, and I want that Helgenburg." He cleared his throat. "I did give Feldman a few bucks for walking-around money."

"How much?"

He looked away. "Chump change."

"Chump change?"

"Don't be deliberately obtuse. I gave him a little taste so he'd be indebted to me and not shop the piece around to the highest bidder."

He looked around for some more Armagnac, forgetting the

bottle was in the sunroom, behind the bar. Then he put his snifter down on the desk. "It's all perfectly legal, if that's what you're worried about."

"I don't care one way or the other," I said. "My job is to find Feldman."

"If you do, there'll be a small commission in it for you."

"No thanks. I already have a client."

He nodded. "I forgot I was talking to the original noble savage. All right, be that way. You'll never get rich."

"So what?" I said. "I'd just spend it on frivolous things like food and rent."

"But considering our longstanding friendship, I hope when you do find him, you'll let me know."

"That'll be up to my client," I said.

He glared at me for a few seconds, deciding whether he wanted to make a fuss about it. He chose wisely.

"Well, I should be getting back to my other guests," he said. "And you should be getting back to Cathleen."

"One question first."

"You're going to ask whether I like it or not, aren't you?"

"I guess you know me pretty well too, Victor. Just how badly do you want this thing?"

"The Helgenburg? Two hundred thousand dollars' worth," he said.

CHAPTER THIRTEEN

Victor and I emerged from the study, and the perfect host, he immediately rejoined the party, making sure all his guests had whatever they wanted to drink. I managed to find Cathleen, who was deep in conversation with Chickie Tattersfield. They were discussing a sale at Chisolm Halle in an elegant shopping center nearby called the Eton Collection.

"Are you finished with my date, Mr. Jacovich?" Chickie said.

"He's yours."

"Did you two solve all the problems of society?"

"Not all of them, no."

"Well then, what on earth is the point?" she said, and drifted gracefully away. Chickie Tattersfield was the kind of woman who seemed to drift or float when she moved, as if her feet never touched the ground. Maybe the huge settlement she'd received when she divorced her husband acted as sort of a cushion of air beneath her.

During my absence Cathleen had acquired a snifter of her own, and I took both hers and mine to the bar for refills. The piano player was singing something from *Cats*, which is what he sounded like.

I brought the Armagnacs back to Cathleen. She took hers and swirled it around, coating the sides of the glass. She glanced over at Victor, who was making sure his uncle was happy and comfortable. "Are you working on a particular case now, Milan?"

"I'm always working on a case. Otherwise the bank comes and takes the car away. Why?"

"Well, I wondered if that's why you're here tonight. You don't seem to be having a very good time."

I shrugged. "Except for Victor and his uncle, and now you, I don't really know anyone here."

"I get the idea that this kind of party isn't your thing anyway."

"You're right about that. Is it yours?"

She shrugged her shoulders rather prettily. "I'm used to it. Cleveland is a very married town, and so when you're single you latch on to any social life you can. It's a way to get through the days and nights. You grow up in a certain circle with certain people, and one day you look around and discover that outside of your work, these little get-togethers are your only form of social interaction. So you keep going to the same old parties with the same old people and kissing the same old cheeks because the alternative is sitting home six night a week watching old movies on cable and painting your toenails."

"I know—I do that a lot," I said.

She smiled and took a sip of her brandy, keeping her eyes fixed on me all the time, and I was sure it was one of the techniques they teach in those how-to-flirt classes they give at the Y. "I hope you'll call me some evening when you have nothing else going on. I'd like to get to know you better."

My heart gave a little jump, but it settled down quickly when it hit its head on reality. "That would be nice," I said. "But we live in different worlds, Cathleen."

"You really are judgmental, aren't you?" She didn't say it with any heat, just as a casual observation.

"Just a realist."

She pushed a strand of hair off her face. "But I think there's more to it than that."

"Oh?"

"Victor told you we used to go out for a while, didn't he?"

I mulled that over for a moment. "Yes, he did."

"That's part of it too, isn't it?"

"Not really."

"Sure it is. I'm thirty-six years old, Milan. Did you think I just stepped out of the convent this afternoon and wriggled into this dress?"

"Of course not. Everyone over the age of six has a past."

"But."

"What?"

"There's a 'but' hanging there at the end. Would you care to share it with the rest of the class?"

All of a sudden my collar felt too tight, and I fought down the urge to claw at the knot of my tie. I suppose my face was getting red. She smiled a sad Madonna's smile and said, "Because it was Victor. Right?"

"You make it sound pretty black and white."

"No, you do. I kept company for a few months with the nephew of an old family friend, a stockbroker, and in your mind I'm some kind of gangster's moll. Okay, fine. I'll only ask once." She lifted her snifter to me. "I don't see any reason I shouldn't think you're a goddamn fool, do you?"

My smile was full of regret. "Not if you don't mind joining a very big club."

The party wound down pretty quickly after that—parties in Cleveland usually do, especially during the week. As soon as it seemed polite to do so I said my thank-yous and goodbyes. Judge Pingitore pumped my hand as if I were a potential campaign contributor and told me how great it had been to see me. Victor thanked me for coming and added meaningfully that I should be sure and keep in touch. Giancarlo D'Allessandro squeezed my face, then slapped it once with what I assumed was affection and warned me to stay out of trouble. And Regina Sordetto lowered her eyelids at me, which seemed to be her all-purpose hello and goodbye. Kind of like *shalom* in Hebrew.

Cathleen Hartigan was distant but pleasant when she took my hand in her very cool one and told me it had been an interesting evening, but I could tell from the lack of interest in her eyes that

I'd once more blown it for myself. I'm very good at that. I've had years of practice.

I waited at the bottom of the portico steps for my car. The hardcase named Angelo came up beside me. He looked mad. I'd embarrassed him in front of his boss, and he was probably going to get into trouble.

"Smart guy, aren't you?" he said.

"Smarter than you. This is a dinner party, not a sit-down of capos. You don't frisk the guests. You're not doing wet work tonight, you're . . . a footman."

His scarred brows lowered over his eyes. "Footman? What's that?" he asked, puzzled.

"A guy who puts both feet in his mouth."

It took him a few seconds to realize he'd been insulted, and then he tucked his prognathous jaw into his chest and shifted forward onto the balls of his feet. I set myself to dodge the punch I knew was coming and counter it with one of my own. I thought I could probably take him without too much difficulty. But I didn't want to.

"Angelo!" The voice cut through the damp evening air, and all the fight seemed to go out of the ex-pug. He stepped back away from me, although he never took his eyes off my hands.

John Terranova came strolling over smoking a cigarette. "Knock it off, Angelo," he ordered.

Angelo looked from me to him, then back again.

"Pound sand," Terranova growled. "This is Mr. Gaimari's friend."

Angelo ducked his head and trotted away, and I relaxed a little.

Just a little.

"You gotta excuse Angelo," Terranova said. "Too many four-rounders on the undercard, too many times makin' it look good goin' into the tank." He slapped the side of his own head. "You know?"

"Thanks, John."

Terranova smiled and flipped his cigarette away. It made a

slim orange arc in the darkness, scattering sparks when it hit the shrubbery.

"Nothin' to thank me for, Milan. Angelo looks mean, but he can't hurt nobody no more. You're a pretty tough guy; you coulda taken him."

"I know," I said as the other pug drove up to the door in my car. "But thanks anyway—I'm wearing my good suit."

I threw him a little salute and allowed the pug to hold the door while I slid beneath the wheel.

Victor Gaimari can collect art and porcelain until it comes out of his ears. He can generously contribute to the Cleveland Ballet and the Museum of Art, he can sit on boards and show up with socialites like Chickie Tattersfield on his arm—but he's still just a hoodlum with an expensive haircut. And keeping guys like Angelo around simply proves it.

I found my way back onto Chagrin Boulevard and headed west. I thought about stopping in at Noggin's or the Italian Cafe for a beer to wash away the lingering taste of Armagnac, but after due consideration I decided I wasn't much in the mood for anything but going home. I was very careful to observe the speed limit through the four-block stretch of Woodmere Village, one of Ohio's more notorious speed traps, even at eleven o'clock at night.

Sometimes I'm my own worst enemy.

Cathleen Hartigan had hit the nail right on the head when she called me judgmental. She wasn't the first to make that observation, and she probably won't be the last.

But it just happens to be who I am.

For instance, when I become emperor, everyone who plays his car stereo loud enough to be clearly audible through both his closed windows and yours will be summarily executed. People who use apostrophes where they don't belong, like the butcher shop on Fleet Avenue whose window sign proclaims "Chicken's," will be clapped into solitary confinement with nothing to read except books on English usage. All car phones will be confiscated and burned. Local business owners will be permanently barred from appearing in their own television commercials. All baseball and football stadiums with artificial turf will be converted to grass. And as for places that put you on hold and make you listen to the music of Andrew Lloyd Webber . . .

My ex-wife Lila used to call it "pontificating" when I talked that way, and I suppose I can be something of a pain in the ass. But I have a very firm sense of what's good and bad—for me, anyway.

And what's right and wrong.

And Victor Gaimari, for my money, is a wrong guy. He's pleasant enough socially, as long as you don't cross him. He keeps his word, which is a rare commodity these days. And I know he gives a lot of money to good causes every year.

But it's dirty money, or money that used to be dirty and has been carefully laundered. It's money that the average Joe will never see because he's too busy working his butt off to feed his family, too busy paying his taxes and tossing a ball with his kids and going to church on Sunday. He doesn't know all the sneaky little angles Victor does and wouldn't use them if he did, because that's not how the game is played.

That's why the idea of dating someone who used to date Victor Gaimari, even casually, goes way beyond my tolerance.

That's why I told Cathleen Hartigan I wouldn't call.

That's why I spend six nights a week watching old movies on cable and painting my toenails.

I got home a little after eleven to find that the red light on my answering machine was blinking the joyful news that I'd had three calls in my absence. I have a beeper that I keep on my belt during the day, but I didn't think it was appropriate to wear it to a dinner party at Victor Gaimari's, so I'd left it on the nightstand next to my bed.

The first message was no more than a dial tone, followed by the recorded voice of an operator telling me that if I'd like to make a call I should hang up and try again. It was probably one of the ubiquitous sales calls that come almost every evening during dinnertime, and they'd disconnected when they heard the machine instead of a real live person.

Then, "Milan? Is Tetka. How you are? You don't call me long time now. Vatsa matter, you die or sometink?"

I smiled at the familiar magpie voice. My octogenarian Auntie Branka, my *tetka*. She lives up in Euclid, half a block from the Conrail tracks, and that's her standard greeting to me when I've let more than three days go by without calling and talking to her. She still wears the widow's weeds she'd donned when my Uncle Anton died about ten years ago, and she's just about the only family I have left. Her son Aloysius, or Loy as everyone calls him, is a Garfield Heights dentist with a BMW and a twelve-stroke golf handicap, and her daughter Helen is married, lives in Parma, and hardly ever visits. Another son, Dragan, had come home from the Mekong Delta in 1971 in a body bag. So I'm one of her last remaining family ties too.

I should call her more often and want to, but every time I do she invites me to dinner, makes me eat the *sarma*, stuffed cabbage, that I've cheerfully loathed since I was three years old, and tries to introduce me to still another of her Euclid widow pals twenty years older than I am. I scribbled *Tetka* on a Post-it note and stuck it on the handset of the phone so I'd remember to call her in the morning.

The machine beeped and I heard a male voice, thick with emotion and worry.

"Mr. Jacovich? Irv Feldman, from New York. I don't know whether this is any help to you, but I found that business card Jeff left in his old room. It's from the Barthalow Gallery on East Sixty-fourth Street." He spelled it for me slowly. "It's not a regular art gallery; I think they specialize in old letters from famous people, and autographs and things like that. I don't know what Jeff was doing there. Maybe he just—well, who knows. Anyway, if you hear anything, please, ah, give a shout. My wife and I are getting concerned."

And then he left his home telephone number, and the machine beeped three times to let me know it was finished.

I wrote *Barthalow Gal.* on another Post-it. Then I stared at it for a while and started singing softly under my breath, as in "Barthalow gal won't you come out tonight, come out tonight, come out tonight . . ." It isn't often I can give myself a chuckle.

Old letters and autographs, I thought. In addition to ceramics, was Jeff Feldman into collecting notes from Dickens? Abraham Lincoln signatures? Maybe pages from former Browns coach Sam Rutigliano's playbook? It was something to consider.

I went to the refrigerator for a beer, but the cupboard was bare. I had to settle for a couple of Toll House cookies. They're better for you, anyway.

It was probably too late to return the professor's call, and definitely too late to call Auntie Branka. So I dialed the number of Jeff Feldman's apartment on Euclid Heights. I figured it was highly unlikely that my young client had already gone to bed—in fact I had serious questions as to whether she was even home.

She was, and she hadn't yet retired for the night, but when she answered the telephone after six rings, she sounded a little punchy, although I could barely hear her over the blast of reggae music that was clanking away in the background.

I had to repeat my name twice before she remembered who I was, and that gave me something to think about. Whenever I give someone fifteen hundred bucks in cash, I usually can recall their name.

"April," I said, "we have to talk. Can you meet me at Arabica tomorrow morning?"

"What time?"

"Ten o'clock."

"Whoa! That's like way early for me."

"Force yourself," I said.

CHAPTER FOURTEEN

The sun was out the next morning, really out, as if it meant business. Maybe spring was coming early to northern Ohio for real, although we all know better than to get complacent in the first week of April; a snowstorm could be just around the corner.

I parked about half a block west of Arabica and made my way up toward Coventry. I'd already had a pot of coffee at home and wasn't really looking forward to any more, but if you go to Arabica, you drink coffee. It's part of the drill.

When I reached the front of the Centrum Theatre I saw that April Delavan was outside, sitting on one of the stone balustrades that attract casual loungers and coffee drinkers alike during nice weather. She was flanked by two young men, one in his mid twenties and another big kid who looked like he might have recently played high school football but was already running to fat. He had a thin gold ring through one nostril and was wearing jeans and a Cleveland State sweatshirt, and he held a twenty-foot-long rope at the end of which was a medium-size yellow dog of indeterminate ancestry—somewhere in the mists of time there had been a German shepherd involved, I thought, but beyond that it was hard to tell. The other guy, the older one, wore an army fatigue jacket a lot like April's.

The dog wagged its tail and bounded over to sniff my crotch as I approached. Its owner yanked it back roughly.

"Hi," April said, lifting a languid finger.

I nodded to the two men. "Hi. Want to go in and get some coffee?"

"Okay," she said, and stood up, uncoiling herself from the stone. I took her arm, and we started into the Coventryard Mall.

"Hey!" the guy with the dog said, and gave the poor animal another jerk.

I stopped and turned to look at him. "Excuse me?"

"Hey, whattaya think you're doin', ace?"

I sighed. It was too early in the day for any overt displays of machismo, especially from a blubbery kid whose face hadn't even cleared up yet. Ace.

"I think I'm going to have a cup of coffee with this lady," I said.

"Yeah, well, tough shit, because we were havin' a conversation here."

I nodded gravely. "Well now you're not," I said, and steered April inside. I didn't look back to see how well he took it, mainly because I flat didn't give a damn.

We got into the serving line, which was a lot shorter than it would have been an hour or so earlier. Arabica was a regular stop for a lot of work-bound commuters in the morning.

"Who's your friend with the attitude?" I said.

She shrugged. "I don't even know his name. He was hitting on me. They both were." She said it matter-of-factly, and I suppose to her it was no big deal. For women who look like April Delavan, fending off would-be romancers has to be a full-time occupation.

April got an enormous pastry covered with slices of almond, we both ordered black coffee, and we took a table in the back where we wouldn't be disturbed. I stuck my head into the other room and looked around. In retrospect I guess I was checking to see if Nicole Archer might have been there. But it was ten o'clock in the morning, and Dr. Archer was probably at her office.

It was just as well. Walking in with Jeff's current lover to find Jeff's former lover might have been awkward—more for me, probably, than for either of them.

And a sudden wave of bitter envy welled up inside me; I could taste it in the back of my throat. Lowlifes like Jeff Feldman seemed to attract the most desirable women, and yet when faced with the obvious interest of Cathleen Hartigan last night, I had to climb up on my high horse of principle and get all stiff-necked. I didn't imagine Jeff Feldman would have thought twice about it.

"So what's goin' on?" April said, pulling my attention back to the present. She was licking an almond sliver off the corner of her mouth. "You find Jeff yet?"

"No. I've got a line on him, but to follow it up I may have to go to New York. Just for a day."

"New York? When?"

"Tomorrow. But I need your okay to spend the money. It'll probably cost around five hundred for air fare and additional expenses. I'll itemize them for you."

She gave her hand a bored flutter. "Whatever," she said.

"Good."

"You could have asked me that on the phone," she said, sounding piqued.

"I wanted to discuss something else with you too."

She slumped down in her chair so that she was sitting on her tailbone. I took that to mean I should keep talking. So I asked a question to which someone else had already given me an answer, just to see if they jibed. "How did you meet Jeff?"

"My father introduced us."

"Your father knows him?"

Her head lolled back on her neck so she was staring up at the ceiling. "My father collects art. Big-time. And Jeff makes it his business to know every collector in town. My father told me Jeff was an artist and a very interesting guy and that I should meet him because I could learn a lot from him."

"And did you?" I asked. "Learn a lot from him?"

She lowered her chin so she was staring right at me. "Yeah. I learned that I should never lend money to a guy I'm sleeping with."

"Somebody ought to put that on a sampler," I said.

She laughed. There was hope for April—somewhere in the far recesses of her airweight brain was a sense of humor.

"I talked to your father, you know."

She stopped laughing. "Why, God damn it?"

"Because his name came up in my investigation and I thought it was a good idea."

"When was this?"

"Yesterday. Don't worry, I didn't tell him you'd hired me. I didn't even say I knew you."

She seemed relieved. "That's good," she said. "He doesn't know anything about the money. It's not his business—it's my money. But I'd just as soon he didn't know about it."

"Why?"

She colored slightly and looked away. "Because I kind of feel like a jerk," she said. Her chin sunk onto her chest, and I thought I heard a sniffle.

"Everybody acts like a jerk sometimes," I said gently, putting my hand on hers. "Be glad you're getting it out of the way early."

"It's out of the way, all right. Because I've learned a good lesson from Jeff—not to let anyone fuck me over! That's why I want you to find him."

I pushed my chair back and stood up. "In that case, I've got some work to do. Come on, I'll drive you back."

"It's only three blocks."

"That's okay, I'm going right by there."

She levered herself up from her chair like a woman four times her age. "Life sucks, doesn't it, Mr. Jacovich?"

"Sometimes," I said. "But consider the alternative."

We started for the door, jostling against the people waiting in line for coffee and pastry. "I mean, sometimes I think it'd just be easier if I'd never gotten born," she went on.

"Shame on you, April. Didn't you ever see that movie with Jimmy Stewart and Donna Reed?"

"Yeah. I thought it was a crock of shit."

We went out onto the sidewalk, squinting against the sun, and I took her arm. The two guys who had been sitting with April were still there, and the dog wiggled not only his tail but the whole rear half of his body. He seemed glad to see me. At least somebody was. His master glared at me as though I carried plague.

"See ya," April said to them with a small wave.

We started down the street to where I'd parked my car. We hadn't quite gotten to the Centrum's marquee before I heard the guy with the dog say, "I'm just too young, that's all. I'm too young to have a date," laying on the sarcasm with a trowel. "I guess I'll have to wait until I get old and fat before I can go out with pretty girls young enough to be my daughter."

"Come on, Larry," the other one said.

"No. I'm just too young. I guess you can't get a date unless you're some beat-up old fart with money."

It just hit me wrong. Things do that sometimes, especially on mornings when I'm feeling a little sorry for myself. Life is all about timing, I think, and this fat kid's was worse than he knew. I stopped and turned back to him.

"Did it ever occur to you, Larry," I said, "that the reason you can't get a date isn't because you're too young but because you're an asshole?"

April was tugging on my arm but I shook her off.

The kid stood up, his nose ring catching the sunlight. He was almost as tall as I am, with a buzz cut revealing the ugly, bullet shape of his head. There were tattoos on the knuckles of the hand wrapped around the dog's rope, but I was too far away to see what they were. "Nobody calls me that."

I shrugged. "Apparently they do."

He took a few steps toward me. "You know this dog could rip the shit out of you? All I have to do is say a word."

I looked down at the dog, whose tongue was lolling out of the side of his mouth. I've seen cats that scared me more.

"And I could rip the shit out of you," I said, "and no one would have to say anything."

His face turned bright red, all except for a stark white border around his lips.

"But I don't hurt little boys, Larry, so run along and play. And next time, watch your wise mouth."

He stood there uncertainly, trying to decide between a loss of face and what he surely must have known by now would be a humiliating beating. He eventually did the smart thing and took a few steps backward.

Good enough. I turned, took April's arm, and continued down the sidewalk. I pretended not to hear the accusation of incest he howled at me when I was too far away to turn around and chase him.

"Wow," April said as I unlocked the passenger side of my car. "Sometimes you're one tough son of a bitch, aren't you?"

"Sometimes," I said, and closed the door.

I don't take a lot of pride in being tough. My genes, over which I had no control, dictated that I'd be big and strong, and in northeast Ohio that kind of size preordains a high school and collegiate football career. It also put me into the Military Police during the Vietnam troubles, and from there it seemed pretty natural to slide into law enforcement when I came back home. I guess I got tough too because to be untough is to doom yourself to the role of perpetual victim, and I'm not comfortable in that role.

So turning the other cheek just isn't in my canon. I've never in my life looked for trouble—but then as big as I am, I've never had to. All I usually need to do is show up.

I don't know—do you just let things go? Do you just allow some punk with his own agenda running around in his head to dump all over you, just chalk it up to bad manners?

Sure the dog owner was just an overgrown kid. And maybe he just caught me in one of my more snarky moods. But I raised two kids, and I know that by the time little ones are four years old they know the difference between right and wrong as well as the rest of us, and their every action after that is a conscious choice. We're raising a whole generation that doesn't know the meaning of the word respect.

I parked on the street in front of my apartment building and went upstairs and brushed my teeth. Then I called my travel agent and booked a flight to New York first thing in the morning, with a return trip the same night. I supposed I could have arranged to stay in the Big Apple long enough to have dinner in one of the legendary restaurants and take in a show, but that didn't sound like something I'd like to do by myself.

Then I called Professor Feldman at CCNY.

"You're coming all the way to New York?" He seemed amazed, and even more worried than before. "Because of Jeff?"

"I want to check with the Barthalow people, but I'd like to talk with you too. Any chance we could meet somewhere?"

"I'll pick you up at the airport," he said.

"That's not necessary; I can grab a cab."

"A cab? What are you, crazy? You don't take a cab in New York unless you speak Farsi. Come on, it's no trouble. It's a Saturday and I don't have any classes, so I can come get you. Where's a better place to talk than in a car? What's your flight number?"

There was no arguing. I did want to talk to him, and almost anything was worth not having to try getting a cab at LaGuardia. I just hoped he'd go away when I wanted him to.

We said good-bye, and then I tapped out Valerie Oakey's number. "I hope I'm not interrupting you while you're working," I said when she answered.

"Not at all. I'm drinking coffee and looking out the window at this beautiful spring morning. Remember, I told you my heart doesn't get started until sometime after noon. Well, unless my watch has stopped, it's just past eleven. What can I do for you?"

"Stretch your memory a little?"

"I'm game if you are."

"Great. When Jeff Feldman was staying with you, do you remember him ever being interested in old letters or autographs, things like that?"

She giggled. "The only autograph Jeff cares about is at the bottom of a check."

"He was never involved with old manuscripts, or collectors of that kind of thing?"

"No. Jeff is a greedy slug when it comes to money, but he's also committed to art, with a capital *A*. I wouldn't think he'd consider any autograph as having intrinsic value—unless it were van Gogh's or someone's. So I don't think he'd bother, if only from lack of interest. He certainly wouldn't go to the trouble of developing sources, if that's what you mean."

"That's what I mean. Did you ever hear him mention the Barthalow Gallery in New York? Or did you ever see any sort of correspondence from them?"

"Barthalow? It's a long time now since he was here, but I'm sure not. That's a funny name. Funny unusual, I mean, not funny ha-ha. I think I'd remember it."

"Well, if anything kicks in, anything at all, you have my number."

"I'm putting my thinking cap on right now," she said.

After I hung up, I made out two more file cards: BARTHALOW GALLERIES and THE HELGENBURG VASE. I looked at the second one and chuckled to myself before I added it to the growing stack in April Delavan's file. It sounded like the title of a Robert Ludlum novel of espionage. *The Bourne Identity. The Gemini Contenders. The Helgenburg Vase.*

I shook my head sadly. I was getting into the habit of telling myself jokes and laughing at them.

I made another call I hoped would at least make me smile. "This is Dr. Archer." The voice was lower than I remembered, mellow and professional-sounding.

I had to clear my throat before I spoke. "Dr. Archer, this is Milan Jacovich. We met the other evening in Arabica."

"I remember perfectly who you are, Milan. What a nice surprise to hear from you."

"I hope I'm not interrupting anything."

"You are, but I'm grateful. Sometimes the natural rhythm of the day can become oppressive. I'm going to take a few minutes and indulge myself and talk to you. I love my patients, my babies, but a three-week-old doesn't offer much in the way of conversation. So I'm glad you called."

"I'd like to run something by you if you'll let me."

She laughed, low in her throat. "You're not going to ask me about your chronic sinus problem like everyone does doctors, are you?"

"My sinuses are just dandy, thank you. I'm not after free medical advice. It's about Jeff Feldman."

She didn't answer, but I could hear a subtle change in her breathing.

"When Jeff was with you, did he ever mention anything about old manuscripts or letters, or autographs?"

"Autographs?"

"Collectible ones."

"I take it you mean like Thomas Jefferson's, not like Vinny Testaverde's."

"Well, yes."

"I don't recall anything like that. At all. But Jeff was only in my life for about a heartbeat and a half—I really didn't know him. He wasn't exactly giving of himself. He didn't talk much about his life. In fact I know less about Jeff than I do about the lady who works at the dry cleaners."

"Something came up about Jeff and a gallery that deals in old documents and things like that. The Barthalow Gallery in New York. Ring a bell?"

"Sorry, no bells." There was one of those weighty silences. "Is that *all* you called for?"

I found my mouth getting dry. "No," I said.

"Whew! You had me worried for a minute."

"Uh, do you like baseball?"

"Sure. I've been a Tribe fan all my life."

"Well, next Tuesday is Opening Day and I have tickets. I was wondering . . ."

"Tuesday? That's a day game, isn't it?"

"One-thirty."

"I can't. I'd love to. But I'm a working woman."

"Sure," I said, feeling really stupid. "I didn't even think of that." I hate it when I sulk.

"But we could have dinner after the game and you can tell me all about it. How does that sound?"

I rubbed the back of my neck where the muscles had started to bunch up. Ed Stahl and I always go out for dinner after the

Opening Day game. It's kind of a tradition, and I've always been a traditional kind of guy.

And then I remembered how Nicole's hair bounced when she moved her head, and how I was my own worst enemy.

"That sounds great," I said, and it was like a big weight lifting off my chest.

We made arrangements to meet for dinner at Johnny's Downtown, a bistro down in the Warehouse District, a fairly new offshoot of my favorite restaurant on the Near West Side, and I hung up and sat there for a while until my stomach stopped fluttering.

Nicole Archer. *Twang!*

Ed was going to be bent out of shape that we weren't going to head from the ballpark to a dark, smoky tavern someplace for our usual dinner of red meat and potatoes. But if our friendship wasn't strong enough for him to handle Nicole Archer . . .

The phone trilled at my elbow, startling me, and I picked up on the first ring.

"Milan Security."

"That was fast," Marko Meglich said. "Were you sitting on the phone?"

"I knew it was you. "What's wrong?"

"You know a woman named Alys Larkin?"

"I've met her."

"When?"

"Two nights ago in a little bar on St. Clair. Why?"

"Because," he said, "they found her this morning at the bottom of an elevator shaft with a broken neck. And she had your business card in her pocket."

CHAPTER FIFTEEN

Marko Meglich leaned back in his desk chair and took a sip of coffee from the custom-made mug that bore his name and shield number. He'd mail-ordered it several years ago from a catalogue specializing in law enforcement items when he'd gotten the wild idea into his head that plastic and foam coffee cups somehow cause cancer. One of the many fringe benefits of the Job is rampant paranoia.

"The call came in at ten o'clock this morning from the guy she shared the studio with," Marko said, and checked the papers in front of him. "Tydings Belk."

"He's the one that found the body?"

"Right." He shook his head. "Is that some kind of a name or what? Sounds like somebody getting punched in the stomach. Tydings Belk. Jesus."

"Any idea yet when she fell? Last night or this morning?"

"According to the patrolman who took the call, his best guess was that she'd been there at least twelve hours.

"Patrolman? Wasn't there a detective there to follow up?"

He shrugged. "We don't have the manpower to send out detectives on an accidental death."

"Accidental?"

"We'll know more after the autopsy, but we're calling it an accident until the coroner finishes doing her thing," he said. "It's an old building, and the woman fell down an elevator shaft that was obviously unsafe, so we have no reason yet to believe it was anything else. But your card right there in her jeans makes me a little bit edgy, and so I thought I should have you come in and talk to me."

"This is an official interrogation then?" I said.

Marko fingered his mustache. "Don't get me irritated, Milan. Nobody's interrogating you. There's no two-way mirror in this office, and there's no tape recorder running. This conversation is routine, and you know it."

I really wanted a cigarette, but the air in Marko's tiny office was so foul with tobacco smoke that I couldn't bear to make it worse. So I contented myself with fingering the pack of Winstons through my jacket pocket. "All right," I said. "Let's converse. As you know, I've been retained—and I'm not going to tell you who my client is unless you make me—to find a ceramic artist named Jeff Feldman who's come up missing. That was what the trip to the morgue was about."

"I remember."

"And I talked to Alys Larkin because she and Belk shared that studio with Feldman. We had a beer at Jerman's, I gave her my card and told her to contact me if Feldman turned up, and that's the sum total of my involvement with her."

He rocked forward in the chair, his forearms hitting the desk. "You sure?"

"Except for when I pushed her down the shaft. I haven't had time yet to make up a T-shirt that says I did it."

He ignored the sarcasm. "What'd you talk about?"

"I asked her if she had any idea where Feldman was, and she said no, and that she didn't much care, either. The whole thing lasted for not quite one beer. Listen, does it strike you funny that three artists share that loft, one of them disappears and another one falls and breaks her neck?"

"I'm not sure funny is the word I'd use, but yes, it did occur to me."

"How do you read it?"

"I don't. Yet."

"But you're calling Larkin's death accidental."

"Temporarily," he said. "That elevator was a disaster waiting to happen anyway. The city should have condemned it a long time ago."

"I don't believe in coincidence."

"Neither do I. So Feldman has disappeared and Larkin's gone down an elevator shaft."

"My read is that they're connected. Maybe Feldman has been hiding out somewhere, just biding his time until he could do Larkin."

"Maybe," Marko said, nodding his head sagely. "Maybe Belk might be next."

"A distinct possibility. Or," I pointed out, "he might be the perp."

He made a sour face indicating he didn't buy that. "You seen him? He's just a little gnome of a guy."

"So was Attila the Hun."

"What?"

"A little gnome of a guy."

He tilted his head to one side and looked skeptical. "Where'd you hear that?"

"I didn't 'hear it.' It's not a rumor, it's historical fact."

He shrugged. "I didn't know that. I always thought Attila looked like Jack Palance."

"That was a movie!"

He almost pouted. "I know it."

"I suppose you think Moses looked like Charlton Heston, too. And Elliot Ness looked like Kevin Costner."

"Elliot Ness looked like Robert Stack."

The hell with the bad air. I fired up a Winston.

"So are you staying on this?" Marko said.

"I still have a client and I'm still looking for Feldman, if that's what you mean."

"Who's the client?"

I sighed. "Cut me some slack, Mark."

He cracked the joints in his thumbs, like a flamenco dancer clicking her castanets. "It seems like all I do is cut you slack. Well, not this time. I want to know what you know."

"I don't know anything, yet. And I wouldn't stay in business two minutes if I couldn't ensure confidentiality to my clients, and you know it."

"We could be dealing with a homicide here."

"We could," I said, "and if we are I'll put my cards on the table face up. But you're calling it an accident."

"At the moment."

"So what are you getting in my face for?"

He leveled a finger at me. "I don't like the way your missing-persons case is dovetailing with a possible murder."

"I don't like it either. And if I come across anything that makes possible probable, I'll certainly tell you. But in case you forgot, I don't work here anymore. And I'm not compromising a client—or my own integrity—just to satisfy you."

He toyed with the handle of his coffee mug. "Then I want you out," he said finally. "Off this case."

"I'm not on this case—not the Larkin case. I'm looking for a missing person privately, and you can't order me off just to satisfy your own ego."

"Ego's got nothing to do with it, damn it! Just let the police do their job for a change."

"Then let me do mine," I said. "I'm looking for a missing guy, who happens to share a studio space with your accident victim. I turn up anything on Larkin, it's yours. Otherwise, no matter how much you sit there and glower and flex your muscles, you can go piss up a rope."

His face grew even more scarlet, and he seemed to bulk up before my eyes, as though someone had inserted an air hose into a handy orifice and forgotten to turn it off. I waited for him to stretch thin and explode. But then his angry face crumpled and all the fight went out of him. He slumped back down in his chair, pinching the end of his meaty nose between thumb and forefinger. "Why does it always end up like this with us lately?"

"Because you're a pain in the ass?" I suggested.

He shook his huge head from side to side in sorrow. "We always fight."

I stubbed out my cigarette in his well-used ashtray. "We argue, because we're coming from different places now. We don't fight. Lucky for you, too, because the day a nose tackle can't clean the clock of a wide receiver will be the day I turn in my cleats and jockstrap."

He stared down at the top of his desk, exposing his bald spot, and I felt a sudden rush of affection for this man I'd known more than half my life. I reached out and squeezed his wrist. "It doesn't have anything to do with our friendship. Hell, if I was in trouble you'd be the first one I'd yell to for help, and you know damn well I'll always be there for you too. That's what friends are all about—not agreeing with each other all the time."

He didn't say anything, but after a moment he gave me a small, almost imperceptible nod. As if it cost him. Marko Meglich, who'd been a top-of-his-voice, boisterous, ebullient kid, now found it difficult to express any emotion south of toughness or cynicism. That's another big bite the Job takes out of a veteran cop's heart.

"Listen," I said. "Can you cut loose from here Tuesday afternoon?"

He looked up at me. "I s'pose. Why?"

"Ed Stahl invited me to the Tribe's home opener, and he said I could bring someone."

He shook his head, his eyes like a basset puppy's. "Ed doesn't like me very much."

"Ed doesn't like anyone very much. He's a journalist. Besides, he'll be too busy making notes for his column, especially if we lose. Come on, Mark. The beer's on me."

He took a while to think it over, and then finally his demeanor brightened. "Okay, good. Sounds like fun. And maybe after we could grab some dinner."

"Uh, I've got a dinner date after."

His face fell again. "See how you are?" he said.

When I got downstairs I stopped outside on the bottom step of the Third District Police Headquarters and looked around at what was familiar territory. There's not a lot of pedestrian traffic on this stretch of Payne Avenue, but an old man was coming toward me down the street, bundled up as though it was winter, in a tweed coat into the pockets of which he'd jammed both hands. A plaid scarf was wound around his neck, and a knit wool cap like merchant seamen wear was pulled down low over his ears. His shoulders were hunched up around his neck, and his weathered features were large and rough. The planes and crags of his face were Slavic, and I figured him for Croat only because he was huffing and puffing up the sidewalk toward the Croatian-Slovenian neighborhood just north and east of the police station.

He was near seventy, about five feet two if he stood on tiptoes, and he walked with a rolling gait, looking like one of those blow-up toys with the round bottoms that keep popping up no matter how hard you knock them down. Some English major with an overactive imagination and a passion for flaming metaphor might have described him as a little gnome of a guy.

Jack Palance, for God's sake.

I walked the block and a half to my car and got in. I knew Alys Larkin's apparently accidental death was in some way mixed up with Jeff Feldman's disappearance. I just couldn't make a logical connection.

I knew something else, too. Feldman was a hot-eyed hustler who wouldn't be above doing something outside the law to turn a buck—or, from what Victor had said, quite a few of them. People have been known to kill for less.

But Mark Meglich was right. The Larkin business was the police department's job. All I was concerned with was Jeff Feldman and where he'd gone with my client's money, no matter how much the body in that old elevator shaft got under my skin.

I drove back east on Superior, the brightness of the late afternoon sky throwing dark shadows on the industrial streets just east of downtown, and pulled into the complex where Jeff Feldman worked and Alys Larkin had died.

The CPD hadn't left any yellow crime-scene tape stretched across the elevator door because they were treating it as an accident, so I felt no guilt about taking a look. Opening the horizontal wooden gates, I looked down into the shadowy abyss of the shaft, about a twenty-foot drop. I shined my pencil flash around but couldn't really see anything, except in my imagination, and I didn't want to think about Alys Larkin down there in the dirt and grease and spiderwebs of fifty years.

The elevator itself was on the top floor at the moment; I could look up and see its cables hanging down beneath it. Probably because of Larkin's death the city would get around to condemning it one of these days. So often it takes some kind of tragedy to get people off their asses.

I went inside and climbed the dark stairs slowly. I could hear music, a violin, sad and sweet. Heartbreak music. There was another sound too, not really a noise but more of a deep rumbling that affected the whole building. When I got to the second floor I realized what it was.

The gas jets of the giant kiln out in the corridor had been turned on, and the blast of scorching air hit me the minute I stepped through the stairwell door. The very air inside seemed to be humming, and the floor beneath my feet vibrated.

I walked past it gingerly, that side of my body almost shriveling from the searing temperature, and turned into the great room where the three artists had worked.

There was only one light burning, a sixty-watt bulb set into a fixture high up in the ceiling, so I didn't see Tydings Belk at first. He was at the far end of the room, near the windows, and he was so still that if not for the pink and indigo western sky silhouetting his large shaggy head I wouldn't have noticed him at all. He didn't even look up when I came in. He seemed to be listening intently to the music, which poured from a big black Panasonic boom box.

"Mr. Belk," I called out.

He didn't move. Perhaps between the violin sonata and the roar of the kiln he hadn't heard me. I called his name again, louder this time.

Slowly he turned his head to see who it was that dared intrude, his shoulders rotating as well, as if his neck was stiff, his eyes camouflaged by the light flashing off the thick lenses of his glasses. After a moment he silently resumed his original position, studying the sunset. It was hardly an invitation to come in, but since he didn't actually tell me to leave I took it as one and walked across the big loft, being careful not to brush against any of the tables and knock over ceramic works drying on the racks.

"I'm sorry to bother you, Mr. Belk."

He turned and looked at me again, frowning as if he couldn't quite remember who I was. The three-quarters-empty bottle of Jack Daniel's on the table next to him might have had something to do with his memory lapse.

Then again, maybe I'm just not a very memorable guy.

Finally he said, "Oh yeah. The rent-a-cop with the J that sounds like a Y." He shifted in his chair. "Come in—oh, you already did. Well, sit down then. Have a drink."

I nodded and sat down across the table from him.

He pushed the bottle toward me. "You get to drink it out of a collector's item," he rumbled, waving his hand toward the work area to his right. "Pick one. One of the last mugs to be made by the late, noted Cleveland ceramicist, Alys Larkin."

"A paper cup will do fine." I took one from the ledge against the window where a Mr. Coffee sat with something muddy and brown and terrible in the bottom, and Belk filled it generously. It would normally take me a week to finish that much. I don't usually drink Black Jack, but I sensed that he needed a little human contact, and that he really couldn't bear the thought of drinking alone.

"L'chaim" he said, raising his own paper cup and emptying it while I just took a sip of mine. His eyes teared, and he coughed as he put the cup down. "Know what that means?"

I nodded. I'd seen *Fiddler on the Roof.*

" 'To life, to life, l'chaim,' " he sang. "Isn't that a bite in the ass?" He tilted the bottle and filled his cup again. Some new medical study ascertained not too long ago that having one drink a day could conceivably be beneficial to the heart; I think Belk was currently working on March 12, 1998.

"You believe in the laws of compensation, Mr. Jacovich?" He pronounced it right this time. "You know, that some ignorant punk who can't find his own dick with either hand can soar through the air like a peregrine falcon and slam-dunk a basketball through a hoop several feet over his head? Or that some geek with Coke-bottle-bottom glasses and pencils in his shirt pocket who had the social skills of a cranberry in high school turns into a scientific genius and winds up inventing the personal computer and makes enough money to buy Cincinnati?"

"I guess I do," I said.

"Or an ugly runt like me is given the talent to make beautiful art." He waved his hand at the racks of his own work. "That's why I'm firing the kiln. I'm cooking up some things. Creating something beautiful in order to compensate for something beautiful that's died. I'm sorry it's so damn hot in here, but that kiln gets up to more than nine hundred degrees Fahrenheit after about forty-eight hours. It'll cook damn near anything to fine ashes—except for the ceramics. The heat's one of the sacrifices we make for art. The many sacrifices."

He stared into the depths of his drink. "And you know what the primo example of the law of compensation is? Humans. Humans have been given the power to think and reason. To laugh. To walk upright, to paint pictures and write books and make lousy movies. To invent the wheel and harness fire and have dominion over the beasts of the field, who just mate in the springtime and piss in the woods and give not a damn about anything else."

He drank some more Black Jack. "Ah, but there's a kicker. There's always a kicker." He scratched his thinning hair and a flurry of dandruff drifted onto the shoulders of his sweatshirt. "Man is also the only creature on earth who is born knowing the inevitability of his own death."

The loft was silent except for the low roar of the kiln. Belk tried to smile, but it came out a death's-head rictus. "Makes you wonder why people bust their humps their whole lives, doesn't it? It's like going to see a movie and knowing the ending."

He heaved himself up and walked the few steps to Alys Larkin's worktable. He ran his fingertips lovingly over a ceramic bowl. "Alys knew she was going to die, too," he said.

"She probably did."

"Just not now. Not like this."

He turned to face me, cradling the bowl in his arms the way

someone would hold a child. The light from the window was fading quickly, but I could still see the tears that had spilled out of his eyes behind his glasses. He shook his head like an animal in pain and wiped his nose with his sleeve. "Alys wasn't easy to be around sometimes," he said. "She was always mad about something or other. Jealous. Most people thought she was . . . abrasive. That's a bad rap for a woman. A man who's abrasive is considered tough, but a woman . . ." He shook his large head in sorrow. "That's when we hear the B word."

He looked at the bowl in his arms. "But there was a vulnerability about her, a tenderness . . ." He stopped and closed his eyes, two fat tears squeezing out from beneath his eyelids and running down his cheeks into his beard.

I cleared my throat to loosen up the thickness that was collecting there. "I didn't know you were lovers."

"Who else would have me?" he said simply.

I couldn't answer that one. I took another swallow of Black Jack, becoming more morose by the minute. Other people's grief is never easy to deal with; I never know what to do with my hands.

"She was a genius, you know. Better than me—certainly better than Feldman. The best. And she barely made a living. A goddamn shame, you know? If she'd lived in another age—say the eighteenth century, when porcelain was given its rightful importance in the art world—she would have been one of the immortals." He opened his eyes and looked at me accusingly. "You don't believe me."

"Of course I do, Mr. Belk. I have no reason not to."

He nodded. "Good. Now at least one more person knows. Listen, I thank you for the company. For letting me talk your ear off. But I feel a real crying jag coming on, and I'd be ever so grateful if you weren't here to watch."

I left a business card on the table. "If there's anything I can do," I said.

He didn't look at it. "How are you at raising the dead?"

• • •

When I got home about seven o'clock I was feeling a bit light-headed from the whiskey—it hadn't been enough to keep me from driving, but I was glad I didn't have to perform brain surgery. I figured I'd better have something to eat to soak up the alcohol. I stood at the refrigerator with the door open long enough to start feeling chilly. I finally chose a big wedge of white cheddar I'd bought at the West Side Market, cut up an onion and fried it up along with a link of klobasa sausage I'd soaked in apple juice and sliced lengthwise, slathered two pieces of Lax and Mandel's pumpernickel with Stadium Mustard, and sandwiched it all together.

Not the healthiest dinner imaginable, I know, but the sad fact is that the only two things that really taste good are foods with fat and foods with sugar. And as Tydings Belk had pointed out, we're all going to die anyway.

It hadn't been Alys Larkin's time to die, though. I knew that because if she'd stepped out into space from the second floor she'd have landed just a few feet down on top of the elevator cab. And if the elevator had been on the second floor and she'd been on the first, she'd only have fallen twenty feet. Far enough to bang yourself up and bust an arm or a leg or an ankle, I suppose, but it was unlikely that she'd have made the false step, turned a complete somersault, and landed upside down on her head. Not impossible, but not likely either. Which meant that in all probability someone had killed Larkin and thrown her down the elevator shaft.

I wondered why.

CHAPTER SIXTEEN

New York is not my favorite city. It used to be, or one of them, anyway. There was something visceral about walking down Fifty-seventh Street that made my blood run a little faster and my senses a little more keen.

Now visiting there is like taking a crash course in survival training. The traffic is impossible, the streets are filthy, pedestrians bang into you all day, and if it's not the panhandlers trying to separate you from your money it's the pickpockets, the transvestite hookers, or the guys trying to sell you a Rolex knock-off from a dirty blanket on the sidewalk or sucker you into a game of three-card monte.

The museums, the Metropolitan Opera, the Knicks, the theaters, and the Fifth Avenue stores are great, but they just aren't worth it to me anymore. Now New York just makes me tired.

My plane landed at LaGuardia twenty minutes late, which in New York is nearly on time. As I came out of what the airlines have coyly named "the jetway," I saw a skinny, bespectacled man with a thick shock of wiry white hair sticking out from beneath a checkered cap. He had a mottled complexion and wrinkled crepe-like skin beneath his chin, and he was holding up a yellow legal pad on which he'd inscribed MILAN sideways across the top page with a Magic Marker. He caught my eye and smiled a tentative welcome. I guess I look like a Milan.

"Professor Feldman?"

He took my hand. His own were small and soft, with delicate, tapering fingers. "I hope you don't mind my using your first name. Jacovich wouldn't fit on one piece of paper."

"Not at all. Let's keep it that way," I said. "I appreciate you taking the time to do this."

"I appreciate you coming all the way to New York. You want to help my son, so I can't do enough for you, all right? You have luggage?"

I shook my head. "I'm only staying till this evening."

"Come on, then," he said, tugging my arm.

We weaved our way through the terminal, and I admired how nimbly he dodged the crowds of fast-moving pedestrians as we headed toward the parking lot. Longtime New Yorkers develop certain skills that people in the rest of the country don't even think about.

"You're lucky it's Saturday," he said as we walked. "Traffic isn't so bad on a weekend, we'll have pretty much a straight shot into town. So. You're a native Clevelander?"

"Born and bred."

"Nice. It's nice to stay close to your roots. Cleveland's a good town. I've spent time there. You've got a world-class art museum—I have some friends on staff, and I know most of the people in the art department at Cleveland State."

He moved very quickly for a man in his seventies, but now his pace slowed just a hit, almost imperceptibly. "Come to think of it, I never visited my son there. He didn't ever invite me."

We went outside into the short-term parking lot. The temperature in Cleveland had been in the mid sixties when I'd left that morning, but here it was about ten degrees warmer, and the air was heavier and harder to breathe. All around us it seemed to thrum with traffic sounds. You could feel the rhythm pounding inside your chest.

"I'm over here," he said, leading me toward a dun-colored two-door Plymouth of indeterminate years. A chrome strip on the passenger side door was missing, exposing a runner of rust. The back seat was piled two feet deep with books and catalogues. "It's an old clunker, but it gets me where I want to go, and if some schmuck on the street steals the hubcaps, who really cares, am I right?"

We got into the car and I buckled the seat belt across my chest. There were a couple of granola bar wrappers on the floor under my feet, and for some reason I tried not to step on them.

"So," he said when we were finally out of the terminal lot and on the expressway. "What's this business with the Barthalow Gallery? You think they'll know where my son is?"

"That's what I plan on asking them, Professor."

"Irv," he corrected me. "Call me Irv. If I'm supposed to call you Milan, you call me Irv. So tell me. How can I help you with whatever it is you're doing?"

"I'm not sure, Irv. I'm pretty much poking around with a white cane on this one."

"Try." Urgency put a rasp in his throat and pulled down the corners of his mouth.

"Okay, I will. First of all, do you know of a porcelain maker named Helgenburg?"

He turned his head and stared at me until the blast of a truck's air horn warned him he was drifting into the wrong lane. Pulling back over quickly, he earned another horn toot from the taxi behind him. Irv raised his right middle finger at the cabbie in the universally recognized salute. New York drivers take no prisoners.

"Have I heard of Helgenburg? Has a painter heard of Rembrandt? Has a composer heard of Mozart? Helgenburg was one of the masters, right up there with Wedgwood and Spode. What little survives of his work these these days is very rare and very expensive. What's Helgenburg got to do with Jeffrey?"

"From what I've been able to piece together so far, Jeff has a line on acquiring a Helgenburg vase and has been shopping it around Cleveland."

He banged both hands on the steering wheel. "That is so much horse-pucky!" The words all but exploded out of his mouth.

"Why?" I asked, startled by his vehemence.

"Because it's out of his league. Way out! Look, I know my son. He thinks he's a big shot, but what he really is is a sneak and a schnorrer who lives off women from deal to deal. Legitimate collectors don't talk to him, and neither do legitimate galleries, to say nothing of the kind of high-level people that would have anything to do with big-ticket art. How the hell is he going to get his hands on a Helgenburg?"

"As I understand it, this particular piece is a rare vase that disappeared in Nazi Germany during the war."

"Oy!" the professor said. "There've been rumors about that thing for the last forty-five years. Nobody even knows if it exists anymore."

"But if it does, isn't it possible that it would turn up in channels that were, well, not exactly mainstream?"

His profile was grim, unyielding, like a throwing ax as he stared out through the windshield. "Say what you mean, Milan. I know what kind of man my son is."

That didn't make it any easier. "Okay, Irv. Isn't it possible that if the vase does exist it might surface on the—what would you call it, the black market?"

"That's what I'd call it, sure. But Jeff? He's a small-time little pisher. He'd have as much chance at getting his hands on a Helgenburg as . . . I don't know what."

He accelerated suddenly, cutting off a slow-moving dry cleaners' panel truck, and the driver beat a Morse code tattoo on the truck's horn. I gripped the dashboard and ran through a quick Hail Mary in my head.

"You're a white-knuckler, eh?" he said. "Don't worry, I haven't had an accident in fifty years."

"It only takes one."

"Ach!" He waved a dismissive hand at me. "They'll have to catch up with me first. Look. My son has a gift. A talent. And I'll take a little of the credit. I nurtured him, I taught him everything I knew about porcelain, and that's a hell of a lot. He could have been a fine artist, a craftsman—he had the hands for it, and the eye as well. He chooses to waste that gift, consciously *chooses* it. Like Vladimir Horowitz deciding to work in a piano bar in Queens playing "Tie a Yellow Ribbon." Instead of using his God-given gift, Jeffrey deals and hondles, too damn dumb to realize it's more work to hustle a buck than make it legitimately. And that makes him pretty small potatoes. If anyone had a Helgenburg—especially *that* Helgenburg, which is highly unlikely in the first place—they'd have to be nuts to give it to someone like him to move."

He wiped the corners of his mouth with his hand. "If he's telling Cleveland people any different, he's conning the socks off them."

I didn't want an anxious father to worry any more than necessary, but I figured that even as arrogant and reckless as he was, Jeff Feldman wasn't stupid enough to try and run a game on Victor Gaimari. "I don't have all the facts," I said. "That's what I'm here for, to get them. Irv, that business card from the Barthalow Gallery—did it have someone's name on it?"

He fumbled inside his jacket and came up with a now bedraggled-looking card, with the gallery name elegantly embossed on beige card stock. "No. But it's probably just a small gallery, else I would have heard of them, so I don't imagine they have a lot of employees."

I took the card and looked at it, smudged and creased as though it had once been stuffed into someone's pocket. Just the name and an address and phone number in black block lettering.

"I don't know what Jeff was doing in a rare document gallery, though," he said. "He never showed any interest in that kind of thing before. I suppose he could have just dropped in on impulse. People walk the streets in New York, take a quick look in places and pick up a card or a book of matches, then go right out again. Urban serendipity, they call it. But my son's never done anything in his adult life that wasn't either going to make him money or get him laid. That's the way he is."

We entered the Queens Midtown Tunnel. The sound of tires on the pavement became magnified, a kind of rhythmic, pulsating roar. It felt as if we'd been swallowed by a whale.

"He just falls off the face of the earth one day," Feldman said, "and then somebody hires a detective to find him—I don't like the way this whole thing smells. He must be in bad trouble."

"He might be. I'll help him if I can."

"You never told me who you're working for, Milan. Who wants him badly enough to hire you? And I think I have a right to know, don't you? I'm his father, for God's sake."

"I can't tell you. My first obligation is to my client."

He threw up his hands, a gesture part exasperation and part despair, and the car drifted over the white line. He quickly regained control of the steering wheel.

"But I can assure you," I continued, "that it's no one that wishes him ill."

He laughed bitterly. "Everyone he's ever known wishes him ill except his parents, who he dumps on the worst. It hurts to say it—it eats out my guts—but Jeff isn't a nice man."

"Don't beat yourself up about that, Irv. Jeff made his own choices, just like the rest of us."

"Choices. So many choices."

We burst out of the tunnel into the light almost as if we were emerging from the birth canal into a too bright, too loud world. We were on the streets of midtown Manhattan now, and the general decibel level was so high that I had to lean toward Irv Feldman in order to hear him.

"Who chooses to be a thoughtless shit?" he wondered aloud. "Who chooses to be a *momzer*?"

"Unfortunately, a lot of people," I said.

"And now his crowning touch, the final stake through his mother's heart. He's just taken a powder and won't tell anyone where he is."

"That's how it looks right now, Irv, but there could be a lot of explanations. And I promise you I'll find the right one, whatever it takes."

He nodded wearily. "Sure. For all the good it does."

"The good is that you'll know."

He turned uptown on Third, almost on a dime, twisting the wheel angrily as if Third Avenue was the cause of all his problems. There didn't seem to be any defined traffic lanes; cars whipped in and out almost at random. Every time we got to a red light,

Feldman stomped hard on the brake, and I was thrown forward. If I hadn't been wearing a seat belt I would have cannonballed through the windshield and wound up half a block ahead of us.

"And what has he left behind for us to remember him by?" Feldman said. He was obviously full of anger and taking it out on the brake pedal. "A grandchild? God forbid he should ever make that kind of commitment. A business? Ha! A body of work to be proud of, or friends who love him? No!" He shook his head. "Just a mother who cries herself to sleep at night with a nervous stomach from worrying about him for forty-two years."

He held his right index finger and thumb up about a quarter of an inch apart, then squeezed them together. "A dot, a feather, a speck of shmutz you wipe off your face leaves more of a mark than my son."

We drove in silence for a while. Then he said suddenly, "You're a Catholic, Milan, right?"

"Well, I don't exactly work at it anymore, but I was raised in the church, sure."

"Catholics and Jews have a lot in common when it comes to family. Jews put a lot of stock in their kids. Sons especially. Sons carry on the name."

His eyes grew wet and I looked away so as not to embarrass him.

"A lot of Jewish parents, they have a son turns out like Jeffrey, they'd say Kaddish for him."

"A prayer for the dead."

He gave me a sardonic smile. "Good for you, you saw *The Jazz Singer*."

"Not the one with Neil Diamond."

"Neil Diamond was nothing in that part compared to Al Jolson." He smiled. "So you saw Jolson?"

"A long time ago."

He wagged his head back and forth and wiped his hand across his face. "A lot of Jewish parents with a kid like Jeffrey, they might just say 'Our son is dead, we have no son.' But my wife and I, we hung in there with him. We kept saying that he just had some growing up to do. We thought eventually his upbringing would kick in, like some kind of a time-release cold capsule. We hoped he'd change, he'd see the light. Didn't happen."

Expectations. They'll get you between the eyes every time.

"But guess what?" he said. "We're still hanging. We're still hoping. That's why I want to help you any way I can, help you find Jeff and get him out of whatever mess he's stepped in. Because for me, for his mother, there's always hope."

"I guess that's the only way to play it."

"So I want to go to the gallery with you."

It was what I'd been afraid of all along. "I wish you wouldn't, Irv," I said carefully.

"Why not? I won't get in the way, I swear to God. I wouldn't even open my mouth."

"I have my own way of working, and I don't want to have to explain you to anyone. And people are more likely to open up to one man than to two." I looked over at him and tried to give him my kindest smile. "Besides, you know damn well you won't keep your mouth shut."

He started to protest but I cut him off.

"If it was my kid I'd feel the same way. But you're too emotionally involved, and you might make a mistake. I'm a professional, Irv, and I came all the way here from Cleveland with a game plan. Don't make me rewrite it at the last minute."

"It's a public place," he said, full of the truculence and anger of a man grown old before he was ready to and whose wounds wouldn't seem to heal. "You can't keep me out, y'know."

"I know. But if you go in there and screw up the works, I've got no place left to look, and you might never find your son again. So it's up to you."

He scowled, his own knuckles white as he choked the wheel. I noticed a few of the joints on his right hand were swollen and arthritic-looking. Finally he nodded his head in unwilling capitulation.

A few minutes later we arrived at the corner of Fifty-seventh Street just as the light changed to red. Irv stomped on the brake pedal harder than ever, and I reached out instinctively to brace myself against the dash.

"Why don't you drop me off and go on home and relax?" I said. "Then as soon as I finish at the gallery, I'll call and give you whatever I have. How's that?"

He sighed a martyr's sigh. "I guess it'll have to do," he said. "But I should tell you that I'm not good at sitting around waiting."

"I'm not sure anybody is," I said. "We all like to feel as if we're in control of our own lives."

He nodded. "It's just an illusion, though, isn't it, Milan?"

He pulled to the curb at the corner of East Sixty-fourth and Third and pointed in the direction of Lexington Avenue. "It should be on this block," he said.

Unbuckling my belt, I opened the door and swung my legs out. "Thanks for the ride, Irv."

"Thanks for the conversation—even though I did all the talking. I guess that's what you call being a good conversationalist, the ability to listen to an old man's nonsense. I appreciate it."

A cab pulled up behind us, and the driver stuck his bearded and turbanned head out the window and shouted in heavily accented English for Irv to move his fucking piece of shit out of the way. It came out "fockin' piss of chit."

"You'll call me, Milan," he said low and intensely, his voice quivering. It wasn't a question. "Jeffrey's mother will want to know." The implied peril to his son was hitting Irv Feldman hard, but it was more comfortably for him to lay the fear and worry off on his wife.

I patted his arm. "I'll call you," I said, and got out of the car. While waiting to cross the street I saw the cabdriver glower as he drove past, giving me the familiar single-finger greeting. I somehow doubted he meant have a nice day.

CHAPTER SEVENTEEN

I crossed the street and headed up Sixty-fourth, buffeted on both sides by pedestrians who were in more of a hurry than I was. I imagine that if you were to stroll the streets of midtown Manhattan all day you'd ache all over your body by evening. I felt like a punt returner fighting his way through the other guys' special team.

The Barthalow Gallery was a narrow storefront in the middle of the block, with a window in which a framed photograph and letter written by Henry James were prominently displayed on a bed of flowing ice-blue satin and lit by two baby spotlights. The gold lettering on the window and the glass door was discreet and elegant, and when I went inside I saw that, narrow as it was, the gallery went back at least eighty feet. A glass counter ran almost halfway to the rear, where it gave way to a series of long, tall walnut shelves, the kind you might see in an old-fashioned library. A skinny, unhealthy-looking man wearing a suit of nubby greenish-brown tweed was behind the counter waiting on a male customer who seemed to be questioning the provenance of the document he was being shown.

A short, slim woman approached me. Her business suit was tailored and medium blue, and her creamy blouse was buttoned clear up to her chin, fastened there by a cameo brooch about the size of a dessert plate.

"Good afternoon," she greeted me in a voice more cheerful than

I'd expected. "Welcome to the Barthalow Gallery. Is this your first visit? I don't remember seeing you before."

"Yes it is. I'm from out of town."

"Oh, wonderful. Where are you from?"

I told her. The clerk behind the counter looked up at me quickly, then back at his customer.

"Ah yes, Cleveland," she enthused. "I'm sorry to say I've never been there."

I thought about suggesting she visit us and maybe take in a ballgame at our new stadium. But not very hard.

"Actually, a friend of mine suggested I come in and see you. One of your customers."

"Oh?"

"Mr. Feldman. Jeffrey Feldman."

A line that appeared to be born of genuine confusion formed between her eyebrows. "Yes, uh . . ."

"You know him, don't you?"

"No, I don't think I recall that name."

"He's from Cleveland too. Or at least he lives there now." I looked back at the male clerk behind the counter. He was ignoring his customer and looking at me. "He was in here a few weeks ago, I believe."

She shook her head thoughtfully. "I can't place him. I'm Freya Barthalow. My husband and I own the gallery, so I know just about all our clients."

I fished her business card out of my jacket pocket. "Feldman gave me this," I said.

She looked at it, a slight sneer curling her lip when she saw its bedraggled condition; I think she imagined I got it by rolling a wino. "He might have picked up one of our cards when he visited," she said, and pointed to an elegant brass holder on the counter in which about fifty of the little suckers were displayed. "But I can guarantee he never made a purchase from us. I'd remember."

"That's funny."

"Yes it is," she agreed. "But no matter, really. May I show you something anyway?"

"I hope so," I said, deciding to take a shot in the dark, and I raised my voice so it would carry. "I'm looking for anything relating to an eighteenth-century porcelain maker named Josephus Helgenburg."

Out of the corner of my eye I saw the clerk jump as if he'd been goosed with a cattle prod. He was listening more closely to our conversation than he was to his customer, who was beginning to exhibit some annoyance. People rich enough to spend thousands of dollars for somebody's autograph like to have attention paid to them.

Freya Barthalow shook her head. "I can't recall we've ever had anything like that. Most of our papers either have to do with public figures, you know, or with the literary world. Do you collect porcelain?"

"No, but I know someone who does." The clerk behind the counter had turned into a perpetual-motion machine, dancing around almost maniacally and shooting looks in my direction that didn't even pretend to be furtive.

"Why don't you check with someone at the Metropolitan Museum?" Freya Barthalow suggested. "I'm sure they'd be much more knowledgeable about something like that than we are here. What was the man's name again?"

"Helgenburg," I told her, but I was really speaking for the clerk's benefit. "Josephus Helgenburg. I'm told that pieces he made two hundred years ago are worth a small fortune today."

"I'm sure," she murmured, her interest waning. "Well, I'm sorry I don't know this person who recommended us, and I'm even sorrier I couldn't help you find what you're looking for."

"You've been more help than you know, Ms. Barthalow." I glanced over at a display case that held a military document signed by Edwin M. Stanton, Lincoln's secretary of war. "This is fascinating. You mind if I look around a bit?"

"Of course not, take your time," she said. "And now if you'll excuse me?" She'd pegged me for a looky-loo and wasn't going to waste another moment on me.

I nearly bowed, she inclined her head, and she left me alone to browse. In the next case was a photograph of the GI's favorite pinup girl of World War II, Betty Grable, and a framed letter signed by her. Quite a place, the Barthalow Gallery, where Betty Grable and Edwin M. Stanton compete for attention. Poor old Edwin didn't much have a chance, I figured.

I walked around with my hands behind my back, looking at the various photos and documents. It only took the clerk about three minutes to get rid of his customer, who didn't buy anything.

I glanced back at him, raised an eyebrow, and strolled out of the gallery, taking care to stop outside and study the Henry James letter with rather more interest than I felt. Then I started walking leisurely down East Sixty-fourth Street—or as leisurely as one can walk in New York—toward Lexington Avenue, where I could pick up a taxi heading downtown.

I didn't get a quarter of a block before I heard a raspy voice calling out behind me, "Excuse me? Excuse me—sir?" I slowed my pace just enough to allow the clerk to catch up with me.

"Excuse me?" he said again, his eyes wide and intense behind the thick lenses to make me think this was all innocent. He was older than I'd thought, at least forty-five, with the unhealthy pallor of a lifetime city dweller.

Maybe I'd been mistaken; maybe he hadn't been far more interested in my conversation with Ms. Barthalow than was normal. Perhaps he'd run out of the gallery and chased me down the street just to tell me he was a member of the Greater New York Browns Boosters. Or maybe he'd misinterpreted my raised eyebrow and was going to ask me to dinner.

"Did I hear you say you're from Cleveland?" he asked.

I smiled as if just recognizing him. "Oh, you're from the gallery, aren't you? Cleveland Heights, actually. It's a suburb." He moved closer to me, invading my personal space.

"You're a friend of Feldman's?" he almost whispered.

"Not exactly a friend," I hedged, feeling strangely noble about not lying.

He jerked his thumb toward his own chest. "Winstock," he said. "Bert Winstock. I'm the one you want to see, not Mrs. Barthalow." He seemed to be breathing too hard from just a quick half-block walk, his narrow shoulders rising and falling beneath the dark gray suit, and there were little dots of white spittle on his lower lip. His neck looked like a garden snake that had swallowed a tennis ball.

"Oh?"

"Didn't Feldman tell you?"

I tried to shrug noncommittally.

"Feldman and I are doing a little business," he said.

"Uh-huh."

"So, uh . . ."

I waited.

Winstock glanced at the stream of pedestrians that was parting around us as though he suspected all of them were passionately interested in what we were saying. Then he moved even closer to me. I think he'd been chewing Dentyne, because his breath smelled kissing sweet.

"You have something for me?" he asked.

I backed up a little. "Am I supposed to?"

"Jeff didn't bring it himself so I figured he sent you instead."

"Bring what?"

He frowned. "Cut the crap, okay?"

"What crap?"

He reached out and bunched my lapel in his fist—a pretty gutsy play for a guy who weighed at least seventy pounds less than I did and was five inches shorter—and pushed his face close to mine. "What do you think you're pulling?"

"Your arm right out of your socket unless you take your hand off me."

He turned several shades grayer and let go, backing a couple steps away from me. "Come on," he said. "Are you sure Feldman sent you?"

"I never said he sent me."

He looked confused and more than a little desperate. "Then who are you, anyway?"

"A friend, and I've got the feeling you're going to need one. Maybe you'd better tell me what the nature of your business with Jeff Feldman is."

He started to answer, and then what little color remained in his face drained away, leaving him with the pallor of a three-day-old corpse. He licked his lips and started to back away from me again. A burly guy in a Knick's jacket banged against the clerk on his hurried way toward the corner, almost upending him.

"Come on, Winstock, I'm trying to help."

"Go fuck yourself," he screamed, loud enough to be heard a block away, and turned and ran back up the street toward the gallery.

Despite the loudness and the virulence of the curse, not a single passerby seemed to notice. Maybe they thought I'd asked him for directions and he'd given me the stock New York reply.

I ate at a little Chinese restaurant on Lexington Avenue. I couldn't decide if it was lunch or dinner, but when I'm hungry it doesn't matter. The place was hardly elegant, but my experience with Chinese restaurants has been that if one has linen tablecloths and a cocktail lounge, the food isn't so hot. The best ones have fluorescent fixtures buzzing overhead, Formica tabletops, and a gruff waiter who hurls the menu at you and asks, "Yeah, wha' you want?" This place looked good and lived up to its promise.

I had a dumpling appetizer, fiery Szechuan beef with tangerine peel, and pork fried rice, washing it down with a couple of Tsingtao beers. It came to something under fourteen dollars, but from what I've heard of the prices in Manhattan restaurants I think I got off easy.

I didn't call Professor Feldman until I got to the airport, mainly because I hadn't determined until then how much I was going to tell him.

I decided to lie.

"It was a washout, I'm afraid," I said, huddling in one of those half phone booths, which was several sizes too small for me, and straining to hear above the constant announcements coming over the airport lounge's loudspeakers. "Nobody at the Barthalow Gallery ever heard of Jeff. He must have wandered in to browse and picked up one of their business cards just for the hell of it."

Feldman didn't answer for a moment, but I could hear his breath whistling through the receiver. It was the ragged, labored breathing of a disappointed and tired old man.

"So what now?" he finally said querulously. "You just go home to Cleveland and quit?"

"I go home and keep looking."

"I'll pay you, y'know. For your time."

"I already have a client," I told him. "Don't worry, I won't stop until I find him."

"But it doesn't look good." He made it a sorrowful declaration of fact and not a question.

"Don't get negative on me. I still have a few ideas."

He pounced on it like a cougar. "So you did learn something at that gallery?" he said, and his voice seemed suddenly energized and alive. "You said this afternoon that if there was nothing at the gallery you had nowhere else to look. Now all of a sudden you've got some ideas."

"Just vague ones. Abstract ones. I don't want to get your hopes up, Irv."

He sighed. "Hopes are about all I've got left," he said.

My seatmate on the flight home was a thirteen-year-old girl wearing fawn-colored jeans with lace at the cuffs, a frilly blouse over a tank top, and a French schoolgirl's hat like the one Leslie Caron sported in *Gigi*. She was as graceful and skittish as a colt, and before we even left the ground she had told me her name was Kristen and asked mine, informed me that she was afraid of flying, or more accurately, of landing, told me she'd been in New York for her father's third wedding, announced she disliked her new stepbrother, and inquired if I was divorced. When I admitted I was, she said gravely, "I hate that."

She dug into her oversize traveling bag, in which I noticed a battered teddy bear, and pulled out a pad of Day-Glo letter paper—her dad had given it to her, she said—and spent the rest of the flight drawing flowery, sinuous vines around the borders. It was just as well. As charming a traveling companion as she was, I needed the time to think.

The visit had given me something to chew on other than tangerine-peel beef. I had the feeling Freya Barthalow had been telling me the truth, but if so, then what business did the clerk, Winstock, have with Jeff Feldman? What did Winstock think I was supposed to deliver? Did it tie in with Jeff's disappearance, and even though it was none of my business, did it have anything to do with Alys Larkin's one-way trip down an elevator shaft?

Whatever it was, I didn't believe Irv Feldman needed to know about it, but I felt lousy for lying to him. He was a nice man and obviously in pain, and I didn't want to add to that anguish. Although if my current thinking was on the mark, I was afraid I was going to have to.

I took out my notebook and jotted down a few random thoughts while I sipped the half cup of Diet Pepsi the muscular flight attendant had delivered from his rolling cart. You'd think with what they charge for an airplane seat they could give you the entire can. And I also remember the old days, when flight attendants weren't muscular. I surrendered my tiny bag of complimentary peanuts to Kristen, who devoured them along with her own.

I made a list of things I had to do and people I had to call before picking up the boys: go to the grocery store, Russo's Stop-N-Shop right across Fairmount from my apartment, because I hadn't done any shopping since April Delavan had shown up in my office early in the week, and I was out of a lot of things, including beer. Stop by the public library. Call Victor Gaimari. And call my client, April, just for the hell of it.

The flight attendant announced we were beginning our descent into Cleveland-Hopkins International Airport, and Kristen asked me to hand her the airsickness bag from the compartment on the back of the seat in front of me. I gave it to her quickly, but a glance at her told me she wasn't anywhere near getting queasy; her color was normal and her eyes were bright. I chalked it up to pubescent dramatics.

As the plane started down through the clouds, she said, "I think I'm going to pee in my pants."

"You're not allowed to pee in your pants *and* throw up," I told her. "You have to choose one end or the other."

That made her laugh so much she evidently forgot about doing either. When we finally deplaned—the airline's word, not mine—I saw her greet her tired-looking mother with a hug in the passenger waiting area. She murmured something to her mother and pointed at me. The woman looked at me with suspicion and nodded rather stiffly.

I ransomed my car from the airport lot and drove home. There were two messages on my answering machine, one from Marko and one from Victor Gaimari. I decided they could wait until morning.

It was only nine o'clock, but I was tired. Plane travel wears me out; maybe it's all that sanitized air. The refrigerator was sorely lacking in the dinner-fixings department, so I splashed water on my face, went across the street to the Mad Greek, and had roast lamb, a salad with feta cheese, and a Greek beer, and then went back to my apartment. The stairs felt a little steeper than ever before.

I flopped down in front of the TV in my little den, watched the news, and then *Saturday Night Live*. The guest host was a fresh-faced young actress in a shapeless dress and clodhopper shoes who reminded me a little bit of April Delavan. Halfway through the program the specialty musical act came on, featuring a lead singer with a shaven head who looked and moved like a dress extra from *Night of the Living Dead*. I was asleep before they finished what, with a stretch of the imagination, might have been called their song.

Except for Bruce Springsteen, Paul McCartney, and the Rolling Stones, in twenty years of watching *Saturday Night Live*, I've never once been able to stay awake through their musical guests.

I don't know anyone who has.

CHAPTER EIGHTEEN

In the morning I gulped down some coffee at home while I checked the sports page to see how the Indians were faring in the last days of spring training. They were playing .500 ball—but anyone will tell you that stats don't mean a thing until there's money on the line.

I rummaged around on the top shelf of my bedroom closet until I found my baseball glove, the one I'd had since I was a teenager. Once a rich tan, it had faded to an uncertain gray that almost obliterated the signature of former Dodger outfielder Willie Davis on the heel and was stiff from lack of use. I hadn't oiled it in at least ten years. I had, however, wrapped it around a worn old baseball and tied it up with string when I'd last used it the previous fall, so it still maintained a serviceable pocket. I was going to pick up my sons later that afternoon, drive out to one of the Metroparks, part of Cleveland's famous "Emerald Necklace," and toss a ball around, a rite of spring shared by millions of families all over America.

I pulled my car out into the April sunshine and drove the few blocks over to the library. Cleveland Heights and neighboring University Heights share an excellent library system, and one of the branches is at the corner of Coventry and Euclid Heights, diagonally across from Arabica. I found myself feeling grateful to the local voters who had recently approved a levy that allowed the libraries to stay open on Sundays.

It's a beautiful library. Built in 1926 of tapestry brick and stone in a combination of Tudor and Jacobean styles, it's a triangular shape and has an unusual chimney with articulated stacks, and an irregular series of multiple windows. In the main hall are two gigantic chandeliers, which are at odds with the fluorescent ceiling fixtures in the rest of the room. It's an officially designated Cleveland Heights landmark.

I didn't quite know what I was looking for, and it's at times like these that I appreciate my college education the most; it allows me to penetrate the mysteries of library catalogues and find what I want with relative ease.

There were several books on eighteenth-century English porcelain, and I lugged them all to a table in the middle of the library and began perusing them carefully, jotting in my notebook as I went.

Josephus Helgenburg's name loomed large in the annals of fine porcelain. In fact one of the books positively waxed rhapsodic, even mentioning the commission from Bonnie Prince Charlie. But it took me about fifteen minutes to find what I was really after.

A full-page color photograph of the twin of the "lost" Helgenburg vase, the one in the British Museum.

It was a fairly unusual shape, round and fat at the bottom with a graceful, narrow neck that blossomed out at the mouth like the bell of a trumpet. And it was covered with an intricate cabbage-leaf pattern, deep red on white, the leaves outlined with veins of gold. I don't know the first thing about porcelain, of course, but even I could tell it was quite extraordinary.

I was sure it was a good photograph, but I was willing to bet it didn't do the vase justice.

I asked the reference librarian if she knew of any other books on the subject, and she told me that the library in Rocky River, an upscale suburb on the West Side, had a state-of-the-art collection of material on ceramics and porcelain, the best in Greater Cleveland. I looked at my watch. It was after eleven, and I had to pick up my boys at two. What I already had would have to do me for the moment; Rocky River was too far to drive. But I made a note of it in case I had need of further information.

Then I photocopied several of the pages that discussed Helgenburg and his techniques, and the picture of the vase. It didn't look nearly as beautiful in the harsh black-and-white of the Xerox machine.

I left my car where it was in the municipal parking lot behind the Medic Drug Store—I'd fed the meter enough for three hours—and strolled across the street past the Sunday morning crowd at the tables and on the steps outside Arabica. It was mostly couples who had obviously just climbed out of bed from under the Sunday papers, and they gave me the kind of twinge young people in love always do.

My bellicose young friend with the dog was nowhere in sight this morning, and it was just as well. I was in no mood.

I stood in the vestibule of Jeff Feldman's building ringing his bell for a long time, my irritation mounting exponentially as the seconds ticked by. Finally I got an answering buzz and walked up the stairs to the second floor, where a sullen April Delavan opened the door wearing a white calf-length nightshirt with tiny blue appliquéd flowers at the neckline. Her exquisite features were still puffy from interrupted sleep, the blue eyes blurry and slightly bloodshot.

"What are you doing here so early?" she grumped.

"Early's a matter of opinion. Got a minute?"

She shrugged airily, as if minutes weren't very dear, and stood aside so I could come in. She hadn't straightened the place up since my visit several days earlier; indeed she'd added to the clutter. And the thick, cloying odor of stale marijuana smoke hung over the apartment like swamp gas.

"I've got a couple of questions you might be able to answer, April."

"Jeez, wait a second, okay. My eyes aren't even open yet." She padded barefoot into the bathroom, peed, rinsed out her mouth, and splashed water on her face. I know all that because she didn't bother closing the door.

She came out rubbing her eyes with a towel that had probably needed laundering days ago, and by the time she dropped it on the floor she seemed to be more or less awake. "What's goin' on?" she said.

"Did Jeff Feldman ever say anything about a Josephus Helgenburg to you?"

"Nuh-uh. I didn't know many of his friends."

"Helgenburg isn't exactly a friend. He was an Austrian porcelain maker who died over two hundred years ago."

"So who cares, then?" she asked impatiently, cocking her hip.

"Think, April, okay? Helgenburg."

She wandered around poking through one ashtray after another until she found a smokable butt. "Sounds familiar, but I can't remember why."

"Did he ever tell you he was in possession of one of Helgenburg's pieces? A vase?"

She shook her head. "We didn't really talk that much, tell you the truth." Maybe the shaking jarred something loose, or at least woke her up a little more, because her eyes took on life for the first time since I'd walked in. "It wasn't Jeff I heard it from," she said. "It was my father."

"When was this, April?"

"Long time ago. Months, maybe. Way before I ever met Jeff. I can't remember what it was about, but I know he mentioned the name."

"Your father wanted to buy a Helgenburg piece?"

"I dunno. I suppose so. For his precious collection. He spends more time on that damn collection than he would if he had some woman stashed away somewhere. He probably does anyway." She walked around picking things up and putting them down again, finally finding a matchbook on the bed under a casually tossed bra. She lit the butt, but it must have tasted terrible even to her, because she made a face and quickly stubbed it out. "He's borrowed from everyone in town just to keep us eating, but he's always got money to buy some damn piece of pottery."

"He's borrowing money?"

April plopped down onto the edge of her bed, her legs sticking straight out in front of her. The bottoms of her feet could have used a good scrubbing—so could the floor. I suppose the two facts were related. "He even tried to borrow money from me," she said. "But no sale."

"You gave eighteen thousand dollars to Jeff Feldman, but you wouldn't loan any to your father?"

"Jeff was my boyfriend," she said by way of explanation, in a tone that dripped condescension. Obviously that was something I should have figured out for myself. She stretched out on the bed and put her hands behind her head. "Another screwup, huh? At least I'd know where to find my father."

"Everybody makes mistakes, April."

"What the hell, it's only money. Hey, you got a cigarette?" she asked, sitting up. "I'll pay you back."

I tossed her a nearly full pack of Winstons. "If it's only money, why have you hired me?"

Somewhere April had acquired the disconcerting habit of not looking at people when she spoke to them. I was beginning to find it annoying. She shook out a cigarette and put the pack on the pillow beside her, and I mentally kissed it goodbye. "I don't like being used, that's all," she said.

She stuck the cigarette into her mouth and it bobbed up and down when she talked. Very Warner Brothers, very Bette Davis. "My father used me to get to Jeff—I'm not stupid, I know what's going on. And then Jeff ripped me off. That's two strikes, you know? So, no loan for Daddy Dearest, and no letting Jeff get away with it." She blew twin jets of smoke through her nostrils and added matter-of-factly, "Paybacks are rough."

"You're pretty young to be so tough, aren't you?"

She regarded me the way one might a particularly rare specimen of centipede in a jar of formaldehyde. "I've been around, Mr. Jacovich. I've gone to finishing school, and I've lived on the streets. And I learned one thing. In this world, you either get tough or you die."

Sometimes even being tough doesn't help, I thought as I drove east out Chagrin Boulevard toward Orange. Alys Larkin had seemed pretty self-sufficient to me, but it hadn't kept her from a broken neck.

But April Delavan had something else going for her. She was

not only tough as well as beautiful, but she was very, very rich. That seemed to me to be an unbeatable combination.

The lovely eastern suburbs were getting green, as if spring really meant it this time. The entire northeast had taken a pretty sound pummeling from winter—we'd had a White Easter—and the balmy temperatures and bright sunlight of the past weeks had gotten our hopes high, as well as coaxing out a few early buds.

It was almost noon when I rang Victor Gaimari's doorbell.

Chickie Tattersfield answered it.

"Good morning, Chickie," I said. "Milan Jacovich, from the party Friday night. Remember?"

"Uh-huh," she said, and for all the interest she exhibited in my presence I might have been delivering a pizza. She was wearing a silk lounging outfit that must have cost as much as a small two-bedroom home. She turned and walked back into the house, leaving the door open. I supposed that was to be interpreted as permission to enter, and as I followed her inside I bit back a number of sarcastic comments I wanted to hurl at her retreating back. I guess a divorce settlement in the mid-seven-figure range buys the right to rudeness.

Victor came up the steps from the living room wearing a white shirt, charcoal slacks, and black loafers with no socks. The shirt was open three buttons; Victor didn't have a very hairy chest. Behind him I could hear opera music pouring from the sound system. I'm not a big opera fan, but it beat *Cats* hands down.

"Well, Milan!" he said. "What a surprise."

"I'm sorry to bother you on a Sunday, Victor."

"No bother at all. Can I fix you a bloody Mary?"

"I won't be staying long."

He tried to look disappointed, indicating the living room with a somewhat dramatic gesture. I went down the steps and sat in one of his wing chairs; it was a lot less comfortable than it looked. He clicked off the music and stretched himself out on the sofa, leaning against the back with both legs up on the cushions; the pose was right out of a Calvin Klein Obsession for men ad and matched the outfit. From the corner of my eye I could see Chickie

Tattersfield moving around in the sunroom, a drink in her hand.

"Did you come for another lesson in porcelain collecting, Milan? Or is there something else?"

"Yes, and yes, Victor. Let me just run a name by you: Alys Larkin."

"Never heard of her," he said. Victor, for all his faults—and they are legion—usually tells the truth, at least to me. And on the few occasions he's lied to me I've found him to be quite bad at it, his eyes shifting and his color turning a bit more ruddy than usual. This time he didn't even blink, and his expression didn't change a whit, so I decided to believe him.

"Who is she, anyway?" he asked.

"A local ceramic artist. A dead ceramic artist."

"Dead?"

"When last seen."

He put his feet down on the floor. "I don't like the sound of that."

"Neither do I. And probably neither would she if she could hear it."

"Are you telling me she met with some sort of misadventure?"

"Misadventure. That's quaint, Victor. Why would you assume that?"

"Because," he said easily, "every time someone in this town gets killed you ask me if I know about it."

"She shared a studio with Jeff Feldman. So there is a connection."

"A tenuous one, but all right. So what?"

"So not much. I was just asking."

"You drove all the way out here for that on a Sunday? You could have called."

"And miss seeing you again? Three times in a week, that's something of a record for us, isn't it?"

He ignored the sarcasm. "I thought Sunday was your day to spend with your kids."

"I'm picking them up when I leave here. And thanks for your concern. But that isn't all I have to ask you."

"I'm all yours," he said. "For a few minutes, anyway." He inclined his head toward the sunroom and lowered his voice slightly. "She doesn't much like being ignored."

"I know how she feels," I said, remembering her non-greeting at the door. "Let's talk about collecting."

"All right," he said. He was easy to get along with this morning, Victor.

"It isn't a tax write-off, is it?" I asked.

"Unfortunately not. Only when you donate something to a museum."

"Then, why? I know you're a very cultured guy; I see the paintings and things. But you could buy a nice house, a Ferrari, toss a three-week orgy with that kind of money. Why spend it on a vase? So everyone will know you can?"

He allowed himself a self-deprecating smile. "Partly, I suppose. Another part is the fun of knowing you own something a lot of other people want." Again he flicked a glance toward Chickie in the sunroom. She was staring out the window and sucking on one of her long acrylic fingernails.

"At least," he went on, "I make use of the things I buy. I'm not one of those people who acquires a painting and keeps it locked up where no one can see it, or a rare book they never bother reading. I'm afraid I'm not very single-minded when it comes to collecting. The purists would probably be appalled. My tastes are eclectic. The paintings, for instance. I enjoy them, enjoy looking at them. But I enjoy collecting other things too. For instance— this should interest you especially, Milan—in my library upstairs I have a first edition of *Lady in the Lake* signed by Raymond Chandler. I'll be glad to show it to you, if you like."

"Some other time," I said, not wanting to give him the satisfaction of knowing how impressed I was. "So you're not really that into porcelain? You don't have a passion for it?"

He considered his answer carefully. "I like it very much and respond to it on some emotional level. It gives me pleasure, certainly. I don't know if I'd characterize it as passion."

"Then you don't know all that much about porcelain?"

His hand went to his open shirt collar, and he fingered the

flesh at the base of his throat. "I'm no expert, if that's what you mean. But I don't go into things half-cocked. I'm knowledgeable. I've done a certain amount of research on it, and I can hold my own in a conversation with people who know a lot more than I do." He touched his mustache, smoothing it unnecessarily. "I'm not some semiliterate dummy with work boots and a lunch pail."

I felt my ears getting warm. "My father was a semiliterate dummy with a lunch pail, Victor."

He flapped his hand at me. "Oh, come on! So was my grandfather." He sighed. "It was probably an unfortunate metaphor. I didn't mean to offend you, Milan, although I seem to do that a lot without even trying. Maybe you're overly sensitive and I'm not sensitive enough."

I just lifted an eyebrow, accepting his truth with a certain grace I wasn't feeling. I can be as supercilious as Victor. I just have to work a little harder at it.

"Chickie and I have plans for this afternoon, though," he said, "so I am going to have to ask you to get to the point."

"Thanks, Victor," I said, "but I think I already did."

CHAPTER NINETEEN

I'm taking a class in dried flower arranging, Milan," Lila was saying as she bustled around at the sink. Most of my memories of Lila are, unfortunately, of her standing at that sink. "I think I have a natural feel for it, and maybe I can make a few extra dollars."

"That's good, Lila." I was drinking a cup of coffee, sitting in the kitchen that used to be mine, nodding and making mindless small talk with the woman who used to be my wife, waiting for my two sons to do whatever it was they had to do upstairs so we could leave for the park.

"The boys are getting older now, and they don't require quite so much of my time, so I figure I'm in a good place to start something new, don't you? And it's artistic. I think it will be very rewarding for me."

"Sure," I said. "I'll bet you'll he great at it."

That was a kind lie that cost me nothing. My ex-wife Lila, with a fiery Serbian temperament that's always smoldering beneath the surface like a volcano, doesn't have anywhere near the patience it takes to do the delicate kind of work required of flower arrangers. The kitchen, which I had painted red about seven years before, was full of potted plants, jade trees and succulents and ficus and lots of other things I couldn't name that had big, shiny, palmy leaves, but they only required weekly watering and an occasional snip of dead stalks. Still, Lila had always considered her thumb green just for keeping them alive, and if she wanted to begin a career in the dried-flora field I wasn't going to be the one to dis-abuse her of the notion.

"Stephen's having a wonderful time with baseball practice," she said. "They made him the catcher."

I'd known that, since I'd talked to Stephen on the phone ear-lier in the week, but I winced anyway. When a father dreams of his kid playing baseball, he imagines a rangy, powerful slugger or else sees the kid standing on the pitcher's mound, staring in with a Bob Gibson glare that automatically backs hitters off the dish. Not squatting down behind the plate with his hat on backwards, wearing the mask and the shin guards and the chest protector—what major league catchers themselves unfairly call "the tools of ignorance." Catching is a punishing and unglamorous job.

The boys came crashing down the stairs carrying their gym bags with books and clothes for school the next day, or rather Ste-phen crashed, which is his usual means of locomotion. Milan Jr., at age seventeen, is far too dignified to express enthusiasm about anything in which an adult is involved, and he stalked storklike into the kitchen, his fielder's glove hanging low on his belt like a professional gunfighter's pearl-handled .45. His greeting to me was "Hey."

I tried not to let it bother me—it's the attitude of teenagers everywhere, the one I've come to think of as faux cool.

Stephen, teetering on that twelve-year-old precipice between childhood and adolescence, looked as if he was glad to see me, though with his catcher's mask tilted back on his head it was hard to tell. He was wearing his uniform, a drip-dry replica of that of the Houston Astros, and he graciously allowed me to squeeze his shoulder.

"How's the Man in the Iron Mask?" I said.

"Come on!" he complained, and punched me in the arm.

It's particularly cruel that the people you love most in the world, your children, reach a point in their development when they deem any overt physical expression of that love to be ob-noxious. I couldn't remember the last time Milan had let me hug him. Stephen was still not completely opposed to hugging his father, although it had to be when no one else was looking, but he chose to punch my arm instead.

Not that I would have really been hugging *him* anyway, what with the mask he was wearing, and the chest protector and the shin guards and the giant pillowlike catcher's mitt.

I take great pride in both my sons, as unalike as brothers can be. Milan Jr., the athletic, serious one who takes after his Serbian mother, with his dark and somewhat somber good looks, and Stephen, all Slovenian smiles and sunshine and boundless enthusiasm, stir such strong feelings in me that often I have to blink back tears of joy when I see them. Not being there all the time, not living in their house and seeing them every day, evokes in me a loving intensity when I am with them that's almost painful.

So I could bear Milan's cool detachment and hope it was a temporary thing, and I could even live with Stephen's mask and pads; better that than to have my parental dreams crash and burn the way Irv Feldman's had. Or Chase Delavan's, for that matter.

Do parents go wrong, or just people? Hadn't Jeff Feldman once been a sunny, active kid playing out heroic fantasies on the playground? Had he ever gone out in the park and tossed a ball with his father? Hadn't he suffered adolescent angst along with everyone else in the world? Why, with loving and cultured parents, had he grown up to be a bum and a hustler and a user? Why, with every material advantage, had April Delavan developed into a cynical, burnt-out Jell-O–head?

Looking at my two loves, I wondered if there was anything a parent could really do, that I could do, that would guarantee them honor and decency and whatever measure of happiness the future might hold. Or is life simply a dangerous crapshoot?

I suffered through Lila's weekly instructions about making sure the boys ate properly, easy on the junk food, and got to bed on time, and seeing that they took their books to school with them the next morning. Sometimes she treats me like a bachelor uncle who lives in another state and only comes to visit at holidays. I think she forgets I'm their father.

It hurts.

It hurts because one of the things I think defines me is fatherhood, and my boys are my number-one priority. My divorce hadn't been my idea, nor was it my fault that I was living in an apartment across town from my kids, only seeing them on weekends or special occasions. So when Lila consistently reminds me that I'm no longer a resident parent, it cuts deep.

And time was running out. As I looked over at Milan Jr. in the passenger seat beside me I saw the shadow of dark fuzz on his chin and upper lip, and the way his cheekbones and jawline were becoming sculpted and defined, and I realized that very soon I'd lose this one, at least in terms of his being a kid. Stephen, jabbering happily in the back, still had a few years yet where spending a Sunday with his father would be considered a treat instead of a duty, but even now I was beginning to have to fight for time with him, away from his friends.

We wound up in the Metropark just off Green Road on the East Side and spent some time tossing a ball around between us. Milan Jr. has a wicked arm, and after half an hour my left hand was sore and swollen; one of the first things any kid learns is that the ball is hard as a rock. I sat on a bench while Stephen, his mask down over his face, squatted down behind a sheet of paper he'd commandeered from my car and put down for a makeshift plate, and watched his brother pitch to him.

The sound of the ball smacking the glove was like a pistol shot. I thought about telling Milan to take it easy, that Stephen was only twelve, but I stopped. When does concern cross the line and become overprotection, I wondered? When does easygoing leniency with a kid become apathy, and strictness become oppression?

No wonder Irv Feldman was wracked with doubt and remorse.

The next morning we were all up early, albeit with pizza hangovers. I threw on a jogging suit and cooked the boys breakfast, hearty bacon and eggs and hot cereal and orange juice for them, to make up for the junk food we'd eaten the night before, and black coffee for me. Then, throwing Stephen's catcher's gear in the back seat of my car so I wouldn't forget to drop it off at Lila's later, I drove them to their respective schools.

Neither one kissed me goodbye—which would have shocked hell out of me anyway—but Stephen socked me on the arm again before he got out of the car.

It wasn't even eight-thirty yet, so I went back home to finish up the pot of coffee, pay a few bills and catch up on some paperwork, and get dressed to start the day. But life so rarely goes according to our plans.

Chase Delavan rang my doorbell about ten minutes after I got home.

"I hope you don't mind my just dropping by," he said as he stood in the doorway. "I called earlier, but you weren't home. I have to be downtown later, so I took a chance."

I invited him in, but I wasn't comfortable about it. The apartment still showed the ravages of two kids having spent the night, and I was hardly dressed for company. The thousand-dollar Brooks Brothers suit Delavan wore spoke volumes vis-à-vis my red jogging suit.

"What can I do for you, Mr. Delavan?"

He looked around the front room I reserve for my business dealings as if he'd inexplicably been dropped into a Moroccan sewer. He was an arrogant and ostentatious bastard, and I wasn't enchanted with his attitude. The scent of expensive men's cologne hovered around his head. "I wanted to inquire as to how your search is coming."

"My search?"

"For Jeff Feldman."

I had to give him credit for chutzpah. And I wondered if he had somehow found out that it was his daughter who was paying me. "You 'just dropped by' to ask me that?"

"Call it insatiable curiosity and humor me." He didn't look at all ready to be humored.

"I don't really think it's any of your business, Mr. Delavan."

"I can see where you wouldn't," he allowed, and then simply

waited with patience and assurance, as if for something inevitable, like a sunrise.

I couldn't think of a reason not to tell him, other than the fact that I didn't like him very much. "I haven't found him yet. And when I spoke to you last week, you didn't seem very interested in Feldman one way or the other."

"True," he said, "but change is the way of the world, isn't it? The one constant."

He folded himself gracefully into one of my client chairs without being invited, crossing one ankle over the other. "Remember I told you that Feldman might have access to a very rare piece of ceramic art?"

I nodded.

"Well," he explained, as if to a not very bright five-year-old, "I can only assume that where Feldman is, the ceramic wouldn't be far away."

I went behind my desk and sat down. "A big assumption."

"Perhaps," he said. "But my acquisitive nature leads me to that conclusion. And I want that piece. It's a superb example of European porcelain, and I want it. Badly. And I'm used to getting what I want."

"I hope you do," I said with half a heart.

He cleared an early morning frog from his throat. "It occurs to me that perhaps you can help me."

"I already have a client, Mr. Delavan."

"I know. But your client has engaged you to find Feldman. I want you to get that porcelain for me. And I'll pay you handsomely."

"Handsomely," I repeated. I have great admiration for people who speak as if they live in the eighteenth century.

He elaborated. "Shall we say, oh, perhaps a five-thousand-dollar bonus?"

"You can say that, sure. But I'm a little confused here. Last week you were afraid to tell me what this pottery thing was for fear I'd tell someone else."

He uncrossed and recrossed his legs, maybe so I could see his silk socks and be impressed. "I realize it's a calculated risk, Mr. Jacovich. But I've decided to trust you." A benison, given freely and from the generosity of his heart. "'This pottery thing,' as you call it, is a vase. A very beautiful, priceless vase." He sat back in the chair, smug and smarmy.

"What a guy!" I said.

"Excuse me?"

"You're going to just haul off and trust me? Just like that? Zowie! I'm proud and humble."

He sniffed. "I came here to talk business. Your business. There's no need to be sarcastic."

"Perhaps not. But I have to tell you I'm not at all interested in your commission, Mr. Delavan. As I said, I'm already engaged in this matter."

"Yes, but since you're trying to find Jeff Feldman anyway, you can pick up a nice piece of change without going even a tick out of your way."

"I'd be going a lot more than a tick out of the way of my professional ethics."

"What if I made it ten thousand?"

Rich people. "You're not listening," I said.

I was obviously straining his already short supply of affability. "Don't force me to play hardball, Mr. Jacovich."

I flexed my left hand. It still hurt from Milan Jr.'s blazing pitches. "You don't know what hardball is."

"You think not? The vase belongs to me by right. I already advanced Feldman a good deal of money for it, and that makes it mine, ethically and morally."

Those were two words I never thought I'd hear issuing from Chase Delavan's lips. "How much money?"

"A substantial amount, and that's all you need to know. So I'm already financially committed, and I won't be held up again. Ten thousand is my offer."

"You can keep your ten thousand," I said. "With a full set of instructions."

He flushed beneath his sunlamp tan. "I'm connected to some

fairly important people around here. I can put you right out of business, you know."

"On what grounds? Rudeness?"

"Possession of stolen property."

"I don't have any stolen property, Mr. Delavan. Oh, wait, there's that towel from Bally's in Atlantic City . . ."

He got up out of his chair and came to lean over the desk, jabbing a finger into my chest. "You obviously don't know who you're dealing with, Jacovich. I can make things very unpleasant for you."

I'm not fond of being poked—less so of being threatened. I uncoiled my six foot three from my desk chair, looming over him. "And I can make things very unpleasant for you, Mr. Delavan."

"Oh?" He seemed amused, confident. "How?"

"I'm bigger than you."

His amusement faded along with his tan, and he backed a couple steps away. "Watch yourself," he warned. "I'm nobody to fuck with, and I won't be thwarted by some two-bit Slovak gumshoe in sweat clothes."

"Mr. Delavan," I said, "you're not only politically incorrect, you're geographically that way, too."

I came around the side of my desk, and that was enough for him. He stalked toward the door a little too quickly to be casual, trailing a bit of his dignity behind him.

When he'd gone, the effluvium of his cologne lingered after him like a bad memory, and after I regained control of my temper I opened all the windows to air out the room a little bit. It didn't seem to do much good, so I lit a cigarette, on the theory that if I couldn't get rid of the offensive odor, I could mask it with a new one.

Delavan was a bully in an expensive suit. I wondered if he'd bullied his daughter April as well, so much so that she'd grown up hard and tough behind that angel's face more out of self-defense than as a matter of conscious choice.

I wrote out a couple of checks and filed some papers that should have been put away a week ago, and then I took out my index cards on the April Delavan case and moved them around on the desk some more. A definite pattern began insinuating itself into my consciousness, but after a few moments I realized that with all that I'd managed to learn and surmise in the last week, nothing had brought me any closer to my original—task locating Jeff Feldman and getting April's money back.

I pondered some things in the shower; the hot water drumming on the back of my neck was not only invigorating and relaxing but inspired a certain clarity of thought. April Delavan had hired me to find her missing boyfriend, who'd ripped her off for eighteen thousand dollars. Her father *and* Victor Gaimari had also given Feldman money for a hunk of porcelain to display on the mantel, and both had offered me a lot more money to find it.

So Feldman had been playing everyone against the middle and had walked away with a substantial amount of cash. It was entirely possible he had wisely disappeared into the ether, perhaps to surface at a future date in some unlikely place like Des Moines. But I decided after putting a lot of the pieces together, including my interesting trip to New York, that both Delavan and Victor were being led down the garden path while Jeff Feldman had dropped off the face of the earth.

And then there was Alys Larkin.

I turned off the water, glanced uneasily at the drain in the tub to see how much hair I'd lost during the shampoo. Not much, thanks be to God. I dried myself quickly. Chase Delavan had managed to put me behind schedule.

Then, after I called Marko and made a lunch date, I dressed in khaki slacks, a brown tweed sports jacket, and a brownish tie over a yellow button-down shirt.

My going-downtown clothes.

CHAPTER TWENTY

When the dirndl-skirted waitress arrived with the main course, Marko Meglich pushed aside his half-finished bowl of soup to make room and dug into the large plate of roast pork with mashed potatoes and lots of good rich gravy. He sighed heavily, once more put-upon. "I hate it when you get into your bulldog mode, Milan. It wears me out."

"Eat your lunch," I urged, regarding my roast chicken. "It'll give you energy."

We were at a table against the wall at Frank Sterle's Slovenian Country House on East Fifty-fifth Street near St. Clair Avenue, only a few blocks from where both of us had been born and grown up. Spring sunlight was fighting its way through the stained glass windows and illuminating the murals of Slovenia that surrounded us. A lot of businessmen, Slovenian and otherwise, find their way to Sterle's for lunch.

"If the department is willing to call Alys Larkin's death an accident, I don't see why you can't." Marko dipped a slice of bread into his gravy.

"Because I think she was dead before she went down the shaft. I don't like the angle at which she fell."

"Probably she didn't either."

"Nice mouth," I said.

He chewed energetically. "The coroner is happy. The department is happy. The only one not happy is you, and that's no reason for us to waste manpower poking around in this."

"Not even if it's a possible murder?"

He shook his head. "That's your tune, not mine. I don't need to go out and look for work, you know. There was a gang killing last night on Central Avenue. Two dead, including a fifteen-year-old girl, and three in intensive care. Some optometrist in Tremont offed his wife with a tire iron. And God knows what new stuff will be on my desk when I get back from lunch. Kids bring loaded guns to school instead of pencils and erasers. We're back to the days of the Old West, when everybody packs iron and draws on whoever looks at them funny." He slurped at his iced tea. "I'm in the only profession that doesn't have to advertise."

"I just think it's worth a look, that's all. You're taking the easy way out, calling it an accident."

"Sure I am," he agreed. "I have to. Nobody's got respect anymore. Not for property, not for other people, not even for human life. When you and I started twenty years ago, things were different. Back then people were taught respect. Now the respect of their peers is more important to a kid than whether their mom or dad is going to be mad at them, and it's a war zone out there. Homicide division's busier than a Wal-Mart on a Saturday, and it's the safest time in the world to be a cop because hardly anyone resists arrest—they just laugh at us. They know they'll be back on the street in a couple of hours, and it isn't worth it to them to kill one of us. Because now we can only afford to put time in on cases that look like they might be solvable, that look like they are for sure homicides, and not accidents. We have to prioritize, just like anybody else."

"Must be tough to breathe with your heads in the sand," I said.

His face flushed, and he wiped at his mustache with a napkin. "That's not fair, damn it! Understand, Milan, we're like any other big-city department; we're stretched too thin, even though the mayor added a bunch of uniforms last year. We don't have the resources to mess around with possibles. We could commit maybe two hundred man hours to this and find out it's what we called it in the first place—an unfortunate accident. In the meantime, somebody winds up in a Dumpster with two bullets in their skull, and we don't have anyone available to check it out because we're chasing the wind on this Larkin thing. It doesn't compute for me."

"There are some very heavy people trying to locate Jeff Feldman and this ceramic piece he supposedly has."

He sopped up some more gravy, shoved nearly a whole slice of bread in his mouth, and looked down furtively at his gold tie to make sure he hadn't dripped anything on it. "I know you're not going to tell me what heavy people, so I won't even ask. But seems to me if it's so—I'm not doubting you, now—but *if* it's so, they'd be after Feldman, not Larkin."

"Pretty shortsighted, isn't it?"

He pointed his fork at me, and I tried to ignore the gravy that dripped from its tines. "You find me Jeff Feldman with a broken neck and maybe we can talk. This way . . ."

"You don't connect it that a guy who's got something a lot of people want real bad disappears into a black hole and his business roommate falls down an elevator shaft?"

"You make the connection and I'll send out a couple of suits."

"I don't know the connection," I admitted.

"Me neither. That's why I can't move on this." He blotted the wet bottom of his glass with his napkin and finished off the iced tea.

"Would you do me a quick favor, then?"

He arched a suspicious eyebrow.

"Look up a Bert Winstock on the national computer and see if he's got a sheet."

"Who's he?"

"A guy I met. Lives in New York."

His eyes raked the ceiling. "New York. Jesus, Milan!"

"It'll take five minutes away from your case load, Mark. And it might tell me a lot."

"What am I looking for on this guy?" he said. "Murder? Arson? Child molesting?"

"I'm not exactly sure. But my best guess would be forgery or fraud, something like that."

"Doesn't exactly sound like public enemy number one."

"You never know," I said.

"Winstock, huh? Why you want a line on him? What'd he ever do to you?"

I ran my finger around the edge of my coffee cup and didn't meet Marko's eyes. "He told me to go fuck myself."

"No!" he said, and threw up his hands in mock horror. "Well, why didn't you say so in the first place? I'm shocked—*shocked!* We're gonna nail that son of a bitch if it's the last thing we ever do!" He wrote Winstock's name down in his notebook.

"Just because I owe you one for the Opening Day tickets," he said, putting his notebook back in his inside pocket. He patted it tenderly, as if saying good night to a child. "Pick me up tomorrow about quarter after twelve, all right? We'll drive to the ballpark in a department vehicle—maybe we can get a decent parking space that way."

I pushed my chicken leg around on my plate. "It just feels wrong to me, Marko."

"Going to Jacobs Field in a cop car? Don't get all noble on me, all right? It's no big deal."

"The Larkin business, I mean. It feels all wrong."

"Then *you* chase it," he said, and looked around for the waitress so he could order dessert.

It's only about a seven-minute drive from Sterle's to Little Italy, but then it's never more than half an hour's drive from anywhere in Cleveland to anywhere else. I found a parking space on Murray Hill, very close to Mayfield Road, so I took the opportunity to stop at Presti's bakery for a loaf of Italian bread still hot from the oven, which I left on the passenger seat. Slathered with Stadium Mustard and wrapped around fried klobasa, it would be lunch for the rest of the week, I figured.

Then I walked up the hill to Dorian's. It's a fairly steep hill, and I didn't like the way I was puffing when I got to the gallery.

I thought for probably the ten thousandth time about cutting down on my smoking.

Today Alphonso Diorio was sporting a bilious green windowpane plaid jacket with squares so big a dinner plate wouldn't cover them, a dark blue dress shirt, and a light blue tie, an ensemble that he might have copied out of the Wise Guy's Dress-for-Success Manual.

He was reading the paper at his desk, giving truth to the *Plain Dealer's* boast that it's "the newspaper you read all day long." It must have startled him to see me walk through the door, because his fat, sweaty face got a little bit more sweaty, and he flicked a glance toward the telephone on his desk.

"Hello, Mr. Dorian."

"Whattaya say?" he greeted me weakly. Amazingly, it didn't hurt my feelings at all that he wasn't happy to see me.

"I know you're busy," I said pointedly, "but could you could give me a few minutes?"

He twiddled his fingers through his thinning hair, blinking his eyes so rapidly I thought he was about to faint. "Uh, sure, I guess so," he said, and looked at the phone again. Then he stood up, bent at the waist as though trying to present the smallest target possible. "I, uh—if you'll excuse me for just a moment . . . ?"

"For Christ's sake, Dorian, I just want to talk. About art and things. I need your professional expertise. Nothing incriminating, okay? You don't have to run back and call Gaimari about it."

He hesitated for just a second and then straightened up, standing as tall as he could, and the lines of his face hardened beneath the rolls of fat, giving me a glimpse of the tough guy he probably used to be. Maybe in his younger days he had been almost intimidating. "As a matter of fact I do, Mr. Jacovich. That's what I get paid for."

I had to cede that point. "Well, tell him hello for me," I said, and waved a hand at him. He nodded grimly and, head high, vanished into the back room with more dignity than I'd given him credit for.

I sat down opposite his desk and helped myself to a wrapped red-and-white mint from a dish on the shelf to my right. I picked up the newspaper, barely noticing the little button on the phone as it lit up. Dorian had been looking at the sports section, which was largely devoted to the probable fate of the Indians for the coming season, which would begin the following day. I hadn't had a chance to peruse it that morning because of Chase Delavan's unexpected visit, so I read it with interest. Offensively, the paper opined, the team was an acknowledged powerhouse; pitching, however, was iffy, and defense more so.

Dorian finally returned, his color more nearly normal, and lowered his bulk into his chair. "So what's the deal, Mr. Jacovich?" he asked. "Oh, and Mr. Gaimari says to say hello back."

Long and hard I considered giving him a bad time about having to ask Victor's permission to breathe, but I decided not to. He was doing his job, just like he said. Besides, I could probably get more out of him if I didn't make him hostile.

"Let's start with how the gallery business works, because I don't have a clue." I indicated the ceramics so carefully displayed all over the room. "Are all these by local artists?"

"Not all of them," he said. "Some of them are from Southern Ohio, a few from the Pittsburgh area, and a couple of others from as far away as New Mexico. But most are by local people. We like to support Cleveland here."

"That's nice," I said. "Hometown spirit."

"Something like that." He smiled uncertainly, not sure whether or not I was baiting him, and leaned back in his chair a bit, which squeaked a protest. "We take most pieces on consignment here. If they sell, we take a percentage. If not, after a certain amount of time we return them, and no hard feelings."

The mint had dwindled to almost nothing, so I crunched up the rest of it with my teeth. "Did you ever take anything from Alys Larkin on consignment?"

A line appeared between his eyebrows that might or might not have been a frown. "Alys Larkin. That was too bad about her, I was sorry to hear that. Those old buildings down there, a lot of artists rent them out, but they really aren't very safe. Yeah, we moved some of her stuff every now and then. Not lately, but maybe about a year or so ago."

"Did it sell well?"

"Pretty good. She had lots of talent. She was wonderful with porcelain. She did quite a few clay pieces, too—candlesticks and earthenware pitchers. But it was with porcelain she really shone. Is that the right word, shone?"

"Why not?" I said. "How about Tydings Belk?"

He shook his head. "Belk's stuff runs more in the tableware department. You know, full sets of dishes, stoneware, things like that. That's not what our clientele looks for."

"But he's talented too?"

He spread his pudgy fingers. "I wouldn't exactly call him a great artist, but he's a good craftsman. He makes a nice buck at what he does, and he deserves it."

"Ever carry any of Jeff Feldman's work?"

I think the sound he made was supposed to be a laugh, but it came out more of a hog's snort. "Feldman is a no-talent hack. I wouldn't use any of his shit for a paperweight."

"That bad, huh?"

"You ever been down near the Texas border, Mr. Jacovich? Brownsville or El Paso?"

"No."

"There are tourist joints there on both sides of the border where they sell clay pots in the shape of frogs and armadillos and things for about six ninety-five. Well, that's how good Jeff Feldman is as an artist."

I nodded. "You know a lot about art? Ceramics and fine china, I mean?"

He beamed with what could only be called hubris. "Sure I do. It's my business."

I took out my notebook, flipped it to the part I'd filled at the library the morning before, and ran my finger down the page until I came to a name that Chase Delavan had mentioned to me and that I'd found in several of the books on rare English porcelain. "Are you familiar with a William Ridgway?"

His brow crinkled. "Should I be?"

"How about Nicholas Sprimont?"

Dorian's frown was full-blown this time as he struggled to

make a mental connection. "No, I can't recall ever hearing that name. Is he a local guy?"

"I don't think so."

"Well then," he said.

"Let me ask you something else. Ever run into a forgery?"

He drummed his fingers on the desktop. "How do you mean?"

"A forgery," I repeated. "A piece that's supposed to be rare and valuable but isn't anything more than a good copy."

"The kind of stuff I carry in here, you know, all contemporary artists, the subject hardly ever comes up. You want to be talking to a fine art gallery, not to me."

"But you'd know a fake if you saw one?"

He bristled a little. "I think so."

"How?"

He started sweating again and gave another furtive look at the telephone. "Well," he said, and coughed. "Well. A significant piece like that, it would come with a provenance. Papers."

"You mean like a purebred dog?"

His laugh was nervous and without mirth. "Sort of."

"Uh-huh. And what if the papers were forged?"

He looked blank.

"I mean, if the porcelain was faked, couldn't the provenance be faked too?"

"That'd be pretty tough to do."

"Why?" I said. "They can forge U.S. currency, why couldn't somebody forge a provenance?"

He sputtered a little. "Yeah, but you'd need the right kind of paper, the right ink, stuff that they don't make any more. Any expert could tell in a minute."

"Could you tell?"

He started to answer but the door to the shop opened and closed, and he looked up, grateful for the interruption.

It was John Terranova, Giancarlo D'Alessandro's driver. When he isn't playing chauffeur, he handles a certain amount of rough stuff for Victor Gaimari, although with a bit more panache than the Neanderthal, Angelo, whom Victor had on the door for his party. Several years before I'd been on the receiving end of Terranova's intensive care, but it had been strictly business, and we had decided at a later date not to hold any grudges.

"How you doin', Milan?" he said. He has what you might call a disarming smile, John. "I was in the neighborhood."

I stifled a laugh. I knew he lived in the neighborhood, worked in the neighborhood, and hung out in the neighborhood. But I was pretty sure he hadn't just dropped into an art gallery to browse. He'd made it over here in about as much time as had passed since Dorian hung up after talking to Victor. "I didn't realize you were such a devotee of the arts, John."

He shoved his hands into his pockets. "Not really. But I know what I like." He turned his attention to Dorian. "How they hangin'?"

"Good. Everything's good, Johnny." Dorian seemed more relaxed now that he had a friend.

"That's good," Terranova said, his smile broadening. "I like it when everything's good."

"Me too," I said. I stood up. I'd gotten all I was going to get from Dorian anyway. He'd been growing uneasy, and I was pretty sure he'd clam up even further with Victor Gaimari's muscle hanging around listening. "Well, I'll leave you two to talk serious ceramics then. Thanks for the chat, Mr. Dorian."

"Just Dorian," he said. Oh goody, now I had a new best friend.

"Don't run off on my account," Terranova said.

"I'm not. Believe it." Terranova is tough enough when he has backup; one on one, I think I could hold my own. Of course I didn't fail to notice the bulge on his right hip under his jacket. But he noticed the one under my jacket too. In the days before political correctness they would have called that a Mexican standoff.

I took another mint for the road and put it in my pocket; the damn things really are addictive. "Just one more thing, Dorian."

"What?" He was preparing to get nervous again.

"Ever hear of a place in New York called the Barthalow Gallery?"

He shook his head, and his pendulous jowls shook too, about half a second later.

"How about a guy named Bert Winstock?"

"Nope," he said. "Sorry."

I believed he wasn't lying to me. Hell, he had a hard enough time keeping a straight face when he was telling the truth.

CHAPTER TWENTY-ONE

I climbed the long, poorly lit stairway to the studio loft again, once more aware of the insistent rumble of the kiln that made the steps beneath my feet shiver like the deck of a moving ship. The steel door to the second floor was closed but not locked. It was a fairly old, inexpensive lock anyway and wouldn't have kept anyone out who had even a touch of determination.

I went through and walked down the corridor past the kiln. My skin was singed by the incredible heat, the membranes of my nose and throat dried up, and I had to blink my eyes several times for moisture. I clawed my tie away from my neck and unbuttoned the top button of my shirt, feeling the heat deep down in my lungs as I breathed.

I went into the big room, where the sun struggled its way through the grimy windows, the light refracting to a kind of dirty brown glow. Classical music was once more pouring from the boom box, but it was sprightly piano music this time, probably Chopin, not nearly as sad as the last time.

Tydings Belk was in the far corner of the room, near the windows, busily engaged in throwing a large ceramic bowl on his wheel. He looked up for just a moment to see who his visitor was and then returned his attention to what he was doing. Belk shaped the spinning, whirling clay, his deft hands caressing it like a lover, sprinkling it with water until it gleamed slick, turning inanimate gunk into living art. He seemed so engrossed I wasn't sure if he'd even seen me until he said, "Back again?"

Feeling as though I were too big and clumsy to be there, I navigated the narrow space between the tables until I was standing right behind him. The kiln had warmed up the air in this room as well, and I could smell his sweat. "Do you mind?"

"Knock yourself out, if this is your idea of fun. As long as you don't bother me. I'm working."

"All right," I said.

"At least I'm sober now. Sort of. How about you?"

"Me, too. All coffeed up is all."

He inclined his head at the coffeepot; there was nothing left there but dark brown dregs and grounds, scorched solid from sitting on the hot plate too long. "Fresh out, I'm afraid. I wasn't expecting company. I can offer you a slug of Jack Daniel's, though. Over there in the metal cabinet. I think there's some left."

"No thanks. I'm still feeling it from the last time."

He nodded, humming softly as he worked. Then he said, "Still on the hunt for Feldman?"

"Yep. And no closer, either."

"Well, keep at it." He sounded almost cheerful. "A person doesn't just disappear into dust, you know."

"Talk to me about Alys, will you?"

The wheel slowed down and then stopped turning. He swiveled around in his seat and stared at me, his head lowered onto his chest, his big shoulders up near his ears. "I'm trying to learn to live with it, Mr. Jacovich. It isn't easy, but I'm trying. Unfortunately I'm not there yet, so as you can imagine, it still hurts a lot. So I'd rather not, if you can understand that." He wiped his hands on a towel and tossed it onto the floor. "What's it to you, anyway?"

"It's what I get paid for. I'm just trying to make a connection."

"Between Jeff and Alys?"

"If there is one. What was their relationship, Mr. Belk?"

"Ty," he said. "Call me Ty. Everybody does."

"All right, Ty."

He clasped his palms in front of him as if he was praying. "Is that what you came up here for?"

"That, and to see how you were doing."

"I'm hanging in," he said. "Nice of you to ask. All right, then. What was Alys's relationship to Feldman, huh?" He looked out the window. "Prickly, at best. You talked to her, didn't you?"

"Yes, I did."

"Then you know." His mouth turned down at the corners, making him look like the theatrical mask of Tragedy. "She thought he was a putz. And he is. But just because he shared the loft, we didn't have to be best friends with him, so what the hell. It was a business arrangement."

"Did he ever help her sell any of her work?"

His face darkened. "Where did you hear that?"

"I didn't. That's why I'm asking."

Now he began tapping his fingertips together, slowly and rhythmically. "I suppose that now and then he arranged a sale for her. Threw her a crumb. Whenever there was a buck in it for him."

"Big crumbs or little ones?"

"There are no big crumbs in the art world," he said, and I was startled by the cynicism that twisted the tone of his voice. "Damn few of them, anyway."

"Did Feldman broker any of her pieces within the last month, do you know?"

"She didn't mention it to me if he did. But I think I told you that I'd been away for three weeks. I've kind of been out of the loop."

"So it could have happened?"

He looked annoyed. "Quit sounding like a prosecuting attorney, will you?"

"Sorry. Do you remember who any of the buyers were?"

He shrugged his shoulders.

"Victor Gaimari wouldn't have been one, would he?"

He cocked his head to one side like a bird listening for the approach of a predator. "I know that name. Uh, society columns, I think. He's some sort of local big shot."

"A stockbroker," I said, and didn't elaborate.

"Yeah. No, I think I'd remember if he'd bought anything of hers."

"How about Chase Delavan?"

His eyebrows shot up toward his disappearing hairline. "That sounds right. Delavan, yes."

"More than once?"

"That I'm not so sure about."

"Do you remember the purchase price?"

He stuck his chin out; there wasn't much of it to stick. "Just because Alys and I were sleeping together doesn't mean we talked about money very much. She got paid a decent price for her work, but never anything that made us dance in the aisles here. And on the rare occasions Feldman was able to put her together with somebody who had some bucks, he took a whopping commission."

"How much?"

"As much as sixty percent sometimes." He shook his head from side to side. "He was a real goniff. That means thief."

"I know," I said.

"And then most of the time he'd nail her for what he called expenses too."

"And she let him?"

"The term 'starving artist' isn't whimsical, Mr. Jacovich."

"Milan," I said.

"Milan, then. Artists pay a terrible price for their independence and autonomy. We live from sale to sale, from commission to commission. There's no retirement, no medical, no bennies, and then we get hit with self-employment tax and double social security, too. So we take whatever sale comes along and thank God for it. That's why she let him move some of her better pieces."

He climbed out of his seat. "I'm lucky I'm not as good as she was—I do more commercial stuff and get paid a hell of a lot better for it. But having great talent took its toll on her. Poverty. Anonymity. Lack of respect. It can make you bitter after a while."

"Was Alys Larkin bitter?"

He blew a jet of air through his nose that might have been a laugh. "You met her. She was angry. Not bitter. Just mad as hell."

"At what?"

He closed his eyes for a moment, then opened them again.

"At the world, I suppose. She was a brilliant, gifted artist. One of the better-known ceramicists in the Midwest—and if she grossed forty K a year it was a big year. Pay the rent on this joint and the other expenses and buy supplies, that forty shrinks down to less than twenty-five. You can live on that, but without many extras."

"Why did she do it, then?"

He looked at me quizzically. "Why did she do it? Jesus. Did you go to college?"

"Kent State. I have my master's."

"Then you could have become a thoracic surgeon, or a corporate attorney, or be right up there humping for CEO in a big company, making six figures a year—which, I imagine, is a lot more than you make now. So why do you do what you?"

I pondered the question. "I guess I like what I do." Then I thought about Jeff Feldman and Alys Larkin. "Most of the time I like it."

"Bingo! Artists and writers and actors and musicians do what we do because we like it. Love it, matter of fact. I can't imagine doing anything else. Answer your question?"

"Not entirely. I understand the creative drive, Ty. But if that's your choice, why be bitter?"

He crossed his arms across his barrel chest. "It grinds your guts when you have to scratch for nickels to put food on the table and some no-talent lox who whores for money makes more in a month than you do in a year."

"Someone like Jeff Feldman?"

He nodded. "Feldman, and others who weren't nearly as good as Alys was. It eats the heart right out of you, little by little over the years. I'd say that toward the end Alys really hated Jeff. Hated several other potters in town too. It wasn't jealousy. Alys truly admired other artists. She just hated the whores." He wiped at his pinched face. "It hurt me to see it, but you can't change somebody's feelings, or their convictions. Even somebody you . . ." He took a ragged breath. "Somebody you love," he finished.

I didn't say anything.

He wiped at his eyes. "Excuse me a minute," he said, and did a pretty good broken-field run between the tables and out into the corridor, presumably to regain control of his emotions. A door slammed down the hall. He was in bad shape, bad enough that he forgot to be hostile. He was an abrasive and angry little guy, but I couldn't help feeling sorry for him.

I wandered around the loft looking at the ceramics. Belk's work was utilitarian and attractively colorful, tableware and serving pieces well suited for the casual lifestyle most of us live. I wouldn't mind owning some of it, although I surmised it would be somewhat beyond my price range.

Alys Larkin's work was something else, though. Elegant and formal, decorated with complicated floral patterns in muted colors. Real works of art, which, sadly, now would have no sequels. Belk was right about her; her artistry was above and beyond the run-of-the-mill stuff that I'd seen in Dorian's gallery, or even in the Wickersham.

There were several bowls and vases on a high shelf against the wall on Larkin's side of the loft, one of a kind and imperfectly shaped, mostly covered in unglazed reddish clay. They were probably Larkin's mistakes, or what Valerie Oakey had referred to as end-of-the-day pots, and would probably be sold, if at all, as seconds.

But one of them, a long-necked vase that seemed more graceful and delicate than the others, caught my eye. And all of a sudden my heart began thudding noisily in my chest, and I was practically hyperventilating.

I stepped back to take a better look and banged my behind into a table. Turning quickly to make sure nothing had fallen, I was relieved to find that the ceramics jiggled but nothing had tipped over. I might have destroyed a masterpiece.

I could hear a toilet flushing somewhere in the bowels of the building. Ty Belk came back then, panting a little, walking in his customary simian crouch, his face white and drawn. He'd washed the rest of the clay off his hands but there was still quite a bit on his faded denim jeans. He didn't meet my eyes as he moved past me.

"Sorry," he said huskily.

"That's okay. I know how you feel."

He stopped and turned to look at me. "No you don't, Milan."

Glaring me down, he went back to his wheel and started tidying up. The bowl he'd been working on was now a shapeless lump of clay. "Well, I think I've had it," he said. "Time to go home."

"I hope it's not because of me."

"Nah. It's because of me. I'm not doing any good here." He shrugged. "It'll pass. One of these days. Maybe I'll work twice as hard tomorrow."

"You leave the kiln on all night?"

"Sure," he said. "You have to. It takes at least forty-eight hours for it to get hot enough for what I do."

"You don't worry about a fire?"

He shook his large head. "No more than you do when you leave the furnace on and go away."

"Got time for one more question?"

"Give me a break, will you?" he pleaded.

"This one's easy. You know who Josephus Helgenburg was?"

"Sure," he said. I was looking at him carefully, and his expression didn't change.

"Have you heard anything about any of his individual porcelains being on the market?"

"Oh Christ yes," he said. "Helgenburg is like the Vincent van Gogh of porcelain. There are always rumbles of some lost piece of his being discovered in a basement in Prague or somewhere."

"Recent ones?"

"Not for about four years, that I can remember. I don't pay much attention, though."

"Why not?"

"Because," he said, "I've never known of one of those rumors to be legit."

We went out together. As we passed the kiln, which was sending visible waves of heat through the musty air of the corridor, I felt my skin crawl. Even the unbearably high temperature couldn't keep me from shuddering.

CHAPTER TWENTY-TWO

I'm not what you'd call a creature of impulse. I always like to mull things over first so I don't do anything silly. My friend Rudy Dolsak, the banker down at Ohio Mercantile Bank, once said I was the most judicious man he'd ever met.

I guess in my business, where often there's a tremendous amount at stake in terms of money, and occasionally even human life, it pays to take a deep breath and think things out. But by the time I got back to my apartment from Belk's studio it was a little after five o'clock, the adrenaline was pumping through me double quick, and I didn't have the time to weigh my decisions.

I figured that if I was going to get my ducks in a row, the time was now.

The first thing I did was to open a Stroh's, which I'd picked up at Russo's before coming upstairs. Then I called Victor Gaimari at his office.

"Did you and Dorian have a nice chat?" he asked when he came on the line.

"With such a stimulating conversationalist, how could I miss? And John Terranova showing up at the end there just put the icing on the cake."

"Ha ha," Victor said. "You caught me on the way out the door, Milan. I have a dinner date."

"Chickie Tattersfield?"

He waited a beat. "As a matter of fact, no."

"Oh."

"So I'm in a little bit of a rush. Can this wait?"

"That'll be up to you, Victor. You remember we discussed a certain item of merchandise at your house the other night?"

I heard the rhythm of his breathing alter. Subtly. Victor doesn't give much away, even when he's caught unawares. "Yes?" he said.

"I think I might have located it."

"Oh? Where is it?"

"Where it's supposed to be."

He chewed on that for a while. "That's a little cryptic, isn't it?"

"I meant it that way."

He paused again. "I see," he finally said. "So what are we going to do about it?"

"I was thinking maybe you could drop by here for a little talk on your way downtown tomorrow morning. Unless of course you're going to have to go home first and change."

He said ha ha again. "I never stay all night, Milan. It encourages unrealistic expectations. Besides, I like the way I make coffee better than anyone else." I could hear him flipping pages, probably in his appointment book. "I have a ten-thirty here tomorrow. Is nine too early?"

"I'll have the coffee on," I said, "and try to live up to your high standards."

"Are you becoming a major player in this now?"

"I don't know about major, Victor. Let's just say that I'm in for this hand."

"You're an interesting man, Milan."

"I'll take that as a compliment," I said.

There was no answer at the Wickersham Gallery; apparently there were no appointments for a late Monday afternoon. So I looked up Edgar Curtin in the white pages. I recognized his address as that of one of a series of big brick condominiums on Shaker Boulevard just east of the square; he was listed as P. Edgar Curtin. I only wasted about a minute trying to guess what the *P* stood for. Percy seemed too obvious, and Peter seemed like a better name for purposes of his business than Edgar. I finally decided on Patrick, figuring Curtin would think that too mundane for someone in his lofty position and therefore would use his middle name instead. I punched out his number. The seven-note melody produced sounded like the beginning of the Looney Tunes theme; I was sure Curtin never called his home phone, or he would have had it changed to something by Haydn.

Someone else answered the phone, a man. He sounded young, and querulous. I told him my name and asked him to call Mr. Edgar Curtin to the telephone. Please.

"Yes, I recall your visit," Curtin said when I had identified myself, and from the way he pronounced *visit*, I figured that he was equating it with a particularly gory traffic accident. "I'm *not* particularly pleased that you're calling me at my home, however."

"You might be when I tell you why I called, Mr. Curtin."

"Hurry, then," he said, sounding put-upon. "I have *plans* for this evening."

"Before I left your gallery last week, you inquired whether you could interest me in some fine old English porcelain."

He sniffed. "What if I did?"

"Now I'm wondering if I could interest you in some."

"Ho ho," he said like Santa Claus. "Where would *you* get your hands on anything like *that*?"

"I didn't," I said. "Jeff Feldman did."

"I'm sure I'm not the *least* interested in doing any business with *Feldman*." He still spoke in insulting italics, even on the phone.

"You're going to do business with me."

"A fine distinction," he said.

"All right. I just wanted to give you a fair crack at it, because you were so kind to me the other day. But it's your loss, Mr. Curtin. It's not often that a Helgenburg vase becomes available in the local market."

I heard him gasp. "Just a *moment!*" he said.

I'm glad that Phone-o-Vision or whatever they're going to call it hasn't become a fixture in every household in America, because he would have seen my nasty grin. I did what he asked and waited a moment, listening to the wheels spinning around in his head in the silence.

"Are you *serious*?" he finally said. "You really have a *Helgenburg*?"

"That's right, Mr. Curtin."

"Well. Well, my *God!* I . . ."

I waited some more while he dithered.

"Of *course* I'm interested. Who *wouldn't* be?" he finally managed to say.

I shook a Winston out of the pack and lit it. I didn't mention all the working guys I knew, the Slavs from the East Side and the Irish from the West Side and the Italians from Murray Hill who wouldn't be interested in buying the Helgenburg vase. Why ruin his day?

"Where is it, Mr. Jacovich? You have it in your *home*?"

"Jeff Feldman has it in a safe place," I said, and then let him process that for a while.

"You located Feldman?"

I didn't answer.

"When can I see it?"

"Give me a call tomorrow," I said. And then, "Oops, sorry, not tomorrow. I have tickets for Opening Day."

"Opening Day?"

"The baseball season, Mr. Curtin."

"*Base*ball?" He sounded even more incredulous than usual.

"The Indians and Boston. To some people, Mr. Curtin, watching a great pitcher is right up there on the level of a Helgenburg. I'll talk to you Wednesday."

I hung up smiling.

Two down, one to go, I thought.

I finished the beer and tapped out Chase Delavan's office number, but his secretary told me he'd already gone for the day. I tried calling his daughter at Feldman's apartment, but there was no answer. It didn't surprise me. April Delavan didn't strike me as the type of person who'd just hang around at home on a fine afternoon in her namesake month.

So I went looking for her.

I drove past Arabica slowly and spotted my quarry sitting outside in a white plastic chair at one of the sidewalk tables. I found a parking space on Euclid Heights Boulevard, an occurrence rare enough to make one's heart sing, and walked back up the street.

April was sitting with two young men. One of them was a stranger to me, but the other was the fat kid who'd threatened to sic his dog on me. Larry, I remembered his name was. He'd left the pooch at home this afternoon, although he was still wearing the same Cleveland State sweatshirt.

As I approached, April was just setting down her cappucino and was wearing a light mustache of foam. She raised her head without much interest, shading her eyes from the setting sun to look at me.

"Hey," she said. Not surprised. Not happy to see me. Not unhappy to see me. Just hey.

"Hey back. Got a minute?"

She shrugged. "I guess."

Dog Boy experienced a shock of recognition, realized I was once more taking April away out of seduction range, and his face turned ugly. Uglier, I should say. He put his hands on the arms of his plastic chair and started to rise, but when he was only halfway up, I nailed him with one of my hardest looks. "Don't even think about it," I warned.

He kind of hung there, eight inches of air between his lard butt and the chair. Then he sank back down, anger glowing like two rouge spots on his cheeks.

April had been sitting with her legs doubled under her, and she uncoiled herself languidly from her chair, giving several onlookers a generous glimpse of light blue panties under her full peasant skirt. She picked up her cappucino.

"You want to go inside?" she said.

"It won't take long. Why don't we just walk?"

She practically recoiled at the suggestion. "Walk?" she said, but I took her arm firmly and steered her around the corner onto Coventry Road.

We strolled for about half a block before she got curious. "So what's the haps?"

Not only did I have to put up with teenage slang from a client, but it was fifteen years out of date. "I need your father's home phone number."

"Why?"

"I have to talk to him." Not a very enlightening answer, but all I was willing to give her at the moment.

She stopped on the sidewalk in front of the Dobama Theatre, Cleveland's answer to Off Broadway, and stamped her little foot. "I don't want you to talk to him! I want you to stay away from him!"

"A little vehement, aren't you?"

"Look," she said, "my business is my business, and I don't want him in it." Bitterness and old, smoldering anger twisted her features. "He never paid a goddamn bit of attention to me when I was little, and now that I'm not anymore I found out I like it that way."

Contrary to the old saw, April was not nearly so beautiful when she was angry.

"It's important," I said.

"Not to me. You're working for me so you'll do what I fucking tell you!"

I felt my back go up like a cornered alley cat's. "Who in hell do you think you're talking to?" I said. "Grandma's trust fund doesn't impress me even a little, April, because there isn't enough money in the world for some spoiled brat to talk to me like that. So how about if I just drag you into Arabica and wash your mouth out with soap to teach you some respect?"

I braced myself for the return fire, but her mouth just dropped open instead.

"You think I'm bluffing? Try me!"

She stared at me in awe and wonder, and then her nose got red and her lovely blue eyes brimmed over with tears. She didn't make any effort to wipe them away, just let them boil out and run down her smooth young cheeks. Maybe it was an act, but if so it was a very good one.

"Shit," she finally sobbed, and threw herself on me, burying her face against my chest. I put an awkward arm around her and felt her shoulders shaking. A little of what remained of her cappucino slopped over the rim of the cardboard cup and onto my shoe. Probably no one in her entire life had spoken to her quite so harshly; that might have been her problem.

I hate it when women cry on me. Especially when I made them do it.

Tough guy, that's me. Hardass. Defender of truth, justice, and the American way.

Bully.

"Come on, April," I said. I patted her back gently and murmured "Shh, shh, shh," into her hair.

That made her cry harder.

People were staring at us as they passed. Coventry is one of the busier pedestrian strolls in the Greater Cleveland area, and we were attracting more than our share of attention. Negative attention. And the dirty looks were mostly aimed at me.

I pulled out a pocket pack of tissues and handed them to her. She extracted one and gave her nose a juicy blow.

"Thank you," she said politely.

I nodded and smiled at her. Now that we understood each other.

She used a few more tissues to dab and pat and blot, shuddered a few times as though shaken from within, and then we continued our walk down Coventry. The homeward-bound evening traffic surged past us from Mayfield Road. I kept my arm around her for support.

"I guess I'm not very rational when it comes to my father," she said by way of apology.

"No kidding."

She sneaked an uncertain smile up at me. "He always treated me like I was part of his collection. He'd trot me out to meet his friends so they'd all say, 'Isn't she a pretty little thing?' and the rest of the time it was like I wasn't there." Her perfect brows scrunched down over her eyes. "Until Jeff."

"Jeff?"

"It was my father's idea that I go out with him the first time," she said. "He thought Jeff had something he wanted, and since he didn't have a lot of cash on hand he figured Jeff would stay close by and interested if I was in the picture."

My gut burned as if I'd just swallowed cheap whiskey. I was too angry to make any reply. I just gave her shoulder a squeeze.

"So when Jeff took the money I loaned him and bugged out on me, I figured that was just about enough. That's why I hired you. As the first step to never letting anybody use me again." She tossed her head, letting her hair fall over her shoulders and looking very much like a model in a L'Oreal commercial, and dabbed at her teary eyes with a grimy knuckle. "And that's why I don't want my father to know anything I'm doing. He'll just fuck it up for me, like he always does."

"I didn't mention your name the last time I spoke to him, April, and I won't this time."

"Why don't you just call his office in the morning?"

"I have to talk to him tonight."

She sniffled herself into total control, and only her red eyes tattled of her emotional outburst. I could almost see the tempered steel reforming in her backbone. "I don't think so," she said.

"You want to get your money back, don't you?"

She gave her hair another toss, as if recovering her eighteen thousand dollars wasn't so important after all. "I suppose."

"Then I want your father's home number."

"At the risk of getting you all pissed off again," she said, "no." She started walking again.

I grabbed her arm and spun her around to face me. "April, somebody is dead—maybe more than one somebody—and it's entirely possible it's because of this whole Jeff Feldman business."

Her eyes opened wide, startled and frightened. "Who's dead?" she said.

"Does it really matter?"

She looked down at the ground and shook her head, twirling a lock of curly blonde hair around her finger.

"I don't have the time or the patience to stand here and negotiate with you, or beg you. I want your father's home number. Right now."

When her initial shock had worn off she became a hostile

child again. She looked down curiously at my hand on her arm, as though the contact involved two people she didn't know very well. "What will you do if I don't give it to you, Milan?" she said teasingly. "Hit me?"

"If I have to," I told her, and the eyes got even bigger this time, a fresh supply of tears bubbling up behind them, ready for the floodgates to open again. She looked at me piteously, but I didn't soften my expression a bit. Then she blinked nervously and looked somewhere else. I think she believed me.

I let her go to jot down the phone number she recited. She rubbed her arm where I'd gripped it.

"Thanks, April," I said.

I put my hand at the small of her back and gently guided her back down Coventry Road the way we had come. She dabbed resolutely at her eyes and used the last of my tissues to blow her nose heartily.

We turned the corner. Dog Boy and his friend were still there at the table in front of Arabica. I'd been fortunate to worm Chase Delavan's home number from her; I guess my luck couldn't really be all good.

April sat down in the lone vacant chair, a bit unsteadily, I thought. Dog Boy looked at her, then at me.

"What'd he, make you cry, April?" he said. He scraped his chair back hard, so that it tipped over, and got nose to nose with me, too damn close, his breath smelling of coffee, a fleck of white spittle on his lower lip. "You motherfucker, did you make her cry?" he demanded, and the spittle flew from his mouth to my face.

I suppose I might have considered it as a case of unwise gallantry if I hadn't known that he was just trying to impress her enough to go home with those pretty blue underpants in his pocket. In any case, I'd just about had my daily quota of profane, smart-mouthed kids.

I wiped my cheek off slowly and deliberately. "Get out of my face, son," I said, "or I'll make you cry too."

He stood there uncertainly, fear that I could and would warring with his youthful desire to look macho in front of a pretty woman.

Fear won.

Quivering with humiliation, he spun on his heel and walked away, around the corner where April's eyes couldn't follow him.

I watched him go, nodded brusquely to my client, and headed back down Euclid Heights Boulevard to my car. Righteous. Proud of myself. I'd gotten the phone number I wanted and vanquished a dangerous adversary.

I was getting this big-bully act of mine down pat. For my next trick I'll be beating up little kids and swiping their lunch money.

CHAPTER TWENTY-THREE

I n our high-tech world we often assume that when a phone rings more than four times an answering machine is about to field the call, and I was just ready to hang up. But my instincts told me to stick with it, and after six rings a woman answered, sounding tired and somewhat hassled. "Delavan residence," she announced.

"May I speak to Mr. Delavan, please?"

"May I tell him who's calling?"

"Milan Jacovich."

She paused, computed her chances of getting it right, and finally decided it was beyond her. "I'm sorry . . . ?"

"*My*-lan *Yock*-o-vitch," I repeated as clearly as I could, and wondered if life would be easier if I'd been born Scott Carter. I was leaning as far back as I could in my desk chair, grabbing a moment of semi-relaxation between what had been a tough day and what was bound to be a hard night. I had all my three-by-five cards from April Delavan's file spread out on display, and I moved them around almost idly, looking for a grouping that I liked.

"Just a moment, please." She put down the phone with a soft clunk, and I heard her say "Chase? It's a—a Milan . . . something."

I shook my head. It was evidently Mrs. Delavan who'd answered, but he had her screening his calls at home like a secretary. He was some piece of work, Chase Delavan.

I had trouble hearing a muffled, away-from-the-phone exchange between them, but I could tell Mr. Delavan was annoyed. When he got to the phone at last he was even more so.

"Yes?" he said. Curt, sharp, irritated. And a little suspicious.

"This is Milan Jacovich, Mr. Delavan."

"Yes. This number is unlisted. How did you get it?"

"I'm a detective."

"Well, Detective," he said, "now that you have it, forget it. You've interrupted my dinner. I suggest you call the office tomorrow morning and arrange with my secretary to—"

"I know where the Helgenburg vase is," I said.

It stopped him cold, and I heard him suck in a mouthful of air. "What?" he said.

"I'm sure you heard me. The Helgenburg vase. Isn't that the piece you were negotiating for with Jeff Feldman?"

He was pausing between each sentence now, calculating, being careful not to say too much. "How do you know about the Helgenburg vase? I never mentioned—"

"As I said, I'm a detective. Are you still interested, sir?"

He found his voice after a moment. "You've found Jeff Feldman?"

"I didn't say that."

"But you have the vase."

"I didn't say that either."

"Well, what are you saying, for God's sake?"

"That I know where it is."

"Where?"

"If you want to hide something," I said, "you put it in the most obvious place."

"What does that mean?"

"I'm being deliberately vague, Mr. Delavan. Clearly. It's not in my best interest to tell you where it is. My question is simply are you still anxious to acquire it? Or shall we just forget it and you can go back to your dinner?"

"No, no," he said, suddenly agitated. "We need to talk."

"All right. When?"

"How about tonight?" He wasn't even pretending not to be eager anymore.

"Tonight is no good for me," I said.

"Tomorrow, then?"

"It'll have to be Wednesday. Tomorrow I have seats for the Indians' home opener."

"Oh, for Christ's sake, Jacovich, I have season tickets just behind the third-base dugout. I'll treat you to as many games as you like."

"But tomorrow is Opening Day. I never miss Opening Day." I was trying to sound as naive as I could. It wasn't easy.

I could tell from his breathing that he was becoming increasingly exasperated. Maybe I was running the country bumpkin act into the ground.

"You pick a time on Wednesday, Mr. Delavan," I said, trying to sound more businesslike, "and I'll accommodate you whenever you like."

"In the morning," he said. "Early."

"Shall I come out to your office?"

"No, I'll come to yours." He paused, and I heard him swallow something. Perhaps his second martini of the evening, or a glass of 1989 Dominus Estate cabernet sauvignon he was having with his dinner.

"May I inquire," he said carefully, "if I'm now to deal directly with you? Or do you represent some third party?"

Good, I thought, I've got the fish firmly hooked. I could go back to being disingenuous again. "No, let's just keep this between you and me. As far as you're concerned, I'm the Man, Mr. Delavan. Numero uno. The big kahuna." I cleared my throat and twisted the knife another half turn. "To be honest, I have to tell you that you aren't the only prospective customer I'm talking to."

"God damn it, Jacovich, don't play with me!" His voice broke like an adolescent boy's asking the homecoming queen to the movies.

"I won't make any decision until I've spoken with all parties concerned," I said. "So don't you worry your head about that. You'll have your chance."

"I really hope we can do business together, Milan," he said, managing to calm down some. All of a sudden I was Milan, not

"Jacovich." We were pals. Made me feel warm and fuzzy. "I was serious about those baseball seats, you know."

Trading box seats for a two-hundred-thousand-dollar vase sounded fair to me. "That's great, Chase. Will you buy me some peanuts and Cracker Jack?"

Another silence. Then, icy and commanding once more, "I'll see you Wednesday morning, Mr. Jacovich."

Whoops! I'd slipped a few notches on the good-buddy scale. "That's fine."

"Don't let me down now," he scolded.

"Perish the thought," I said. "Mr. Delavan."

I hung up, tapping my fingers on the handset for a second, deep in thought. And the first thing that occurred to me was that I was hungry.

I ambled into the kitchen to see what surprises the refrigerator held. The freezer yielded two individually packaged chicken and cheese chimichangas I vaguely remembered buying for the boys several months ago. Not really to my taste, but it was getting on in the evening and I had too many things to do to bother going out to eat. I punctured the chimichanga wrappers with a fork and stuck them in the microwave for two minutes.

I've learned to expect little from frozen foods, but the chimichangas abused the privilege. I washed them down with beer, trying not to taste them much.

Stripping off my clothes, I took a quick shower, just enough to wash off the residue of the day. Then I put on a black knit turtleneck over a T-shirt and squeezed into a pair of too tight black jeans Mary had bought for me a few years back because she thought I'd look sexy in them. A lot of good it had done me.

I slipped on some dark tube socks and a pair of dark gray running shoes and studied the effect in the full-length mirror on the bedroom closet door. Not too bad, I thought. Cary Grant in *To Catch a Thief*.

Well, almost. Cary Grant without the cleft chin. Cary Grant with a receding hairline. Cary Grant carrying an extra fifty pounds.

It's why I rarely look in the mirror except to shave.

I took a dark blue windbreaker down from its hanger—it was the closest I had to a black jacket, and though in some circles I might be in danger of fashion arrest, I figured it would serve my needs quite nicely. Then I went back out into the front room to my desk.

The .357 Magnum I always keep in the top right-hand drawer gleamed in the light from the desk lamp. I checked to see that it was clean and oiled, although I'd never in my life put it away in any other condition, and loaded it. At one time it had always been loaded and ready to go, but because of my sons' visits I opt for safety and keep the ammo in another drawer.

I went to the front closet and took down the boot box where I kept my holsters. A dark brown leather hip holster, and a tan shoulder harness Marko had bought me years ago when I was still a Cleveland policeman and he'd had hopes of my making the plainclothes detail. It was by far the more uncomfortable to wear, but I chose it anyway. Drawing a weapon from my hip always made me feel a little bit like Matt Dillon.

I'm old enough to mean the marshal of Dodge City from *Gunsmoke*, not the young actor.

I looped the strap over my shoulder and fiddled with it for a while so it wouldn't cut into me, making adjustments until the Magnum nestled comfortably under my arm. Then I put on the windbreaker, leaving it unzipped far enough so I could get to the weapon with relative ease.

Next to the boot box was a metal strongbox I always keep locked. I lifted it down gently and set it down on the desk to open. Inside was a Saturday night special, a .22-caliber pistol that was unregistered and from which the serial numbers had been carefully filed and acid-etched. Illegal, of course. I'd never had occasion to use it, although I always keep it cleaned and oiled. I didn't think I'd need it tonight.

Next to it, carefully wrapped in a chamois cloth, were a gleaming set of lock picks. Also illegal. They had been a gift from one Clarence Pruzaniec, a burglar and cracksman I had helped put into the correctional facility at Mansfield when I was still wearing a badge. He served three years and a cup of coffee and had emerged a changed man, setting up a high-priced home-security-systems company in Ohio City just across the Veterans' Memorial Bridge and giving lectures and seminars about safeguarding your home. Since we were now in related fields, he'd looked me up, bought me lunch, and gifted me with the lock picks just to show there were no hard feelings.

I slipped them into the pocket of my jacket, along with a penlight that I checked to see was in working order. Then I replaced the strongbox on the shelf.

I was as ready as I was ever going to be.

I stopped at my desk on the way out and regarded the index cards laid out there for a moment. Then I scooped up all but three and put them back into April Delavan's file.

I lined up the ones that remained, almost compulsively straightening the edges.

EDGAR CURTIN. CHASE DELAWAN. VICTOR/DORIAN.

In alphabetical order, I noted. I'm becoming more anal-retentive the older I get.

I switched off the desk lamp and went downstairs to my car.

It was still early, just past nine o'clock, and although in the homes of the steel puddlers and factory workers of ethnic Cleveland that was getting close to bedtime, I figured I had at least an hour to kill before things began falling into place for me. Maybe more.

But I hadn't wanted to sit around the apartment all evening getting edgy. I like my apartment; it's convenient—four minutes from University Circle, ten from the ballpark, fifteen from where my boys live. And I've got it set up so I can live and work in it without one spilling over into the other. But although I've grown used to living alone, sometimes, with nobody to talk to, the walls close in on me.

So I stopped at Vuk's.

Louis Vukovich served me my first legal drink of alcohol at that bar. I guess I've known him as long as I can remember. His tavern, near East Fifty-fifth and St. Clair, is a hangout for a lot of the Slovenian working people in the neighborhood, serving honest drinks, cold beer, coffee strong enough to eat the chrome off a trailer hitch, and a decent klobasa sandwich if he knows you and isn't too busy to cook. Best of all, he's always ready to talk if you are, and he has enough sense to leave you alone if you're not.

I moved out of the old neighborhood a long time ago, and I don't get to Vuk's as often as I'd like. When I walked in on this particular evening, there weren't too many familiar faces at the bar; I'd been away too long.

There was one face I recognized, though, and wished I didn't. Joe Bradac. My former wife Lila's current . . . companion, I suppose, is as good a word as any.

He saw me about the same time as I saw him. It was an uncomfortable moment, but more for him than me.

Because Joe Bradac is scared to death of me.

I don't know why. I've never threatened him. I caught him cheating on Lila a couple of years ago, and I didn't blow the whistle on him, so that should have been his first clue that I wish him no harm.

Then again, I don't particularly wish him any good, either.

I nodded stiffly to him, which is my usual greeting on the rare occasions that I run into him; the East Side of Cleveland is just too small to altogether avoid people you don't like. Then I sat down at a stool toward the other end of the bar and proceeded to ignore him. He was watching *Murphy Brown* on the TV behind the bar anyway.

Vuk came over, moving slowly the way he always does, as if waiting on his customers is strictly his own idea and not a necessary part of his job. He has Popeye forearms, one of which is adorned with a tattoo of a three-dimensional cross, and a nose too big for his face hanging over a substantial mustache, now flecked with gray. What little hair he has left is the color of gravel, and he combs it artlessly across his head to look like more.

"Milan. Haven't seen you around since Christ was a corporal," he said, skillfully combining a greeting with a guilt trip. "You been doin' okay?"

"Sure, Vuk. How about you?"

He wrinkled his nose. "The legs are goin'. Standin' on my feet behind this damn bar for thirty-six years, and the legs are finally goin'." He frowned a little and moved only his eyes in the direction of Joe Bradac. "You aren't lookin' to start any trouble in here, are you?"

"How many years I've been drinking at your bar, Vuk? When did I ever start trouble?"

He flexed his shoulders rotating his thick neck as though he had a crick in it. "Always a first time, isn't there? 'Specially with that bulge under your jacket."

"It's my American Express card—I never leave home without it."

"Just keep it where it is then, all right?"

I nodded. Then he nodded back. The fact that I was carrying a weapon didn't make him nervous; nothing makes Vuk nervous. He's handled worse problems without ever coming out from behind the bar. He was just letting me know that he knew I was carrying, that Joe Bradac was sitting in the back near the rest rooms, and that he didn't want any hassles.

"Stroh's?" he said.

"No, just a black coffee."

He gave me a disgusted look. "What's this look like to you, Milan? Denny's?" He turned to the glass carafe on the hot plate behind the bar and poured some coffee into a brown mug. I could swear it thunked when it went in.

He set the mug in front of me on a cardboard coaster. I put a dollar bill on the bar, but he shoved it back at me. "Come back when you can afford a real drink," he said.

I took a sip. It rotted my teeth, burned my tongue, and ate out the lining of my stomach. It was good. Coffee gets most people wired; for me, it's relaxing, a kind of leveler. And I sure needed one of those because I wasn't sure what was coming in the hours ahead.

And I'm not a guy who likes surprises.

Down at the other end of the bar Joe Bradac hurriedly finished what was left of his beer, climbed down off his stool, and started for the door.

"Whattaya say, Milan?" he mumbled as he passed my stool.

Then, blinking his rabbit eyes behind his thick glasses, he bustled out into the street.

I set my mug down on the cardboard coaster. "Sorry to scare away your paying customers, Vuk."

He blew a raspberry in the direction of the door. "Guy's a jerk anyway," he said. "I never knew how Lila could—"

"Neither did I," I said, anxious to change the subject. "Baseball tomorrow, hey, Vuk? Been a long winter."

He brightened a little. Unlike the majority of working-class guys in the neighborhood, Vuk is not enamored of football in general or the Cleveland Browns in particular. Baseball, however, is something of a passion. Vuk has been an Indians rooter since the Tribe played their games in old League Park, two ballparks ago. Prehistory.

"Yeah. I think we can maybe do good this year."

"I'll be there tomorrow to cheer them on."

"Jeez, how'd you get tickets? Ever since they move to Jacobs Field it's like pullin' teeth."

"My friend from the newspaper," I said. "We always go to the opener."

He compressed his lips into a straight line. "I hope you're healthy enough to use the seats."

"What?"

He looked pointedly at where my jacket was pushed out of shape.

"Don't worry about that, Vuk. It's a Justin."

"Huh?"

"Justin Case."

"That's pretty funny," he said, and wandered down to the other end, where one of his customers was hollering for him.

I drank my coffee and watched *Murphy Brown* for a while. Miles was acting hysterical, and Murphy was cutting him up for it. Being April, this was a rerun, but I hadn't seen it the first time around. Monday nights in fall when the networks trot out their new episodes, I'm usually glued to the football game.

Vuk came back wiping his hands on a bar towel that might once have been blue but had faded to gray after years of washing.

"You oughta find yourself another racket, Milan. Get yourself a real job."

"I have a real job."

"One where you don't have to run around packin'—an American Express card."

"Do you still have your sawed-off Louisville Slugger under the bar?"

"Sure."

"Why? You've never used it except to bang on the bar and get everybody's attention. What do you keep it for?"

"Well, if—"

"To be ready, right?" I asked.

"Yeah, but—"

"The defense rests," I said.

He was going to be stubborn. "I still say you're too old for that shit anymore."

"Forty's not old."

"Not for an insurance salesman. Or a bartender," he added wryly. "But you got kids. They're growin' up now, Milan. They need you now more'n ever." He leaned against the backbar and crossed his huge forearms over his chest, his fierce eyebrows forming an arch. "You don't want Joe Bradac raisin' your boys, do you?"

I don't think he realized how hard that was going to hit, because when my face fell he immediately looked remorseful. He took a deep breath and moved quietly away again to talk to some of his customers.

I just sat there letting my coffee get cold and brooding over the low blow.

When *Murphy Brown* was over and a new show had begun, I got up quietly and left without saying goodbye.

CHAPTER TWENTY-FOUR

There was a fine haze in the air when I walked out onto St. Clair. It could have been mist or it could have been fog; I only knew that it was cold and damp and chilled me right through my clothing, and I zipped up my jacket all the way to the neck. Or maybe what I was about to do was making me shiver.

The last time I checked, breaking and entering was against the law.

And I'm a guy who's lived pretty much within the law. A good part of my life has been spent upholding it, I was raised to respect it.

But there are laws and there are laws.

We've all exceeded the speed limit and gotten away with it. We've all littered. Some of us have gambled. Some of us even keep unregistered firearms in a metal box on the top shelf of the closet.

Murder is quite another story.

So I guess I could justify a little harmless B&E in my own mind if it meant catching a killer.

I got into my Sunbird and keyed the ignition, listening to the even rumble of the engine with satisfaction. I'd had it tuned a few weeks ago, and it was running smoothly—I have a great mechanic. Switching on the wipers for a few seconds to clear the moisture from the windshield, I put it into gear, pulled out of the muddy vacant space between two buildings on East Fifty-fifth that is Vuk's de facto parking lot, and headed downtown to the Feldman-Larkin-Belk loft.

I left my car next to a Dumpster on a side street off Superior, halfway down the block so it wouldn't attract too much notice; there weren't many cars parked in that neighborhood at night. Then I cut through a couple of alleyways and empty parking areas until I came to the building that housed the ceramics studio. The big dark factory, deserted now and without a single light visible, loomed like a medieval redoubt, or maybe a jail. It had certainly imprisoned more than one person behind the invisible bars of their own greed.

I slipped through the big open compound in the center, thinking as I did so that it would make a hell of an exercise yard for the inmates. The dark, soot-stained walls provided excellent camouflage, and I stayed as close to them as I could.

I moved out of the open and into the cavelike alcove that was tucked away to one side of the compound, the asphalt and mortar stalactites hanging above me like little blunt swords of Damocles. There were no cars parked there, which I supposed was a good sign. In front of me the cement wall that held up the defunct railroad spur line rose up to taunt me with its crude graffiti: KOOLS RULE '91 was almost faded away, a sad historical artifact proclaiming the past supremacy of a street gang who had lost their leaders and their power to the natural attrition of time. LASHONDA FUCKS might have been of the same vintage but had probably retained much of its timeliness.

I pushed on the steel door that provided an entry to the building; there was no give at all. My penlight illuminated a shiny new lock, probably the only thing in the compound that wasn't ancient or falling apart. I took out the set of lock picks, switched off the tiny beam of light, and began to work by feel alone.

It was a good sturdy lock that had been installed in that dented and battered door, and I inserted each of the picks in turn, applying delicate pressure the way I'd been taught, but I didn't hear any tumblers click. I wished for a wild and fleeting moment that I had Clarence Pruzaniec at my side—he probably would have had that sucker open in seconds.

It took me about twenty minutes, and when I finally was able to push the door open with a creak, my turtleneck was damp with perspiration despite the evening's chill.

I closed the door behind me and was plunged into complete blackness, and I felt around for the lock and turned it until it clicked. The elevator was to my right, the stairway somewhere straight ahead. Not wanting to chance using the flashlight, I moved very slowly and carefully in the darkness, shuffling my feet and trying to make as little noise as possible, but beneath the rubber soles of my sneakers the grit on the floor made a scratching sound. One arm was stretched blindly in front of me.

After several uncertain steps my hand finally made contact with a wall, and I felt my way along it slowly, the accumulated grime sticky under my fingertips. The wall ended and I extended a careful foot in front of me. I had found the stairway.

I moved up with care. There was no handrail so I had to maintain contact with the wall. At the landing I remembered to turn right and nearly tripped over the first step leading up to the second floor.

Through the soles of my sneakers and the palm of my hand against the wall, I felt the ominous rumbling of the kiln as I climbed.

I got to the second metal door at the top of the stairs and risked shining my flashlight on the lock. It wasn't as new or sophisticated as the one downstairs. Since I'd be sure to hear anyone coming up the stairs behind me, I left the light on, holding the penlight between my teeth, which made me want a cigarette very much. Practice had made me more proficient with my burglar tools, and it only took me about three minutes to spring the lock. I pushed open the door and found myself in the long corridor beside the ceramics studio. Again, I closed the door and locked it behind me.

There was plenty of illumination coming in through the entire wall of windows, the lights of nearby downtown reflecting in the hazy sky. And hunkered down in the middle of the corridor, growling and pulsating, the kiln glowed red, sending out blasts of intense heat.

I've fallen a long way off from my Catholic upbringing at Saint Vitus Parish, but if I still believe in the concept of a Hell, with fire and brimstone and apprentice devils running around jabbing sinners with their little pitchforks, I don't imagine it would need to be much hotter than that kiln. It hummed and grumbled with a kind of malevolence that made it seem alive, and I hurried past it before it dried up all my mucous membranes, trying not to look at it, the way you avoid looking directly at a dead animal on the street. I couldn't suppress a shudder.

I went through the double doorway. It was up over eighty degrees in the studio, and I was regretting wearing such a heavy sweater.

As I walked across the floor my footfalls sounded like the seven-league boots of a giant. I found a battered wooden chair, brushed off the cobwebs, and sat down in a dark corner against the wall on the side of the room where Jeff Feldman's ceramics were still arrayed, now gathering dust. From my vantage point I could see the kiln through the windows. The door I had come through was just out of sight. If anyone were to enter that way he wouldn't get by unnoticed.

I took off my windbreaker and draped it over the back of the chair; it made me only marginally cooler. I would have removed my turtleneck, too, but it would have meant going through the shoulder harness business all over again.

And I waited, hardly moving, in the shadows. The only sounds in the room were the muffled roar of the kiln and, every sixty seconds, the startling click of the old clock on the wall as it jerked away the minutes.

Every time I heard it I was faced with the realization that I was one minute older. It made me impatient.

I'm not good at waiting.

It's a definite failing in my line of work. Maybe it's a holdover from my football days, when as a defensive lineman I had a specific assignment on every play, a reason to move. Or perhaps it's just my nature. Keeping still for long periods of time is alien to me and so makes me nervous.

But I sat there anyway, wishing I had chosen a more comfortable chair, if there was one in the studio. And the ticking minutes turned into an hour. Then more.

Much more.

The white face of the clock was showing 11:43 when I heard a door being pushed open and then closed, and light, careful footsteps getting closer. A softball-size dot of light knifed through the windows and played across the opposite wall of the studio, like Tinker Bell in a production of *Peter Pan*. It was coming from the opposite end of the corridor, almost behind me, and I realized with a start that there must be another entrance onto the second floor from inside the building somewhere. I was getting careless—I should have figured that out.

Every muscle in my body tensed and tightened, and I sat as still as I could, even though the adrenaline was racing through me and making me slightly giddy as I realized that my case was nearly over. I had already figured out the what, the why, and the how. The only piece still missing was the who. And within scant seconds, that piece would be walking in the door and completing the puzzle.

A silhouette of a man appeared against the wall of windows, a stream of light emanating from the large flashlight he held in his hand. He was moving cautiously. From where I sat, all I could tell for sure was gender. I took a deep, calming breath and remained motionless.

He came through the doorway to the loft and stood there a moment, waving the light around and trying to get his bearings. Then he went directly to the middle of the studio, where Alys Larkin had worked.

I'd expected that.

He moved quickly but methodically, examining each ceramic piece on the tables and then going on to the next. His actions were impatient and, understandably, nervous.

When he got near the windows some of the ambient city light from outside reflected off his silver hair. Slowly I let out the breath I'd been holding in my lungs. There were three suspects I'd liked for the murders of Jeff Feldman and Alys Larkin—the people whose names were on the cards neatly arranged on my desk at home. But I was glad it was who it was. Relieved, almost. "Mr. Delavan," I said.

He whirled, whipping the light around, and I ducked down behind a table as the beam stabbed through the dark just over my head.

"Who's there?" Chase Delavan rasped. "Who is it?" I didn't favor him with a reply.

And then he said something that knocked all my carefully arrived at theories right out of the ballpark.

"Feldman? Is that you, Feldman?"

It took me a second to process that one. I was suddenly confused, disoriented. I hadn't expected that.

I stood up slowly. "It's Milan Jacovich," I said.

The beam of light wavered and then found me, shining right in my eyes. "Get that damn thing out of my face," I ordered.

It didn't move. I took the .357 from beneath my arm and pointed it in the direction of the light. "Turn it off!"

The flashlight clicked off at about the same moment the hand of the clock jumped to 11:46. Dots danced on the surface of my eyeballs, looking like a transcription of a Charlie Parker solo.

"Jacovich." Delavan's voice was hoarse, as if he'd been yelling all day. "What are you doing here?"

"Waiting for you," I said, dropping my gun hand to my side. "To try and steal the Helgenburg vase."

He was moving now, getting closer to me. "That's a heavy accusation," he said. "And actionable."

My vision was returning to normal now; the dots had grown smaller and were fading. "You're big on threats, aren't you, Delavan?"

He squared his shoulders, remembering his lofty position in the community, I suppose. "I'm not stealing anything. The vase belongs to me."

"By divine right?"

He shook his head. "I paid for it. I gave Feldman money to get it for me."

"How much money?"

"That's none of your business."

"I have a .357 Magnum in my hand that says it is." I showed it to him again.

He leaned against a table, trying to seem casual, but I think he really needed the support. "I don't see that it makes any difference."

"It does to me. And I'm the one with the vase," I reminded him.

"So this is a shakedown. I thought your story smelled bad when you first came to my office."

"Talk about smelling bad, Mr. Delavan, at least I didn't pimp my daughter to a slime like Jeff Feldman just so I could acquire a work of art. Feldman sold you a bill of goods about the Helgenburg vase, and you tossed him April as kind of a door prize so he'd stay close."

He straightened up, head high, like an aristocrat going to the guillotine in a tumbrel. "That's a disgusting thing to say, and I resent it. Be assured my lawyer will take that remark into consideration too."

"I think your lawyer is going to be pretty damn busy keeping you off death row."

His head shook a little, like a man with palsy. "Death row?"

"The authorities take a dim view of tossing people down elevator shafts."

He came around the last table that separated the two of us. Now I could see him more clearly, even in the shadows of the dark studio. He was wearing an elegant green and gray zippered silk jacket over a plaid shirt, and his face looked haggard and drawn. And frightened. He cleared his throat, but it didn't ease the strain in his voice. "That's absurd," he said. "You're dreaming this. You're bullshitting some more."

"I think I could make a pretty good case for it. You're a desperate man, Mr. Delavan. You're what they politely call overextended. You chopped down a bunch of trees to build houses that nobody seems to want. You even tried to borrow money from your daughter."

His whole body jumped as if from a mild electrical charge. "How did you . . . ?"

"You got the money from April to give to Feldman so he'd

search out the vase and obtain it for you. A vase you couldn't possibly pay for."

"My finances—"

"Are in the toilet," I finished for him. "That's why you wanted Feldman to get you the vase: so you could sell it to someone else and bail out April Homes until you could figure out a way to unload them and get your money out."

"Are you on some drug, Jacovich? This is the most ridiculous flight of fancy."

"The flight of fancy was thinking you could get your hands on something like the Helgenburg for pocket money," I said, "because you certainly couldn't afford to pay market price for it. You were going to get it away from Feldman any way you could. Maybe even by killing him."

"I never . . ."

"I know you didn't. I figured for a while that you did, but when you found me in here, you thought I might be Feldman. It doesn't matter, though."

"Easy for you to say," he said. He slumped weakly against the table behind him, both hands gripping the edge. I thought he was about to faint.

"Somehow the control of the vase passed from Feldman to Alys Larkin," I went on, "and you found out that she was even harder and tougher than he was, and dealing with her was going to be a much more expensive preposition. A proposition you could no longer afford. So when you couldn't reason with her, you lost your temper and got physical with her—and probably by accident, you killed her. Right here in this room, I imagine. And then you panicked, the way most inadvertent killers do, and you threw her down the elevator shaft to make it look like an accident."

"You'll never prove that," he said. "Not in a million years. They've called Alys's death accidental."

"So far, yes. But when I tell the police what I know, I'd be willing to bet they can put the pieces together the same way I did. It's over, Mr. Delavan. And the sad thing is, it was all for—"

I never got the last word out; it was going to be *nothing*.

I should have seen it coming. I've been across the street too many times to allow myself to get sucker-punched. But while he was supporting himself against the table, he'd picked up a heavy clay pot with his right hand, and he swung it around so quickly, shattering it against the side of my head, I never had a chance to duck.

It didn't even hurt at first. I was only conscious of the impact, and of everything going out of focus all of a sudden, like when the TV director switches shots too fast during a football game and the end-zone cameraman isn't quite ready. My vision was further impaired by something dark and wet that trickled into my left eye. The Magnum slipped out of my hand and hit the floor, and I followed it pretty quickly.

The pain kicked in then, and through a reddish haze I saw him reach for the gun I'd dropped. I was too dizzy to stop him, but I batted at it with my hand and it went skittering off, to come to rest under one of the tables halfway across the room.

I tried to raise myself off my face, but he slammed me on the back of the neck with the edge of his open hand—I'd been right when I guessed he was trained in martial arts—and I went down again, and almost out.

I was in a kind of conscious blackout. I couldn't see anything, but I was aware of everything: the gritty linoleum pressing against my cheek, the vibration from the kiln, the pain in my head, and Chase Delavan's feet moving around me. I just couldn't seem to do anything about any of it.

Delavan grunted as he flipped me over on my back. Then he went around behind my head and grabbed me under both arms and started dragging me across the studio. My heels bumped along on the uneven floor. He was strong, probably in good shape from workouts with a personal trainer.

The roar of the kiln grew louder and the heat became more intense, almost unbearable. Then he let go of me.

I fought to open my eyes, to sit up, to make my body work. To defend myself.

And then I was pummeled by a fiery blast that blistered my skin and dried up the inside of my nose. Delavan had opened the door of the kiln.

He was going to burn me alive.

CHAPTER TWENTY-FIVE

Tydings Belk had said that man is distinguished from all other living things by his awareness of the inevitability of his own death. But here, inches from the most unpleasant demise I could imagine, I thought of my boys, I thought of my own little life, I even thought of Lila—and then, crazily, my mind went to Jacobs Field, where the Cleveland Indians were going to play their opening game of the season in about thirteen hours. Without me. And Belk or no Belk, I wasn't ready to go, not yet. And certainly not in agony. Not in a fiery furnace.

Chase Delavan's hands were on me again, rough and unyielding, dragging me closer to the searing heat. I could hear my own hair sizzling, turning to ashes. With a burst of desperate strength I didn't know I had in me, I forced open my eyes, wrenched my body into a sitting position, and reached out with one hand to grab him by the throat.

He looked stunned for a moment; he'd thought I was out. He gurgled, his face becoming engorged with blood, his eyes bulging. Then he tried prying my fingers from around his neck, but I held on, choking him with both hands now, pulling him down on top of me until we were almost in an embrace on the floor, in the red glow and the heat of the open kiln. I could smell the acrid stink of burning hair.

He was hammering on my arms with brutal karate chops to loosen my grip, but with his breathing restricted, there wasn't much steam behind the blows. And then, his arms reaching out to the sides almost spasmodically, his hand found a pile of broken slats from a packing crate that had been carelessly tossed against the wall. He grabbed one, raised it, and plunged it down toward my face like a spear.

I let go of him and rolled my head to one side, and the jagged end of the slat struck the floor next to my ear and splintered. He was able to raise up off me and give himself some leverage, and this time he swung the slat like a baseball bat. It connected painfully with the front of my shoulder, making the left side of my body go numb.

And then he was up and running, down the corridor toward the door I'd come through. I had locked it behind me, and he had to fumble with the lock a few seconds before he could swing it open and run out into the vestibule where the elevator and the stairs were.

I managed to get to my feet, reeling dizzily for a few seconds until I was able to regain my equilibrium. My head was hurting big-time now, the pain waxing and waning with every heartbeat, and I wiped the blood from my eyes so I could see what I was doing. Then I started down the corridor after him, each running step sending a knife thrust through my skull. He had a good start on me, but I was younger and could probably run faster.

The vestibule was still very dark, but with the door open the rosy light from the kiln made it easier to see. He evidently hadn't gone down the stairs in the blackness; the door leading to the outside was open.

I went out onto the flat tarpaper roof, the cool air a shock after the heat of the corridor, and my sweat-drenched turtleneck felt cold and clammy. I listened and looked, all my senses vibrating, but there was no sign of him anywhere.

The squat, square shed that housed the elevator shaft stood darkly at one end of the roof. I went to it quickly and pried open the gates. The elevator was moored in the basement, having been condemned by the city inspectors after Alys Larkin's death, and I could see its pulleys and cables some twenty-five feet below me.

And then a great weight fell onto my shoulders and drove

me backwards to the surface of the roof. Delavan had evidently climbed up on top of the shed to hide, and I'd played right into his hands; he'd landed on me hard with both knees. *I was* getting stupid—a crack on the head will do that to you.

While I was down he punched me in the back a few times. It hurt like hell and drove the breath out of my lungs, and it sounded like timpani. Then he started rolling me, shoving me toward the edge of the open shaft. I don't know how he figured he was going to get away with two bodies in that shaft, but I don't suppose he was thinking all too clearly either.

With a guttural grunt he pushed me over the edge.

For a fraction of a second I had the giddying sensation of free-fall, but I managed to hook my leg around the side of the shed that housed the gate and grabbed with both hands. Then I swung myself back up onto the roof, hitting him with my shoulder, all my weight behind it. He was on his knees, so his center of gravity was lower than I would have liked, but I outweighed him by a good bit, and I managed to topple him off balance so that he was resting on one hip and one elbow, like the woman in Andrew Wyeth's painting *Christina's World*.

But he was fast and lithe, and before I could throw myself on him completely he was on his feet. He swung a fierce karate kick at my head, but I was able to duck enough that it grazed my upper arm instead, almost knocking me back into the elevator shaft. I grabbed the edge of the shed and held on, and Delavan took off running again, across the roof, past what was left of the pigeon carcass. He reached the edge, made a graceful leap across the three-foot space between the building and the railroad spur, and headed north along the tracks of the trestle.

I don't know where he thought he was going. Even if he got away he was finished as long as I was alive to tell about it, and I suppose if he hadn't been so frightened he would have realized that.

But I didn't know where the tracks ended, either, and I was angry enough and banged up enough to want to stop him anyway, just for the hell of it. I struggled to my feet—it was getting harder every time—ran to the edge of the roof, sucked in a gulp of energy, and leapt the three feet onto the tracks. The landing jarred every place that already hurt, and I fought down a wave of nausea and followed him.

Delavan was about twenty feet ahead of me, running smoothly and quickly for a guy his age, and for a moment I didn't think I'd be able to catch up to him, since moving was so difficult and painful for me. But the tracks were uneven and strewn with debris, and when he'd run about the length of a city block along the trestle he tripped on something, stumbled forward a few steps, and almost fell on his face. Struggling to keep his feet, he recovered nicely and took off again.

It gave me the few seconds I needed to overtake him. He was still a few feet ahead of me, but I propelled myself forward, pretending he was an enemy running back, and tackled him around the ankles, skinning both my knees painfully in the process.

It wasn't a clean tackle; he was moving too fast. So he slipped out of my grasp at the last second, and I found myself clutching air and chewing on cinders. But I'd broken his rhythm and sent him careening off his course, his arms windmilling crazily, his feet searching for a solid purchase on the uneven tracks. He stepped between two of the railroad ties, twisted his ankle, and plunged off the edge of the trestle headfirst, screaming all the way down.

He hit the pavement some thirty feet below us with a sickening sound, like a watermelon dropped out of a third-story window, and then he wasn't screaming anymore.

A bored emergency room physician took three stitches in my scalp while a homicide detective sat on a high stool swinging his legs like a kid, watching with detached interest. When I'd been properly patched, he drove me down to Old Central for a chat. There are more felicitous places to spend all night than at the police department talking to detectives. I'd phoned them from the studio and called Marko Meglich at home too, just because I thought I might need a friendly face at the interrogation. So when my escort and I arrived he was there in the squad room, wearing jeans and a sweatshirt and in a very bad humor. My call had apparently interrupted something more interesting than sleep.

But that's SOP for Marko.

Some of the things I had to say to him surprised him right out of his lousy mood, and even though he found my conjecture a little hard to swallow, he promised to send a forensic team to the studio loft first thing in the morning to check it out.

When they finally finished with me it was seven A.M., and the wispy clouds in the bright blue eastern sky were streaked with pink. It looked like a gigantic nursery. But as a uniformed patrolman drove me back to my car, it gave me much comfort and pleasure to think that the weather for the first day of the Tribe's season was going to be perfect. Blue skies, green grass, and the unique sound of a hard ball thwacking into leather.

The uniform bade me good night and drove off in his squad car, but I didn't go home right away. I waited until he was out of sight and then went back up to the loft. I'd already retrieved my windbreaker and the .357 before they took me to the emergency room; this time I was souvenir-hunting.

After finding what I'd been looking for, I got back to the Sunbird and started it up. The red light on the dash came on indicating that there was a problem with my electrical system, and a yellow light warned me to SERVICE ENGINE SOON. And I'd just had it tuned, too. It was all I needed to cap off a fun evening.

All I know about cars is how to drive them, but I could tell there was something seriously wrong. The Sunbird was driving like a World War I tank, requiring almost more effort to steer than I was willing to expend, and by the time I got up the hill to the Heights, the needle on my temperature gauge had peaked and another red light was glowing. The control panel, dancing with multicolored warning lights, looked almost festive. I drove directly to my mechanic's shop and waited until he opened at eight o'clock.

"What happened to you?" he said, pointing at the bandage.

"Not much. The car's in worse shape than I am." I explained what was wrong and he nodded gravely.

"Sounds like a busted belt," he said, and opened the hood. Sure enough, there was a busted belt. Three of them, in fact. If only doctors were as sure of what they were doing as automobile mechanics.

"Your alternator isn't locked up," he said, spinning it with his hand. "I can't figure out what's wrong. Let's take a look."

He got the car onto the lift, peered under it, and recoiled.

"Gross!" he pronounced.

"What?"

He shook his head in disgust. "There's a rat in here the size of a pussycat. You park by a restaurant?"

"No, a Dumpster," I said.

He nodded. "It must've crawled into the engine to get warm, and when you started the car up you sliced and diced it pretty good. Come here, take a look at this."

"I don't need to look at the damn thing. I've seen dead rats before. Just get it out."

"I don't want to touch it," he said.

A spirited discussion ensued between him and the two men who worked for him as to which of them had the honor of extricating my visitor. I told them to work it out between them and called a cab to take me home.

A giant rat, for God's sake.

Maybe it was an omen.

CHAPTER TWENTY-SIX

When I got back home I showered quickly, dabbing the dried blood out of my hair with a washcloth and avoiding the neat surgical patch that had been affixed over my stitches, and put on clean Levis and a sweater. Then, remembering that I was expecting company, I made a pot of coffee, measuring enough into the basket to ensure it would be strong and hearty, and shook a sprinkling of powdered cinnamon into the grounds before turning the coffeemaker on. Not only did I need a pick-me-up after a night of no sleep whatsoever, but it would never do to serve Victor Gaimari a substandard brew. Not a gourmet like Victor.

He was prompt, I'll give him that. My kitchen clock showed one minute past nine when my doorbell rang. Maybe he was just anxious.

I hadn't expected him to bring John Terranova with him, though. The two of them stood framed in my doorway, Terranova slightly to the rear and looking mildly embarrassed about being there. I always get the feeling that Terranova really wants to be legitimate, but he has neither the education nor the smarts to figure out how.

"Good morning, Milan," Victor said, smiling, as usual, like a cheerful shark. He was in his businessman outfit, a lightweight wool topcoat over a dark gray pinstripe suit and a colorful red and green tie. John Terranova was wearing a gray suit, too, almost black, but his looked like it came from KMart. Victor moved confidently into my front room as if he paid the rent, Terranova following.

"What happened to your head?" Victor said.

"I cut myself shaving. Make yourselves comfortable."

I took Victor's coat and hung it in the front closet while he and Terranova sat down in my two client chairs. Then I went into the kitchen and brought out a tray with mugs of hot coffee for everyone. Victor and I took it black, but Terranova had to make it complicated, he wanted cream and sugar. All I had was Coffee-Mate, and he shrugged his acceptance as though he was used to better.

I sat down behind my desk and toasted them with my mug.

"Mmm, this is very good," Victor said, taking a sip and actually smacking his lips. "It's strong—has a nice body to it. And I like the touch of cinnamon." He sounded like a television commercial.

"Me, too," John Terranova said. He would have agreed with anything his boss said even if I'd brewed the coffee with water I'd scooped from the Cuyahoga River with a rusty can.

"How was your date last night, Victor?" I said. "Have a good time?"

It threw his timing off a little. He said, "It was fine, thanks."

"Dating is such a pain in the ass, isn't it? I mean, you never know what stories you've told who, what good lines this one has already heard. I guess it's a real art, being good at dating."

I saw the ridge of muscle at the joint of Victor's jawbone tighten with impatience. He took another sip of the cinnamon-dosed coffee and set the mug down on the desk with an authoritative click. "So, Milan." He folded his hands in his lap like a debutante at a cotillion waiting to be asked to dance.

"So, Victor."

"You mentioned you've located the vase."

I nodded.

"Did you find Feldman, too?"

"No," I said. "I'm pretty sure he's not findable."

"Pity," he said. "Well, maybe some of my people can look around."

"As long as he doesn't have the vase, what's the difference?"

He unlaced his fingers, spread his hands about six inches, then reclasped them. "I gave him some money to do something for me and he didn't do it. I'd like to get my money back."

"You told me it was just chump change."

He nodded. "It was. But that's not the point. If I let Feldman rip me off for a few bucks this time, the next time some other guy nicks me for some more, and pretty soon I'm the biggest patsy in northern Ohio. It's the principle of the thing."

"Ah," I said. "Principle. Of course."

A small frown creased his forehead. He knew when he was being put on. Victor's mother didn't raise any stupid children. "About the vase, Milan. Where is it?"

"It's in the bedroom."

"You're joking!"

I put on a phoney British accent. "I never joke about my work, Double-oh-seven."

He didn't smile; maybe he wasn't a movie buff. John Terranova lifted an eyebrow in acknowledgment of the quote, but that's all he was willing to risk.

"Would you like to see it?"

Victor's dark eyes glittered, and he leaned forward just a little in his chair. He always plays his cards pretty close to his vest, but at the thought of his proximity to the Helgenburg vase he was practically salivating.

"Let me get it for you," I offered.

I went into the bedroom and took the object I'd carefully wrapped in a terrycloth bath sheet that morning from the floor of the closet. It felt fragile in my hands. I brought it and the nine-by-eleven envelope in which I'd put some related documents out into the front room and went back behind my desk, placing the towel-wrapped little item ceremoniously on the desktop, nearer to Victor than to me.

He stared at it like a cobra watching a mongoose, almost as if he were waiting for it to make the first move. Then he licked his lips quickly; I guess in the presence of such a treasure he'd gotten a little cotton-mouthed. "Unwrap it," he said.

"You do it, Victor. I have these big, clumsy fingers."

His eyes flicked from me to Terranova. Then he inched his chair as far forward as it could go, bending from the waist.

"Careful, now," I teased. I'd never seen Victor Gaimari so discombobulated, and I was getting a huge kick out of it. The Duke of Cleveland wasn't acting very ducal; instead he was behaving like a small boy who'd sneaked downstairs on Christmas morning to see what goodies are under the tree.

Victor laid the vase gently on its side and began unfolding the towel. Very slowly. He was playing a game with himself, stretching out the suspense. Kind of the way my ex-wife Lila scratches off her instant lottery tickets—she does one space at a time, then puts it aside for a few minutes before scratching off the next one. I've known her to take a whole half hour seeing whether she's won five bucks.

Victor worked slowly but deftly, unrolling each layer of towel with loving care until he had the object completely exposed. He hefted it and set it upright again, staring at it in dismay.

"What is this piece of shit?" he said.

"What does it look like?"

He sat back in his chair, eyeing the rough, unglazed red clay vessel and looking pissed off. "It looks like something a sixth-grader did in Saturday morning ceramics class. What's going on here, Milan?"

"Doesn't the shape suggest anything to you?"

He cocked his head quizzically. "No."

I carefully opened the envelope and extracted the Xerox copy of the photograph I'd made at the Coventry Library. "Take another look."

He did. "All right, so the shapes are similar."

"They're identical," I said.

"What are you saying?"

"I'm saying that under that ugly surface is the item you paid Jeff Feldman to find for you."

"You're . . ." He'd been about to say "joking" again, but wisely thought better of it. Instead he simply said, "I don't believe you."

I slid a white eight-by-ten envelope out of the larger envelope and passed it across the desk to him. "Here's your proof," I said. "Be careful, the paper is really fragile. It's ready to fall apart."

He opened the flap and pulled out three sheets of paper as if he were surgically removing someone's liver. The sheets were thin and parchmentlike, brown with age, and scalloped around the edges where tiny bits of the brittle paper had disintegrated. The writing on them was in black ink, flowery, old-fashioned calligraphy that might have been produced by the shaky hand of an elderly man or woman. One of the papers was written in German, the other two were in English. The sheets rustled slightly from the shaking of Victor Gaimari's own hands as he read them.

"The provenance for the Helgenburg vase," I said.

He read them all carefully, even the one in German. Then he took a leather case from his breast pocket and removed a pair of tinted aviator glasses and read the provenance again. I was impressed; I'd never seen Victor wearing glasses in public. For him to cast aside his prodigious vanity meant that this was pretty big stuff to him.

He laid the papers down on the desk but he didn't take his eyes from the vase. "What's all this clay crap on it?" he said, his voice as unsteady as I'd ever heard it.

"Camouflage. It wouldn't do to have something like this just lying around where people could see it, so it was covered with that clay to disguise it and rebaked for a bit. I imagine if you got a skilled diamond cutter with a steady hand to chip the clay off very carefully, you'd be pleasantly surprised. You must know a good diamond cutter."

He didn't answer me. He was running his fingertips over the vase with a feathery touch, as though caressing the breast of a woman.

"Too bad I won't be there to see it emerge," I said. "I've gone through quite a bit to get this."

"From where, Milan?"

"I got it," I said.

"Jeff Feldman . . ."

"Is out of the loop."

He looked up at me, confused. "Then to whom does this belong?"

To whom. He's very classy, Victor. I like that in him. "Possession is nine tenths of the law, isn't it?"

He leaned back in his chair and crossed his arms across his chest. "This is very out of character for you. You've always been such a straight arrow."

"What makes you think I'm not still?"

"Just . . ." He waved vaguely. "All right, Milan. Let's deal. How much do you want for it?"

I scratched my chin, pretending to ponder, and frowned. But the frown was really because the stitches in my head were beginning to tighten up. It hurt.

Victor pulled out a leather-covered checkbook and a Cross pen. It was a tribute to the skill of his tailor that he could carry his glasses, a checkbook, a pen, and God knows what else in his pockets and still look as though his suit had been painted on by a Flemish master. "I don't want to haggle with you, it's undignified. Name a fair price and I'll write you out a check right here. You know I'll be square with you, no questions asked."

I sighed. "I can't do it, Victor."

"What?"

"I can't sell it to you."

"I know you've had other offers," he said, and I nodded. "But I'll better them, every one of them. Besides, you and I are old friends. We've been through a lot of crap together. That should count for something."

"That's the problem, Victor. We're friends."

"What are you talking about?"

"My conscience. It would bother me if I sold this vase to you. And you know how I am about conscience."

"Milan, this is not the time or place," he said, a dangerous edge in his voice. "I'm running out of patience. What's your price?"

I slid open the top right-hand drawer of my desk. "I don't think I can let you have it, Victor."

His eyes narrowed, and his face became taut, and all of a sudden he looked exactly like what he was. "I can just take it, you know," he said evenly. "We can just walk out of here with it.

John Terranova shifted in his chair and brought one hand up near the lapel of his jacket. His suit wasn't cut nearly as well as Victor's, and I could tell what he had under his coat.

"You can try," I said.

"What does that mean?"

"It means that I'm not stupid, Victor, and if John there doesn't put his hands back in his lap right now, I'm going to blow a hole in you big enough to—to hide a vase in." I wrapped my fingers around the .357 and took it out of the drawer so he could see it. "I'll do it if I have to. You know I've done it before, right in this room."

The cannon relaxed his hand, his face bland. But his eyes were wary.

"And that would be too bad, Victor. Because of our longstanding friendship. And because it would be for nothing."

"For nothing?"

"The vase is a fake, Victor."

He blinked. "What?"

"A fake. A counterfeit. Under that clay coating is a work of very fine art, an exact copy of the real vase designed and made by Josephus Helgenburg, complete with the gold leaf and right down to Helgenburg's individual mark on the bottom. But it's as bogus as a drag queen on Prospect Avenue."

Victor turned pale under his sunlamp tan. "How do you know?"

"I know. Because I know the artist who did it. Alys Larkin. The late Alys Larkin."

He tapped a finger on the papers. "This provenance . . ."

"Counterfeit, too, done by another fine craftsman. Aged paper, aged ink. And a damn good job, don't you think?"

Victor slumped back in the chair like one of those inflatable sex dolls that had sprung a slow leak.

"And if I sold a counterfeit like that to my good friend, my conscience would bother me something fierce."

He put the checkbook in his lap and played with the pen, thinking hard.

"There never was a Helgenburg vase," I said. "At least not that Jeff Feldman had anything to do with. It was a scam from the beginning, cooked up by him with Alys Larkin. He picked up some operating capital from you and a few other people and spent it on the forgeries, and then he was going to sell it to the highest bidder. He'd make a small fortune, even after he repaid the ones who'd given him the front money."

Victor shifted his shoulders nervously. "Who told you all this, Milan?"

"Nobody. I just put all the pieces together, and this is how it came out."

"Are you sure?"

"Sure enough to kick a field goal with this thing and never bat an eye."

He shook his head in disbelief. "How did Feldman ever expect to get away with it?"

"He didn't take me into his confidence, Victor. But I imagine he thought he could because you and the other people he'd been stringing along don't really know that much about porcelain."

He glanced at Terranova. A flush turned his face a dark red, and the line of his lips almost disappeared. The Duke of Cleveland wasn't used to being shown up, especially in front of one of his underlings.

"I know you're a dedicated collector," I went on, "but you're not an expert. Few collectors are. And like everybody else, they believe what they want to believe."

He didn't like that, and he chewed on the inside of his cheek for a minute. "How do you come to have the vase?" he said, spending the words reluctantly, the way a miser doles out hoarded gold coins.

"What the hell is the difference? It's garbage, Victor. Very artistic garbage, made by the loving hands of a real artist, but in terms of historical importance and collectibility, garbage just the same. It's probably worth two hundred dollars retail in a gift shop. Maybe Dorian could get a little more for it, but not much."

He worried a piece of dead skin at the side of his thumbnail. He must have been overdue for a manicure. "Are you positive that it isn't? . . ." He shrugged, looking down at his lap. "Of course you are," he murmured almost to himself.

"Sorry to be the bearer of bad news," I said.

He nodded. "It isn't your fault." He took a deep breath that whistled through his nose. "Who knows about this, Milan?"

"The people in this room. So far."

He nodded, not looking at me. "I'd like to limit it to the three of us, then. You understand that."

"Sure," I said. I could afford to be magnanimous. Sometimes I'm such a big person.

Victor rose slowly from the chair and wandered around the room for a few moments, not paying attention to either of us. Terranova looked at me with an almost beatific smile. We watched Victor pace.

He wound up at the window, looking down at the Cedar-Fairmount triangle, which at that hour of the morning is clogged with traffic bound westward for downtown. Whatever was going on down there seemed to engross him, as he stood slapping his leather checkbook against his palm, but I knew he wasn't seeing any of it.

He turned around slowly and looked at me with eyes as dark as a coal mine, the sunlight outside the window bright behind him. "How much do you want for the vase, Milan?"

CHAPTER TWENTY-SEVEN

One thing about Victor Gaimari, he's never predictable. For as long as I've known him he's been a tricky and manipulative bastard, full of surprises that are often less than pleasant.

But this time he really had me nonplussed. And since I wasn't expecting the question, I didn't have an answer ready.

"Come on," he coaxed, "I'm standing here with my checkbook wide open."

"Victor, you're not listening. It's a counterfeit."

"I'll pay you whatever you want—within reason," he said. "Partly for the vase, and partly for your discretion."

"My discretion?"

He looked rueful, but more than a little amused. Victor has always had the rare gift of being able to laugh at himself. "I'm afraid I've been made to look pretty foolish. I wouldn't want that getting around, naturally. But in the past I've always been able to trust your discretion—especially when I pay for it."

"You don't look foolish—you didn't actually buy a phony work of art. And you don't have to bribe me not to tell anyone."

"Please understand," Victor said. "I want the Helgenburg. I want it very much."

My voice rose out of sheer frustration. "It's not a Helgenburg!"

"But only the three of us know that. To the rest of the world, it will be."

Now it was my turn to be confused, and I said so.

He smiled now, really smiled, one of the few times I've ever seen him do that. "You're right about collectors, Milan," he said. "We don't really know much. We're just greedy and acquisitive shits by nature. But if the copy is as good as you say it is—and I have the provenance right here, which looks good too—no one will ever know. It would have to be tested, X-rayed, exhaustively examined before anyone realized it was a fake. And I'm not about to let them do that." He belched out his funny little laugh, "Ha ha. All the other collectors in the Midwest will be eating their guts out because I got the Helgenburg and they didn't."

"But that's dishonest," I said.

Even John Terranova laughed out loud at that one.

"Milan," Victor said, "you are truly a rare specimen. Hell yes, it's dishonest. But the fact is that fully ten percent of all the works of art in museums all over the world are counterfeit. And the curators know it, too. But after they've been displaying the pieces for fifteen years or so, they're too damn embarrassed to say so. The art world is funny that way."

He came back to his chair and sat down again, arranging the crease in his pants. "Look at it this way. You go to a museum, you stand transfixed in front of a Vermeer or a Rembrandt. You're thrilled by the artistry, moved by the emotion, touched and transformed just by being there in what you think is the presence of greatness, of immortality. If you think it's the genuine article—and of course you do, because there it is in the museum, after all—it doesn't change the profundity of your experience if in reality the painting is a phony, does it? It's still great." He inclined his head to one side. "Am I right or wrong, Milan?"

"I don't know, Victor. I don't know about things like that."

"Well, I do. And so I'm willing to pay you a good price for that vase—not what the genuine article would be worth, of course, but a very fair price. So name it."

"I can't take your money, Victor."

"Why not? You're not selling it to me under false pretenses. I know exactly what I'm buying."

"It just doesn't—feel right."

He ran a cupped hand over the front of his hair, another one of his almost patented gestures. God forbid his neat little pompadour should be out of place. "Responsibility to your client?" he said. "Is that it?"

"No. My client isn't even aware of the Helgenburg vase."

"Then what's your problem? You think my money's dirty?"

"The thought crossed my mind."

"Milan, Milan." He shook his head sadly. I was a great disappointment to Victor. "You and your ethics."

"They're my ethics."

"I know." He thought some more. "How about this, then? Take the money and give it to feed the homeless if you want. Put it in the collection plate in your church. I don't really care. I just want—what I want." He clicked the button on the silver pen, as if the sound would seduce me. "What do you say, Milan?"

I thought about it. I thought about Alys Larkin. I thought seriously of taking the phony art masterpiece and throwing it out the window. I thought about a lot of things. None of them were pretty.

I gestured at the vase on my desk. "Does it matter to you that two people are dead because of this damn thing?"

"That has nothing to do with me. People die every day, unfortunately, but the world keeps turning. Come on, now. There's been a lot of misery over this already. This way at least I'll be happy. And nobody else will get hurt."

There was something to his argument. I gnawed at it for another minute. Then I threw up my hands and pushed the vase closer to him. "You're a very persuasive guy, Victor."

That pleased him. He sat back in his chair. "You surprise me. I thought it would take more coaxing." He looked over at Terranova for approval, and of course he got it. "All right, then. How much? Go easy on me, okay? It's been a bad week in the market."

We locked gazes for a moment. Then I said, "The vase is yours for eighteen thousand dollars."

He didn't move. "Eighteen?"

"That's my price."

"Done," he said.

I nodded.

He opened his checkbook. "You're a sucker," he said. "I'd have paid twice that."

"I'm like you—I don't want to haggle. Eighteen grand."

His pen hovered, then he rested his fist on his thigh. "I'm curious, though. Why eighteen thousand? Why not twenty? Or fifteen, for that matter? I like things to come out even."

"Me, too, Victor," I said. "Eighteen thousand dollars, right on the nose. That comes out even in my book."

"Your book," he said, amused. He began writing. "Some day if I live long enough, I'm going to have to read your book, Milan."

"I hope not," I said. "Then I won't have any secrets left." I saw him fill in the three zeroes.

"And Victor," I said. "Make the check out to April Delavan."

I've been accused on more than one occasion of being old-fashioned. *Retro* is a word that's been applied to me, by a lot of people. I'll take the rap—I do tend to like things the way they used to be.

But I'll admit it: Jacobs Field, the new ballpark the Indians moved into in 1994, is not only state-of-the-art, it's intimate, the way baseball fields used to be. I always get a kick out of going there; it's certainly an improvement over the moldering old Cleveland Stadium several blocks to the north, where the Browns still play football.

And this Opening Day was everything a die-hard baseball fan could ask for. Sunny skies, a slight breeze blowing out, to favor the hitters, and a home lineup all of whom were capable of taking any pitcher in the league downtown. It could have been warmer, I suppose, but this *is* northeast Ohio; we'd already suffered through a White Easter, with the bronze statue of Bob Feller covered with snow, and I was grateful they were getting to play the opener at all. I was wearing a tweed sports jacket over a sweater and shirt, and the breeze was getting to me a little. I usually wear more sensible clothes to a ballgame in April, but I'd thought about my dinner date later and was a little more dressed up for it, a fact that neither Ed nor Marko failed to comment on.

Ed Stahl's tickets were beauties, field-box seats right off third base. It had been an adjustment at first, seeing the Indians coming out of the third-base dugout, but I got used to it.

I was sitting between Ed and Mark Meglich, munching on a bratwurst sandwich and washing it down with a beer. The warming rays of the sun felt good on the back of my neck.

On the other side of Ed was his companion; he had managed to get a date for the day. She was Carrie Howarth, a feature writer for the *Plain Dealer* I'd met a time or two before. Unfortunately for Ed she was married, with a year-old baby, but hey, a date is a date, and Opening Day seats shouldn't go to waste no matter what.

Since I was temporarily carless, Marko had driven up to the Heights to get me, after laughing hilariously at my rat story. I imagined I'd be hearing about that one for a long time.

The game hadn't started yet; the ground crew was still dragging the field. But Ed was working; his beer between his feet, his kosher hot dog balanced on his lap, he attempted to scribble in his notebook.

"Some of this stuff you can't print, Ed," I told him. "I've made some promises."

"I still don't understand how you made all the pieces fit, Milan." He gave Carrie a superior, knowing look—the kind that only passes between people who share similar jobs and experiences. This was the smug, journalistic, we've-heard-it-all look. "And don't tell me it was intuition."

"Don't tell me what not to tell you, Ed, or there won't be any story at all." When he was properly chastened, I went on. "I went to New York with only one lead—the Barthalow Gallery, which had nothing to do with ceramics but everything to do with old documents and letters. When I mentioned Josephus Helgenburg to the owner, it was pretty obvious to me that she didn't know what in hell I was talking about but that her clerk did. Bert Winstock, his name is. And when he chased me down the street and asked if Feldman wanted me to give him anything, I figured out that Feldman's business had been with him personally and not with the gallery, and that it could only be document forgery.

"That's when I got the idea that if there was a vase kicking around somewhere, it was a counterfeit."

Carrie leaned forward to look around Ed at me. "Wouldn't it take a hell of a craftsman to counterfeit something like that."

"Craftswoman," Mark said.

"Craftsperson," Carrie corrected him, "if you're going to be like that."

The announcement of the starting lineups came booming over the public address system, and I had to raise my voice to be heard. "From everything I knew about Jeff Feldman, that kind of fine work was way beyond his skill. Tydings Belk's, too. So I figured that Alys Larkin must have counterfeited the vase for Feldman."

"Big jump of logic," Ed observed.

"It was, until I realized Larkin had lied to me. She told me she'd never let Feldman broker her pieces, and then Belk told me she had."

"That has nothing to do with counterfeiting."

"No, but it got me wondering. She'd been brutally honest with me about everything else, though—including a one-night stand with Feldman a long time ago." I held up a hand. "That's also off the record, Ed. I don't think Belk knows about it, and it would just hurt him more." I glanced at Carrie. "Off the record to you too."

"Hey, I don't care," she said, shrugging. "This is Ed's story. I just write movie reviews and warm-and-fuzzy profiles of elderly couples who do ethnic folk dancing." She took a bite of her hot dog, getting mustard on her mouth.

"So," Ed coaxed, "Feldman didn't have much to do with it."

"He had everything to do with it," Marko chimed in.

"Jeff Feldman had the connections," I said. "He had the customers on the hook, and also the New York forger to make it all look legit. He couldn't have done it without Larkin, but she couldn't have pulled it off without him, either."

"How did you know Chase Delavan killed Larkin?"

"I didn't, until I went fishing. I kind of hinted around to all the potential buyers that the vase was somewhere in the studio.

Then I just went up there and waited. Delavan was the one who showed up to look for it."

"With Feldman out of the way," Marko said, "Delavan had to deal with Larkin, and she was a lot more greedy. So they argued, it got physical, and probably by accident he killed her. Then he tossed her down that old elevator shaft to make it look like an accident." He ran a hand through his thinning hair, then rubbed the back of his neck where the sun was hitting it. "What I can't figure out is what was Delavan going to use for money. According to Milan, he was Tap City."

"One can only conjecture," I said, "but I think Delavan was planning a little rip-off of his own. He hadn't known about Alys Larkin being in the mix—from the start he'd been dealing directly with Feldman. So my guess was that he was going to get the vase, get Feldman out of the way somehow, and sell the damn thing himself to one of the other collectors."

"Who were they?" Ed said, pencil poised.

Marko nudged me in the ribs. "I'd kind of like to know that myself."

"What's the difference?" I said.

Marko glowered at me, but I was going to stick to my guns. "They were honestly involved in trying to buy what they thought was a genuine work of art. They weren't implicated in any crime."

"We can subpoena that information out of you, Milan."

"No you can't, Mark. No judge would sign that kind of an order. And you start making innocent citizens' names public, you're looking at some nasty lawsuits."

"Whoa, wait a minute, back up here," Ed said. "Why was Feldman out of the way? What happened to him?"

"Jeff is dead," I told him. "I figured Delavan was responsible for that, too. But when I confronted him in the loft last night, he thought at first I was Feldman, so I knew someone else had taken care of him."

"Who?" Carrie wanted to know.

"Larkin," I said. "She hated his guts anyway. And she really didn't need him anymore. Through him, she had the provenance from Bert Winstock in New York, and she knew who the big-bucks guys were that wanted the vase. And it was her artistry and craftsmanship that was making the whole deal possible, and Feldman was going to take the lion's share and leave her with peanuts, so she got him out of the way. It's called eliminating the middle man."

"How did she kill him?"

"I don't know," I said. "My guess is we'll never know."

The Indians took the field to a loud roar from the assembled faithful. And I mean loud—the game, as are most of our home openers, was a sell out. After the playing of the national anthem, the pitcher stalked out to the mound, looked in to the catcher for his sign, and whipped a knee-high curve ball past the Boston leadoff man for a strike. Another baseball season was underway.

Ed was not to be put off. "If Larkin wasted Feldman, then where's his body?"

Marko shifted in his seat as if he were a princess sitting on a pea. He looked at me nervously.

"Lieutenant Meglich here has kindly sent a police forensic team up to the studio loft this morning," I said. "And unless I miss my guess, as we speak they're discovering whatever remains of Jeff Feldman by sifting through and analyzing the ashes at the bottom of that kiln. It gets almost twice as hot as the fire in a crematorium's oven. More than enough to completely obliterate a human body."

Carrie Howarth turned a little green around the gills. "Eeeeyew!" she said, and tossed what was left of her hot dog under her seat.

The leadoff hitter laced a bouncing ball to the second baseman, who scooped it up and tossed him out.

"Jesus, Milan, that's incredible!" Ed said.

I ducked my head modestly. "Oh, come on, Ed. It was only a groundout to the infield."

CHAPTER TWENTY-EIGHT

Sometimes things work out and the good guys win. This was that kind of day—Indians 6, Red Sox 3.

Ed and Carrie had gone back to the office, Ed to write his column on the fall of Chase Delavan and swearing not to violate the promise I'd made to Victor Gaimari. It was still early, so Marko and I went across East Ninth Street to the Taverne of Richfield Cleveland Style—a mouthful of a name for a restaurant, but a pleasant place for a postgame drink. The lounge was packed with fans wearing Indians caps and jackets who had the same idea we did, but we were able to find two stools at the bar. We ordered beers and then Marko excused himself to go call his office.

When he came back, his face was pale.

"Bingo," he said as he sat down on the stool.

"What?"

"They won't know for sure until they run DNA tests, but the forensic guys found what they think might be shards of human bone in the bottom of that kiln." He wiped his face with his hand the way Brian Keith used to in *Hardcastle and McCormick*.

I felt a wrench in my gut. I wasn't looking forward to my next talk with Irv Feldman. It wasn't my responsibility to tell him— but I knew I was going to do it anyway.

"How did Alys Larkin think she could get away with something like that?" Marko said. "It must have taken a certain amount of time for the body to burn up completely."

"She had all the time in the world. Tydings Belk was on a

three-week vacation, and it's not the kind of place that encourages walk-in traffic. And I got close enough to that kiln, thank you, to know that it's not likely anybody would voluntarily stick their face into it when it was hot."

"Still a risk."

"The whole venture was risky," I said.

He looked balefully at me over his beer. "You're really not going to tell me the names of the other prospective buyers?"

I shook my head. "They didn't do anything wrong."

"Buying stolen property? That vase certainly didn't belong to Feldman."

"They didn't buy it."

"They were thinking about it, though."

"If thinking about a crime was a crime, you'd have to lock up everybody in town."

A couple of high-spirited victory celebrants wearing old-fashioned Tribe sweatshirts jostled Marko in the back as they stormed by us, and he gave them a look that could melt lead.

"Besides, there was no vase—no real one, anyway," I went on. Just a counterfeit. And if they'd bought that, they'd be victims, not criminals."

Marko drummed his fingertips on the bar and then took one of my cigarettes and lit it. The woman on the other side of him stared at him as if he'd exposed himself and ostentatiously waved the smoke away from her face.

"This is a bar, lady, not church," he growled, and she turned away from him to complain to her companion.

"We smokers are an endangered species," he lamented. "You can't even light up at the ballgame anymore, and they built the damn stadium on cigarette taxes."

"It's the new world order," I agreed.

He studied the glowing end of the Winston. Then he said, "You told these buyers you had the Helgenburg vase."

"I told them I knew where it was," I corrected him. "That was a lie, to smoke the killer out. There *is* no Helgenburg vase."

"But there is a phony."

"Uh-huh."

"So where is it?"

I looked up at the TV set above the bar. Beautiful, elegant Vivian Truscott, the Channel 12 news anchor, was reporting a fatal residential fire on the East Side that could have been prevented if the smoke detectors in the house had been working. "Chase Delavan never had the chance to find it," I said carefully.

"But you know where it is. Don't you." It wasn't a question.

I put on my most innocent choirboy face, the one I hadn't used since I was in fourth grade. "Well, I certainly don't have it."

He took another puff, and the smoke drifted up into his eye, making it tear. He wiped at it angrily. "You're such a pain in the ass, Milan."

It was a long walk from Jacobs Field to Johnny's Downtown—up East Ninth Street and then across Public Square to West Sixth. My body was aching from my exertions of the night before, and sitting still in the cool air hadn't helped any, so the exercise felt good.

Dr. Nicole Archer was already at the bar, looking beautiful in a maroon pants suit of some clingy material, and I felt that little twang! inside my chest again. She was sipping a glass of white wine. I'd rightly figured her for a white wine person—I don't know why.

She put her cheek up for me to kiss. I liked that. Her skin was warm and she smelled of lilac.

"Are you making some sort of new fashion statement?" she said, looking at the bandage on my head.

"Kind of brings out my eyes, don't you think?"

"Some bad guy do that to you?"

I waved it off. "I'm a fast healer. It's my rugged Slovenian genes."

"Did this have something to do with Jeff?"

My heart dropped into my stomach. I'd been so wired about Opening Day at the ballpark and so excited about our dinner date, I had forgotten how and why I'd met Nicole Archer in the first place.

"I'm afraid I have some lousy news, Nicole."

Her eyes went blank for just a moment, as though someone inside her head had pulled a curtain over them. Then she said, "He's dead, isn't he?"

"I'm sorry," I said.

She took a deep breath and didn't speak for a moment. "It's okay," she said finally. "It makes me sad, naturally, but it was another lifetime." She sipped at her wine without much gusto. "He wasn't really a very nice human being—and that's an understatement. I suppose he crossed one person too many."

"I'll tell you about it if you like."

She considered it. "I wouldn't like. I don't want it to spoil our evening." Then she brightened. "Good game?"

"Great," I said.

"The Indians won?"

"Six—three."

"Then you're happy?"

"I'm glad," I said. "It takes more than a baseball game to make me happy."

"Let's eat," she said, "and you can tell me what."

She brought her wine with her, and we approached the maître d'. He knew me from Johnny's Bar on Fulton, where I'd eaten often with Mary, and greeted me by name.

Nicole looked impressed as we were led to our table. "I had no idea I was with such a BMOC."

"Big man on campus?"

"Big man of Cleveland."

"You better believe it," I said.

Johnny's Downtown had taken over the space long occupied by the late Burgess Grand Café, and their remodeling has kept the old elegance while achieving a kind of new intimacy. We sat at a booth against the wall and admired the Romanesque murals.

"Those stitches hurt?" she said.

"Yes, but I've already been warned about asking for free medical advice."

Her gaze was direct, her eyes sparkling. "I've never met a private detective before."

"Sorry, but I can't say I've never met a doctor before."

"Yes, but you probably can say you've never met a neonatologist."

"I can hardly say ne-o-na-tol-o-gist."

"You're doing fine," she said.

"It must be rewarding, working with the little ones the way you do," I said.

"It is." She looked thoughtful for a moment. "I have to wonder, sometimes, how they'll grow up. If they'll be good people, or turn out rotten."

"Chances are they'll be good," I said. "Most people are. Every once in a while somebody gets bent, that's all."

"And that's where you come in. Straightening them out again."

I felt myself coloring. "You sound like I'm the Caped Avenger."

She put up a cautionary hand. She had graceful hands, long fingers. "Don't disillusion me, okay? I like heroes. There aren't enough of them left."

"No one's a hero to his valet, they say."

"How about yours?"

"My valet? He worships me. As a matter of fact, I hold the bad guys while he hits them for me."

Nicole giggled. "You're a kick in the head," she said. "You make me laugh."

"Is that good?"

"Mmm. I think this is going to be interesting."

"What?"

She put her hand on top of mine. "This."

I was blushing again, but that yammering voice inside my head was urging caution. The doctor and the private detective didn't exactly compute, and my naturally suspicious nature was yanking hard on the reins. But I remembered Cathleen Hartigan and how I'd blown it. I remembered Mary and how wonderful that had been for a while and how I'd blown that too. Life is full of bad judgment calls, but they don't mean a damn thing unless you can learn from them. So I took a breath, counted silently to ten, and asked her, "Is that what this is? A 'this'?"

She gave me that direct, intense look again. "There are no guarantees, but I think it might be. Why don't we see?"

I leaned back in my chair and pantomimed pulling back the string of a bow. "Twang!" I said. And she laughed again.

I believe I mentioned this before, but I think it bears repeating. Sometimes things work out and the good guys win.

ACKNOWLEDGMENTS

The author wishes to thank Laura S. Sherman of the Bonfoey Co. in Cleveland, Helene Morse, and James O'Brien for their valuable technical expertise.

Milan Jacovich returns in:
COLLISION BEND

A NOTE FROM LES ROBERTS . . .

I try to stay eclectic, if only for my own sanity; I'd hate writing about the same thing, book after book. So for the next Milan Jacovich novel, Collision Bend, I revisited a world in which I made my living for many years: television.

I wrote and produced television in Los Angeles mostly on the network level and in the entertainment division, so I knew next to nothing about news, especially local news. Before starting to write the book, I contacted Wilma Smith, the lovely and capable six o'clock anchor of Fox 8 News, and invited her to lunch so I could pick her brain about how a local TV news operation worked.

Who says research is a drag?

Every once in a while I'll come across a name that, to a writer, is irresistible. So it was with Nikki Scandalious, who works in the public relations office of the fabled Cleveland Orchestra. I did a little juggling, however, and in the book Nikki becomes Nicky, an egotistical TV station manager. That didn't stop her friends and acquaintances all over the country from contacting her to tell her she was now a character in a book, albeit with a gender change.

Collision Bend is not, as many believe, another name for Dead Man's Curve on the Innerbelt. It is the hairpin turn on the Cuyahoga River just below Jacobs Field and across from Tower City. And I moved Milan's office down there as homage to Jim's Steak House, one of my all-time favorite Cleveland "joints," now, alas, gone.

I hope you'll follow Milan to Collision Bend.

-- Les Roberts

Now available in quality paperback: the Milan Jacovich mystery series . . .

PEPPER PIKE

Introducing Milan Jacovich, the private investigator with a master's degree, a taste for klobasa sandwiches, and a knack for finding trouble. A cryptic late-night phone call from a high-powered advertising executive leads Milan through the haunts of one of Cleveland's richest suburbs and into the den of Cleveland mob kingpin Don Giancarlo D'Allessandro.   1-59851-001-0

FULL CLEVELAND

Someone's scamming Cleveland businessmen by selling ads in a magazine that doesn't exist. But the dollar amount hardly seems worth the number of bodies that Milan soon turns up. And why is Milan being shadowed at every turn by a leisure-suited mob flunky? One thing's certain: Buddy Bustamente's fashion sense isn't the only thing about him that's lethal.   1-59851-002-9

DEEP SHAKER

Ever loyal, Milan Jacovich has no choice but to help when a grade-school chum worries his son might be selling drugs. The investigation uncovers a brutal murder and a particularly savage drug gang—and leads Milan to a relic from every Clevelander's childhood that proves to be deadly.   1-59851-003-7

THE CLEVELAND CONNECTION

The Serbs and the Slovenians traditionally don't get along too well, but Milan Jacovich makes inroads into Cleveland's Serbian community when an appealing young woman convinces him to help search for her missing grandfather. Hatreds that have simmered for fifty years eventually explode as Milan takes on one of his most challenging cases.   1-59851-004-5

THE LAKE EFFECT

Milan owes a favor and agrees to serve as bodyguard for a suburban mayoral candidate—but these politics lead to murder. And the other candidate has hired Milan's old nemesis, disgraced ex-cop Al Drago, who carries a grudge a mile wide.   1-59851-005-3

THE DUKE OF CLEVELAND

Milan dives into the cutthroat world of fine art when a slumming young heiress hires him to find her most recent boyfriend, a potter, who has absconded with $18,000 of her trust-fund money. Turns out truth and beauty don't always mix well—at least in the art business.   1-59851-006-1

COLLISION BEND

Milan goes behind the scenes to uncover scandal, ambition, and intrigue at one of Cleveland's top TV stations as he hunts down the stalker and murderer of a beautiful local television anchor.   1-59851-007-X

THE CLEVELAND LOCAL

Milan Jacovich is hired to find out who murdered a hotshot young Cleveland lawyer vacationing in the Caribbean. Back in Cleveland, he runs afoul of both a Cleveland mob boss and a world-famous labor attorney—and is dealt a tragic personal loss that will alter his life forever.   1-59851-008-8

A SHOOT IN CLEVELAND

Milan accepts an "easy" job baby-sitting a notorious Hollywood bad-boy who's in Cleveland for a movie shoot. But keeping Darren Anderson out of trouble is like keeping your hat dry during a downpour. And when trouble leads to murder, Milan finds himself in the middle of it all.   1-59851-009-6

Get them at your favorite bookstore!